Praise for

THE STONE ARROW

"A thoroughly absorbing novel."

Asbury Park Press

"IN EVERY WAY A REMARKABLE ACHIEVEMENT... This novel deals wholly convincingly with an ancient culture. I read it with great enjoyment and instruction."

Anthony Burgess

"Author Herley... knows his setting from the ground up and provides a realistic adventure story that ranks high in that genre."

Augusta Chronicle

(more)

"A GRIPPING THRILLER set convincingly in neolithic Sussex. Herley resurrects this time with such panache, the gruesome bits of Tagart's vendetta seem justified."

The Sunday Times (London)

"The action is nearly nonstop and if the setting is unfamiliar, the characters and their motives are not. . . . What keeps the reader enthralled . . . is the sincerity of the author's attitude toward his characters and the passionate attention to detail Herley provides in his imaginative recreation of the everyday life of neolithic people."

The Houston Chronicle

"Margaret Mead would have found nothing to dismay her in this novel, and Ian Fleming would certainly have envied the derring-do."

Publishers Weekly

"This book is full of great action and woodsy lore along with some really neat characters. It's a vicarious thrill."

The Star Banner

"What is remarkable and convincing about the book is its description of a way of life and a landscape. The place at a distance of five thousand years, yet recognizably Sussex, is shown with beauty, force, and care . . . A highly satisfactory first novel."

Financial Times

"I found it a most remarkable evocation of a prehistoric age; and the author's pen pictures of nature—flowers, trees, and animals—are quite outstanding. A great imaginative feat."

George Shipway

THE STONE ARROW

Richard Herley

BALLANTINE BOOKS • NEW YORK

First published in Great Britain 1978 by Peter Davies Limited

 Published in the United States of America by Ballantine Books, a division of Random House, Inc., New York, and simultaneously in Canada by Random House of Canada Limited, Toronto.

Library of Congress Catalog Card Number: 84-22705

ISBN 0-345-34326-3

This edition published by arrangement with William Morrow and Company, Inc.

Manufactured in the United States of America

First Ballantine Books Edition: August 1987

TAGART CAME OUT OF THE WOODS AND STOOD FACING THE broad downhill sweep of the cereal field. The feeling of openness seemed strange and sudden after the embrace of the trees; he sniffed at the smell of the evening, almost cloudless now after the storm, a soft wind coming off the sea, bending the stunted ears of barley, fluttering the leaves of hazel and whitebeam.

A hundred yards away the laborer stood upright and leaned on the handle of his mattock. He had only just become aware of another's presence; yet Tagart had heard the man at work minutes ago, from the depths of the wood, whose floor he had traversed without so much as the snap of a twig.

Tagart, or Tugart, or Tergart, was twenty-five years of age, tall and fine in the face, with dark hair and watchful brown eyes that knew the value of patience. His skin—for it was now the height of summer—was well tanned, his frame hard-muscled and long-limbed, with an economy of movement that seemed like slowness to those who had never been with him in the woods and tried to keep up. Chance had endowed him with stamina, and a wry intelligence which the teachings of his elders had turned into solid skill and a command of the necessary knowledge. Of all the young men in his tribe, it was Tagart who had been regarded as successor to the leader, Tagart who had taken the most beautiful bride, Tagart whose small son would in turn one day be chief; and Tagart whom the others were beginning to look upon with more and more respect and love as each season went by. But now, in the course of a single night, all that had changed: beauty made foul, cleanness made filth. Everything changed; everything raped and defiled.

Not quite everything. Tagart was still alive. He was still alive, and behind the grief he was still himself. The plan, flexible in detail but rigid in outline and purpose, lay like a cold network in his brain.

It was time to begin.

"I come in friendship," he called out, leaving the protection of the trees and starting across the field.

The laborer made no reply. He stood shielding his eyes against the west, his body held nervously, right hand taking a firmer grasp on the polished ashwood haft of his mattock.

Tagart went on. In the edge of his vision he was making a second survey of the field, making absolutely certain that he and the laborer were alone. The farmers' village, which he had studied the previous day, was a cluster of stone and timber buildings inside a wooden palisade, hidden from this field by the rise of the land. It was only a quarter of a mile away, too close, asking for trouble; but then he'd had no choice. He had been forced into the open by the shape of the forest and by the way the fields sloped. Without revealing himself there had been no way to be sure that the laborer was alone; and to waste such an opportunity would be madness, so he had accepted the risk. But that did not stop the tingling between his shoulder blades, nor an almost irresistible urge to check more overtly behind and to the sides.

He halted just beyond the swing of the mattock, and smiled. "The soil needs more rain than this. After the drought she drinks it like a pigeon."

The farmer said nothing. He stood impassive, expressionless.

"I have come along the coast from Valdoe," Tagart told him, speaking more distinctly. He indicated his leather pouch. "My master wishes an exchange of barleys."

The farmer's eyes flicked to the pouch, and back to Tagart's face.

"I see barley is your crop here on this acre."

No reaction.

"I was told to ask for a man with no beard," Tagart said. "A man of importance in your village. Do you know him?"

The farmer grunted. There was no meaning in it.

"Is he your head man? Will you take me to him? I want to talk trade."

The laborer took his hand from his brow and changed position so that he no longer faced the sun. He was a short, broad man, with stumpy legs and wide shoulders filling a stained and streaked doeskin jacket, with beaver leggings bound by thongs, and on his feet alder clogs carved with lines and circles. Round his neck was a talisman of some sort, a flat stone striped with bands of color—cream, brown, maroon—hanging by a cord that passed through a hole drilled off-center. Greasy black locks showed beneath a hare's-skin cap and hung in a tangle at his neck. Years of weather had left his skin leathery and his eyes wrinkled almost shut, yet his was a face devoid of animation or humor, the kind of face under a low forehead that frowns blankly as the brain behind it struggles to assimilate something new. Clearly the man was low in the order of the village, sent out to the fields to do some small task on his own. He had been digging up stones and heaping them to one side, making a tilth of what once had been a barren patch. This was the kind of work reserved for the losers, those at the bottom of the village hierarchy.

He nodded at Tagart's pouch.

"Seed barley," Tagart said, holding the pouch forward.

The offer was disregarded. "You say you come along the coast."

"From Valdoe."

"From Valdoe?" For the first time he showed a sign of interest. It was as if Tagart had not already mentioned the word. "Valdoe? From Valdoe? Are you sent by the Flint Lord?"

"By my master, one of the Trundlemen."

"And he sent you trading barley?"

"Yes."

The farmer's eyes narrowed cunningly. "You will know the flint sellers. They will be here soon with flints: it is time for their trade. Fallott, Bico, and the rest."

"My trade is not in axes," Tagart said. "It is in seed." More mildly he added, "There are many at Valdoe. A mere slave cannot know them all."

"You are enslaved?"

"Building my freedom."

"Why go back? You are far from the Trundle. They could never catch up."

"That is not my way," Tagart said. "My master trusts me and I am grateful."

The farmer forbore from comment. He turned and took a long look to the west, across the curving line of the field, beyond the distant green scrub on the clifftops, to the golden path where the sun was coming down on the sea. The wind pushed wisps of hair at the sides of his face. Tagart heard corn buntings and skylarks, and glimpsed the flash of a jay's wing as it emerged from and returned to the security of the wood. He swayed slightly. Exhaustion was threatening to overtake him. His body wanted to yield and sag to the ground. Sections of his mind were faltering, blinking on and off. He was aware that his strength was draining away; with its loss came the panic of realizing that he might be left with too little when the moment arrived. He had foolishly eaten nothing that day, and the day before he had felt too ill to contemplate food. His stomach had been emptied anyway, in the gray wet dawn with his arms and legs covered in ashes, slime and blood, the back of his throat burning and his eyes watering with each useless retch as he sprawled across their bodies on the riverbank.

His mind drew back suddenly. He must not think of them. Not of them, and not of the tribe. He must think only of the immediate, the practical, what had to be accomplished in each moment. Only thus could he see it through. Fleetingly the whole vista stretched before and behind. In a sense the end of it was hazy and unimportant, the rest of his life a mere contingency as long as he got through the next few days intact; there was no point considering a future which, whatever happened, could for him have no meaning or color.

"You must talk to Sturmer," the laborer said.

"Sturmer? Is he your chief? A man with no beard?"

"Sturmer does our trading."

"Will you take me to him?"

"I will not. We have rules." The laborer scratched his chin. "You say you bring seed. What of it? Our barns are full of seed."

"This is different," Tagart said. "My master wants a barley for the salt wind; the Flint Lord desires new ground opened up along the coast."

"So you were sent to villages by the sea to trade. But why should we give our secret to the Flint Lord? If he wants them he must pay, as we must pay for the tools his traders bring. Flints, livestock, clothes—these are the things we want. Of barley we have plenty."

"No—this seed is different. It's special." Tagart pointed out to sea. "It comes from there, across the water. The yield is double."

"Double."

"That is what my master says, sir."

"Not possible."

"It must be possible or the Valdoe farmers would not sow it by the score of bags."

"Show it to me."

"There is nothing to be gained by that."

"Show me."

"My master said I was only to offer it in the presence of a head man. Take me to Sturmer. I will talk with him."

"Show me." The laborer stretched out a hand. "Show me or be on your way."

"I should not do this."

The laborer moved his fingers impatiently. Tagart gave him the pouch, which was tied at the neck with a draw-string. Two hands were needed to get it open.

Seeing this, the laborer tried to loosen the string while

keeping a grip on his mattock-handle, picking with a fingernail at the bunched leather, which Tagart had drawn especially tight before leaving the woods. After a few fruitless moments, aware that he would make himself look foolish by asking Tagart to open the bag, the laborer released the handle, lodging it in his armpit, and freed both hands for the job.

That was the instant Tagart chose to kill him.

Later, Tagart had time to wonder what went wrong. It may have been weariness, making him slow. Tagart was not sure. He knew only that the man had put up a struggle which made his end more protracted than it ought to have been.

When it was done Tagart searched the body for personal effects. With his flint knife he cut through the cord, releasing the talisman, and slipped the stone into his pouch. Tagart worked quickly, apprehensive now that someone might come from the village and discover him. The sun had dropped more to the west, going down over the trees, casting long fingers of shadow that advanced downhill in a hurry to be night.

A name formed on Tagart's lips, a word without bidding. Sturmer. He said it again. *Sturmer*. A name to go with the beardless face, the face in the firelight.

Picking up the mattock by its blade, he thrust the haft into the ground. Beside it he arranged lines of stones taken from the pile the laborer had made, forming an arrow pointing in the direction of the wood; he finished it with three stones for each barb, and grasped the corpse by its armpits.

It seemed much heavier than a man's body. Ideally he needed a sledge. He forced a smile. Ideally, he needed help for what he planned to do, the help of a hundred men. Or if not a hundred, then ten of his friends from the tribe, who were better than any hundred taken from these slab-faced peasants.

The tribe. He must not think of the tribe. Anger would only slow him down, ruin his chances. He held a duty in sacred trust: the honor of the tribe had devolved upon him and him alone. Nothing must be allowed to stand in his way. If he was to discharge his duty he could ill afford the luxury of rage.

But it was with a fierce renewed energy that he took up the corpse again, pulling it toward the forest.

PART ONE

1

STURMER OPENED HIS EYES AND LAY LISTENING TO THE blood pulsing in his ears. The chimney-hole in his roof was blind, blocked for the summer: the blackened rafters traveled up and met in gloom. There were five, like the arms of a starfish, speared by the central pillar that held up his house. From them, on pegs and hooks, hung clothes, netting, tools, pouches of flints, water bags; seed of wheat, barley, and a dozen other crops; jars of lamp-fat and bundles of rushpith for lighting; baskets, cooking utensils, pots suspended in nets, leatherware muzzles and straps and tackle, fire-making kits, and all the other possessions that were better kept off the ground and away from the vermin and the village animals which ranged free in all the houses.

Sturmer's was the largest and best-appointed dwelling, with three other rooms besides this, where his children slept and he kept further stores. The doorway, which was low and broad and looked out across the village compound toward the Meeting House, gave onto a small area paved with stones from the beach. Behind the doorway and a short tunnel-like porch, which contained a miniature effigy of Gauhm set in a wooden casket, the passageway opened into a pebble-floored kitchen with a sooted hearth, above which was another chimney aperture. To the side was the room where the children slept; to the front another chamber, and beyond that the main room with the tall roof, which from the outside appeared as a cone of weathered timber, caulked with plant fibers and clay, in places tufted with burnt grass and clumps of weeds. That flat part of the roof toward the front of the house was turfed, on a base of planking, and the porch was covered with skins that could be drawn across the entrance. A few small windows—simple apertures—had been left in the walls, which were made of selected and interlocked stones, the gaps and chinks filled with pebbles and the remaining cracks plastered with clay. Against the wall were piles of kindling-wood, logs, a wooden water butt, a number of digging-sticks and mattocks, a stack of wattle panels used for temporary animal pens, and an old bench where the people in the house could sit in the evening and face the Meeting House opposite. It was here that Sturmer sat to answer informal questions and settle small disputes. He was head man of Burh village, and had been so for twelve years.

He was in his late thirties, of medium height and build, with unexpectedly soft features and a mild manner edged by the perceptive gaze of pale blue eyes. Sturmer kept his beard neat and favored subdued clothing: pigskin and goatskin dyed with subtle patterns of yellow and gray. His hair, which was glossy black, he tied in a bun. Triple lines of blue tattoo ran the length of his right arm, flank, and leg, culminating in pentacles on his instep and the back of his hand: for he was also a priest.

He turned on his side and watched the contours of his wife's back. His eyes explored her shoulders and the tiny humps of vertebrae, and the light and shade and texture of her black hair, which he found girlish and endearing where it grew from her nape. He extended a forefinger and almost touched the bumps of her spine, moving his hand slightly to compensate for her breathing. It was no use making plans any more. The matter was out of his control; the spirits had taken over. The drought showed no signs of coming to an end. Starvation, the breakup of Burh, was beginning to look inevitable.

The previous winter Sturmer, like all the villagers, had become uneasily aware that too many dry days were following one another, and that the rain, when it did come, was light and sporadic. A single snowstorm in early spring, with a week of bitter frost, had been the only hard weather the whole winter, when usually Burh could expect heavy drifts and blizzards for days or weeks on end. And there had been no sign of flooding from the river: usually the farmers had to work through the night to protect their village. At the end of the spring and for the two months of low summer the clearings had been filled with blossom—of elder, blackthorn, whitebeam, hawthorn, cherry—to an extent which no one had ever seen before; many plants had gone on flowering through the winter, when normally there was no color to be seen. Even the spring birds seemed earlier and more numerous than usual, supernaturally numerous, and the woods and grassland near the village and on the cliffs were alive with butterflies: blue, red, orange, yellow, white, and brown, flying up in clouds from every bush and clump of nettles. The yellow lilies in the river bloomed profusely long before their time. The ditches and banks were choked with frog-spawn. One night they saw shooting stars over the sea, and Sturmer knew that Aih had been disturbed.

The farmers divided the year into six seasons, each of two moons or months, beginning on the shortest day with winter, followed by spring, low summer, high summer, harvest, autumn, winter again. It was now halfway through high summer, when the crops should have been making their fastest growth and all was to be got ready for harvest. Normally on such a morning Sturmer would long ago have been up and with the rest of the village in the fields. But today there was no work to be done. The crops were dying. For six weeks there had been no rain at all. That alone would have been enough, but Sturmer had other worries too.

During his tenure the village had enjoyed an increase in prosperity and population on an unprecedented scale. Apart from its thirty-three stone and timber houses, Burh now had a threshing shed, granary, two silos, and a general barn, bakery, a bear-proof palisade, and, to Sturmer's pride, a long Meeting House where met the village council. The most important crop was emmer, a kind of wheat that Sturmer had substituted for the old einkorn used by his predecessor. From wheat and barley and honey they made ale; broomcorn, millett, and oats were grown partly as winter fodder for the animals—goats, cattle, and sheep. Crops like lentils and broad beans, kale and rape, were grown in plots beside each house. The wealthier families owned pigs; most kept a dog, medium-sized hounds derived from the yellow hunting dogs such as once had been used by the nomads.

Sturmer had been having trouble with the land. He disliked burning the forest, and would have preferred to go on using the same fields for the village crops: long ago he hd begun to guess at the value of manure, and now regularly changed the location of the animal pens. Some of the beasts were allowed to wander more or less at freedom, grazing on the wild leaves, bringing back their goodness to the village; he tried mulching with leaf-mold from the forest, and gathering seaweed from the shore, a mile to the south, and using that to enrich the ground. The Earth Spirit Gauhm, Sturmer knew, needed help if she was to deliver up her best bounty. But as the years passed it was becoming plain that the ancestors had been right: to grow good crops you must clear forest. Clear the forest, burn it, plant the ground, and move on when the goodness has gone. That was the old way. Sturmer's new way seemed to be wrong. He was disappointed to find it so, because what he yearned for was stability. With a stable village, more elaborate buildings would become possible, more children, more families in one place. More people could be freed from working on the soil. Goods could be fabricated, goods for sale to other villages, and possibly, one day, Sturmer might grow wealthy through trading, like the great Flint Lord at Valdoe.

The vision was moving further and further out of reach. In spite of all Sturmer's efforts quite large areas around the village, once excellent land, were useless and reverting to scrub.

Others in the Council, led by Groden, kept pressing for a return to the old order. They wanted wider forest clearance, a change of site for the village; more, not fewer, acres under cultivation. Sturmer felt it unwise to resist too strenuously. He was thirty-six—getting old. His position as leader was becoming precarious. It was only a matter of time before a younger man—and who else but Groden?—made a thrust and forced the issue, and Sturmer was not sure that Groden would not win. The younger and rasher men in the village supported him: they favored an aggressive approach to the forest and the countryside.

This worried Sturmer in another way. As far back as memory would go, there had been a nomad summer camp by the river some three miles upstream, well inside the forest. The nomads were hunters, in winter foraging in the marshes to the north where they were guaranteed plentiful wildfowl and game, in spring coming over the downs to the forest by the sea coast. In some years they came not at all; in others they stayed a few days or weeks and moved on again. This summer, the nomads had been present all season.

They were rarely seen in person by the villagers. The odd goat or pig missed from its pen, and even tools and skins stolen from the fields, were never closely pursued. The farmers hated and feared the nomads, and they feared even more the magic the nomads controlled. Their god was Tsoaul, Spirit of the Forest. Through the nomads he worked evil on Gauhm; even now he was struggling to win back the village fields, as he always did, working stealthily and by degrees. First he rendered the land infertile for crops, making its cultivation pointless. Next he sent weeds. When these were established he sent hawthorn and birth, which soon become impenetrable scrub. From scrub it was an easy step to forest. Not a square yard of the village was safe from Tsoaul's work; he infested good land as well as bad; he even wanted the very roofs on the houses.

Sturmer was worried because each tree that fell effectively brought the nomads a little closer. Every clearance fire reduced the extent of forest available to the nomads and increased the chance of trouble between them and the villagers.

In other summers there had been trifling incidents. A scarecrow was burnt. Excrement appeared on the Shrine at the cliffs. A pair of youths from the village went to the nomads' camp for a dare: both returned badly beaten and unwilling to talk. Nets had been stolen from the river; a coracle dragged downstream and left wrecked. A beacon fire, set up on the cliffs for the mid-summer festival, was prematurely burnt and the ashes thrown about.

But this year, in this strange summer, the nomads had been here longer, and there had been many more such incidents. Overshadowing them all was the drought.

Sturmer had gone to the Shrine, where the word of Gauhm was breathed. She told him in a dream of Tsoaul and his new onslaught. The drought was the nomads' work: obeying Tsoaul, they had seized the advantage of the dry winter and spring, and by their incantations had awoken Aih the Spirit of the Heavens. Tsoaul had tried to persuade Aih to combine with him, that both might overcome Gauhm. Aih had refused, but said that during the contest he would not intervene. This had left the Forest Spirit alone, goaded by the nomads into greater and greater feats. But in time Tsoaul would overreach and exhaust himself, and then Gauhm would collect her victory. The villagers were not to interfere: to meddle would upset Aih, and then the rain, which was under his control, would never come again.

Sturmer had explained all this in detail, standing on the steps of the Meeting House. It had done little to help. Was he not head man? Was he not supposed to be in Gauhm's favor, her priest, her chosen one? Surely if he were a better man the spirits could be won over, persuaded to end the drought.

Sturmer sensed that Groden might try to use the situation for his own ends. Everything depended on the drought. If it went on much longer, Sturmer's real troubles would begin.

He rose without disturbing his wife and pushed aside the flap of leather at the doorway. His eyes painfully adjusted to the light: the sun was already hot, the sky a white glare only two hours after dawn.

The previous afternoon there had been cloud, and the hope of rain; toward nightfall the air became very close and sultry, with thunder heard far away on the hills. It had seemed as if it must rain, but by dawn the clouds had gone and the emptiness returned.

Everything in the village seemed dusty and old, all the life baked out of it by six weeks of total drought. Since the longest day, over a month ago, the heat had intensified so that even the nights were unbearable. Most of the village had taken to sleeping out of doors, on the stones by the thresholds to their houses. There was even talk of sleeping on the beach, but no one dared to leave the palisade at night.

The water in Sturmer's washing tub was warm and the color of clay. Bits of straw floated on the surface. He bent and held his head submerged for a few seconds before straightening up, expelling spray and wiping his eyes. It was then that he noticed a party of people among the buildings, coming toward him, and for a moment, in spite of the sun on his body, and for no reason that he could understand, he felt cold.

They were walking slowly. In front was Hernou, Groden's woman, slender and dark, with gray eyes in an intelligent face, her tumble of lustrous black hair drawn back and held by a wooden brooch. Once Sturmer had slept with hr; she was only a few years his junior, much older than Groden, to whom she had borne a dead baby in the winter. She and Groden lived in a house by themselves, rather further from the Meeting House than their status and their ambition seemed to warrant.

Behind her came old men, women, some of the older children: twelve people in all. Sturmer folded his arms and stood with his body weighted on one side; he remained silent as the deputation stopped. Hernou looked up at him.

"Look what the nomads have done."

She was holding out a dead dog for his inspection. Its jaws gaped, the side of the top lip folded back and glued to the gums by a frothy crust of dried saliva. A brown trickle of blood had caked hard on the fur from the nostril to the eye. Otherwise there was no sign of the damage done inside the dog's head by the hazel-shafted arrow, tipped with flint and flighted with mottled quail feathers, that slickly and with tremendous power had burst the animal's eye and tunneled through bone, brain and muscle to come to lodge on the inside of the lower jaw.

With the tips of three fingers he stroked the quail feathers, making the dog's head move slightly against Hernou's wrist.

"The arrow need not be theirs."

"The dog is Uli—my husband's dog."

Sturmer acknowledged it.

An old man spoke up. "What do they seek by this?"

"Tsoaul is getting stronger every day," another said.

"They attack and we do nothing, we stand helpless."

"Aih must let us defend the village, if nothing else."

"We must do what was said by Groden in the Council."

"No!" Sturmer said angrily. "That was turned down by decision!"

"Decision? Whose decision? Yours?"

"Or Tsoaul's?"

Sturmer rubbed one forearm with the other hand. A suspicion was growing in his thoughts. "Where was the dog found?"

"On the Shrine path, by the ash tree."

"And when was it last seen?"

"Yesterday," Hernou said. "Yesterday night. We ate with Morfe and Deak. Groden threw it scraps."

"And afterward? Did you see Uli in the night?"

"I cannot say." She bent and placed the animal at Sturmer's feet. Its head lolled on one side. Rigor had not yet begun.

"It is newly dead," Sturmer observed. "This morning, early."

The dog had been shot either at very close range, or by an extremely accurate bowman. The arrow seemed to implicate the nomads, as did the place where the animal had been found, but something jarred, something was wrong. In all the past troubles with the nomads there had always been an explanation, however outlandish, for the things they had done. Sturmer might have understood had the dog been stolen, or even butchered and eaten. He might have understood had the dog represented any threat to the nomads or any conceivable symbol of trespass on what they regarded as exclusively theirs. But for the nomads wantonly to shoot an animal of any kind and leave it to be found, for them to indulge in casual and irrational killing

—that went against everything Sturmer had learned about the people in the forest and their attitude to life.

There was only one explanation. Now Sturmer knew why he had felt cold. He opened his mouth and heard himself speaking the words.

"Where is Groden?"

✢ 2 ✢

ZEME WAS THIRTEEN YEARS OLD, ONE OF THE CHILDREN who by miracle had survived, her open, questioning face partly obscured by the thick dark hair which fell across her shoulders in a shine, smelling clean from her morning swim. Like her sister Mirin she wore her hair loose. Her eyes were black, with a shy glance, the eyes of her ancestors. She loved the sunshine, this summer of perfect weather: for weeks there had been no rain, days on end filled with blue sky and light; and though she did not say it in words to herself, she loved the forest and the incredible plenty it so freely gave. The woodlands at this season seemed benign and calm, smiling on the nomads and the camp site, in graceful, patient acceptance as the preparations for the summer feast went on. To Zeme it was only natural that her sister should be the center of the feast, the first woman of the new tribe, the chief's daughter, mother of his grandson: Tagart's woman.

Today was feast day. Zeme had been looking for flowers since sunrise; they had made fun of her at the camp because they said she was jealous of Mirin, so before dawn she had left to find flowers for garlands which would show them how she really felt. She knew all the flowers, and which were right for each occasion. This morning she had found many appropriate kinds: clary, milfoil, vervain and a dozen others.

Her arms were full of them as she passed under the trees, returning to the camp. Her sister was in her mind, and Tagart, and the funny things he said; the way he pretended to be solemn and talked in a low voice and then he burst out laughing and he'd been joking all along. She thought about him as a brother, and the way he hunted, with traps and spears and arrows. Tagart was the best marksman in the tribe. He had the straightest eye and the strongest arm. He could even impale a snipe as it zigzagged up from some marshy path, or bring down a speeding teal over one of the meres at the winter camp. His bow was so strong that Zeme could only bend it an inch. And his arrows, which he made with a flint shaver, he polished with tallow and fletched with goose quills to make them run faster. Sometimes, when preparing for large quarry, Tagart used wolfsbane posion on his arrows, but he preferred more passive methods: he said that tracking was hard work. Tagart was an expert in strategy, in waiting. He knew precisely where to dig the pits with spikes in the bottom, where to place the beaters and fences in a drive, how to use the long soft ropes to make booby-traps and nooses that could suddenly hoist a stag from the ground and leave it dangling; he lived with the habits of the prey and could tell what they were going to do before they knew it themselves. Much, Zeme conceded to herself, he had learned from Cosk and the other elders, but now Tagart's word was always sought, his advice always listened to and acted on, his intelligence and inventiveness recognized for their constant part in keeping the tribe well fed and safe. Tagart had no fear of the aurochs, the wild oxen with their big horns; when they charged he merely seemed to dance round and round and they fell down dead. Nor had he any fear of the wild boars, nor the lynx, and he had no fear of the wolves, although he said it was wise to leave them in peace and they would do the same for you.

The only animals to avoid, Tagart said, were the brown bears. The bears were unpredictable, moody, and you were never to go near a bear or its cave, and never ever when there were young ones inside, because that made the bears fiercer than anything in the forest, or in the marshes, or along the white seashore.

Sometimes Zeme wished she could go out hunting with the men. It was unfair being a girl. Instead of hunting she had to go out with the women gathering plants. There was a lot to know. Even her mother, Sela, the chief's woman, said she was still learning and would be a pupil of the forest until the day she died. The women went out nearly every day with their hazel and osier baskets, collecting fruits, nuts, fungi, tubers, fleshy stems—whatever was in season. They knew the plants to pick for medicines that soothed pain and helped wounds heal. There were plants to know for dyes, for perfumes and essences, and for seasonings to add to meat and drink; plants to poison arrowheads and spears and spikes; plants to keep the shelters dry, to make a soft bed, to keep insects away; plants to burn for any kind of heat and flame; plants for charcoal, or carvings, or for making toys. Sela and the others had taught Zeme how to twist fibers into strings and ropes, how to peel bark, how to use plants to know where squirrels or jays had hidden their winter stores. The men had shown her how to read the ground by the grasses and sedges that grew there; whether the ground was wet and unfirm, dangerous to traverse; when there had been a fire, even years before; what animal or bird had fed or left its droppings there. And Zeme was learning, like the others, the plants for decoration and for favorable omens and the plants for happiness and long life.

She came to a stream she knew and walked beside it, allowing it to lead her back to the river and her father's camp.

The nomad party had been together in its present form since the early spring, when the large camp in the marshes broke up into smaller units, the families staying together or regrouping as changes in friendship and loyalties dictated. Before the first catkins the nomads were beginning to leave, some spreading north into the great river valleys, others moving westward along the hills, eastward toward the low coast, or, like Tagart's tribe, south over the downs to the chalk cliffs and the vast oak forest which every year seemed to suffer further incursions from the farming people of the south. These were a different breed from the nomads, only partly native, with ideas and blood imported from across the sea. In the west at Valdoe was the largest settlement of them Tagart had heard of: a prison filled with slaves, commanded by one man who had established an army to protect his trading empire along the coast and far inland. The nomads knew of Valdoe because many of them had been captured to work there; a handful had escaped and told stories at the winter camp. The tales were worse than the imagination could make. Yet the farmers were pleased to trade with Valdoe and tacitly to accept the protection it gave them from the foreign raiding parties that would otherwise cross the water whenever the weather allowed.

Tagart's party was led by Cosk—which meant an owl, from the silent way he moved—a man of forty who had led the Owl tribe for ten years or more. This summer the Cosks were forty-one people: nine couples with fourteen children between them, two old men and three women beyond child-bearing age, a woman whose husband had caught a fever and died, and three young men of marriageable age. Cosk and his wife Sela were without sons, but their eldest daughter had brought them a boy, now three years old.

His name was Balan. In twenty years, after Tagart, if he survived, he might be chief. But, before then, Tagart's time was coming. In the years since his wedding to Mirin his acknowledged place as natural successor to Cosk had slowly been confirmed, and now it was certain. To Tagart and Mirin had gone the honor of the summer feast, a celebration of the forest, of renewal and the future. The preparations had been going on for weeks. Young bison were allowed to survive their parents in the hunt and were brought back to camp alive to be tethered nearby until needed. Hares, trapped along the field edges, were kept in cages made of woven sallow; larks, lapwings, pipits, wheatears, nightingales, finches, and wagtails had been snared or limed or brought down by whirling lures and stoned with slingshots. In withy baskets in the water were frogs and newts, and writhing masses of fish: river trout, eels, mullet, perch, pike; and the skill of one boy, who seemed to have a gift for finding them, had bought in more than a hundred crayfish, which now crouched in baskets at the water's edge, their claws and feelers and eyes distorted by the ripples. Along the banks, in rows and racks and wrappers of leaves, were edible flowers: lime, elder, knapweek, hop, dog rose; roots of reed-mace, rampion, parsnip, water lily and flowering rush; stems of burdock and reed; leaves of dead-nettle, plantain, sorrel, comfrey, and nettle; hazelnuts and pignuts; and fruit: whitebeam, red currant, black currant, barberry, blackberry, raspberry, strawberry, sloe, crab apple, and cranberry. There were carved wooden boxes of beetles, lizards, caterpillars, shrews, voles, woodmice, and moles; hedgehogs tied by thongs to stakes; slabs of honeycomb taken from the hive; mints, thyme, fennel, and many other herbs; wooden and clay flasks of liquor steeped with crushed leaves of wormwood and cicely. From the beach and estuary the women had collected seaweed: dulse, kelp and bladderwrack; and shellfish in tubs of salt water: clams, cockles, winkles and scallops. It had taken a fortnight to prepare the feast, and to build a new shelter, and to find all the flowers and leaves for dressing the couple and the camp. Now, at midmorning, Emis and Varl were building up the cooking fires with hornbeam logs; the clay ovens were being prepared, and into them went joints of beef, fillets of hare and venison. The heat of the fires made faces red; across the flames, the air shimmered and made people unrecognizable, trees and branches swirl.

Those who had finished their duties were getting ready for the ceremony, with dyes and pastes and special costumes which after the ritual would be consigned to flame. They wore leather and fur striped and studded, or tasseled and plumed in all colors, especially gray and brown and white. Blue streaks and chevrons on faces and backs, applied with meadowsweet and dog's mercury dye mixed with fat, were displayed by those sharing Tagart's blood, for he was derived from Waterfall people; Mirin and her family were decorated with ash-gray and black, with black and white capes and bunches of owl quills at elbow and knee.

Cosk, the chief, was dressed in a long cloak of owl feathers fixed to deerskin in exact rows that formed patterns in various ways: diagonals, rings, zigzags, verticals, stippled and mottled effects which had taken many hours of work to get right. He carried a carved and stained ceremonial mace, predominantly black with a crest of black feathers, which tapered and continued halfway down its length. Chalk-dust had been rubbed into his hair and beard, and all his skin painted white. He wore a beaked mask made of owl feathers, with tall plumes and a shaggy ruff that extended across his shoulders and blended with the cloak, and feathered footwear with three toes before and a spur behind, taloned like the feet of an owl; oxhide shinguards with the hair left on, dyed and patterned with angular streaks like those on an owl's legs; and a broad leather kirtle, white, radially marked from the belt with lines of dark-brown, ash, and black.

The others were dressed, some almost as elaborately, according to their family and tribe.

One by one they were emerging in the sunshine.

Groden halted, half turning and slightly raising his hand.

It was hot. Even under the green gloom of the trees the air felt stifling and oppressive. Ragged sunlight fell through the high canopy of leaves, sending coin-sized spots of light to the bracken and brambles on the forest floor. A blackbird turned over litter, making a furtive rustling sound. The silence was almost complete. No birds sang: the summer molt had begun.

The oaks here were old and massive. Great gnarled boughs turned this way and that. Here and there in the distance a tree had crashed, and in the space so formed saplings were thrusting upward, greedy for the light. Their roots spread widely, wherever they could, worming through the soil, in places coming to the sides of a stream as it purled through the trees toward the river.

Groden listened carefully. He was twenty-two, lean and tall, with coarse swarthy features and blue eyes as cold as a gull's. He shaved his face, not just from vanity, but because he wished to mark himself out; he meant to be head man one day. Helped and advised by Hernou, he was already a voice in the Council.

He turned and looked at the others, young men like himself: his friends Morfe, Deak, Feno, and Parn. They had covered more than two miles from the village and were far from the usual pathways, much deeper into the forest than anyone ventured in summer when the nomads were about.

"Do you hear anything?" Feno said.

Groden shook his head. The others were waiting, waiting for him to tell them what to do.

"We're too far into thc trees, Groden," Parn said. "I think we should go back. If we go on we'll come to their camp."

"Parn's right," said Deak.

Morfe grinned, white teeth against his beard and the tan of his skin. "If you're scared, go home to your mothers."

"It's not that. You know it's not that."

"Keep a still tongue then."

Groden treated Parn and Deak to a moment's glance. "We go on," he said.

"Your hound is dead, Groden," Parn said, "and we know how you feel. But do you want our corpses added to Uli's on the Dead Ground? We're too close to the river. We've seen none of them. Let's go back."

"We are only five," Feno said. "If they catch us we'll have no chance."

"Cowards," Morfe said. "You talk like old women."

"Come with me, or go back," said Groden indifferently.

Parn and Feno and Deak looked at each other. They all knew that Sturmer would not last for ever. The question was—how important was this moment? It was impossible to tell from Groden's face. He kept his thoughts locked up; they came out only in actions. By then it might be too late to get back into his favor.

"Down there," Morfe hissed. "Something moving."

"By the stream," Groden said, in answer to Feno's questioning glance.

They watched. Coming between the trees, now visible, now obscured by piles of overtowering bracken, in and out of the sunlight, a small figure was following the line of the stream, a child, a young girl dressed in skins. She could not have been more than thirteen. In her arms she carried a bulky bundle of plants, stems and leaves and flowers of many colors.

"One of the nomads," Feno whispered.

"Get behind her," Groden told Deak. "Parn, Feno, go ahead and close in. Morfe, across there."

"What do you mean to do?" Feno demanded.

He was ignored. With Morfe at his side, Groden was already striding through the bracken, moving downhill to head the child off. For a moment the others hesitated, and they too set off as directed. The girl was less than two hundred paces away. A blackbird shrilled its alarm call: the child looked up, her face changing to consternation as she saw them coming. She faltered in her step . . . looked from side to side . . . and the bundle of plants tumbled piecemeal from her hands. Some of the flowers fell in the stream and the current started bearing them away.

Groden and Morfe were running now. The child moved a few paces along the bank, saw Feno emerge and block her path, turned to go the other way, only to see Deak coming from behind.

Groden was beside her on the bank. Morfe at her rear had grasped her shoulders, and before she could scream his sweaty palm was clamped across her mouth.

Groden examined her closely. His eyes traveled down her body, lingering in places, returning to her face. There was no doubt of what she was. The nomads' camp was less than a mile away.

He nodded at Morfe, who took his hand from her mouth.

"Why did your people kill my Uli?"

The girl was too frightened to answer. Her black eyes darted from side to side; she was trembling with fear.

"Can't you speak?"

She opened her mouth. No words came.

"Why do you hate us? What do you hold against our village? Why do you plot with Tsoaul to withhold rain? Why do you blight our fields and make spells near our Shrine?"

"Let me ask," Morfe said. "I'll get it out of her."

Groden nodded. "In a while."

The girl was trying to speak.

"What was that?" Groden said.

"My . . . friends are coming."

He looked at his companions in turn. "She says her friends are coming."

"Let's take her back to the village now," Feno said. "She might be telling the truth."

"Which way are they coming?" Morfe said into her ear. "And are they all as pretty as you?" He tightened his grip across her throat. "Which way? Along the stream? From the ridge?"

"They—"

"Why take chances, Groden?" Feno argued. "Get her away from here."

"Which way?"

The girl cried out.

Groden watched, saw her skin, the shape of her thighs where they were exposed. He had originally planned to make a hostage of a nomad, to take one back to the village. But now he reached out and put his fingers to her neck, spread his hand and gently caressed the softness of her cheek.

"Which way do your friends come?" he asked her quietly.

"They—"

"Tell me."

"They've been hunting . . ."

"Hunting?" His fingers explored the back of her neck, winding themselves into her tresses. "Hunting what?"

"Boar. They're hunting boar."

He yanked viciously on her hair and she screamed.

"Truth," Groden said.

"Truth," Morfe said. "Tell us the truth."

"Why do your people hate us and wish us dead?"

The girl looked from face to face. She seemed unable to

answer. Morfe's hand slid down her belly, pressing her up against him. He bent his head; she turned and suddenly met his eye.

"Tell us the truth," Groden said. "That is all we ask."

"This one is no use to us," Morfe said, lifting her deerskin with his other hand. "She can only speak lies." Without warning he tried to rip away her dress and throw her to the ground, but before he knew what was happening she had sunk her teeth into his arm and the blood was welling out. She wriggled past Feno and leaped across the stream.

"Catch her!" Morfe shouted.

It did not take long.

✣ 3 ✣

THE SHRINE ON THE CLIFFS HAD BEEN MADE MANY YEARS before, a dome of chalk with a central alcove holding the stone altar slab on which rested the carved stone figure of Gauhm, Spirit of the Earth. Only the priest was allowed to come here freely; only he was allowed to pray at the Shrine and listen to Gauhm's word.

It was early afternoon, two hours after the Council meeting when everything had started to crumble in Sturmer's life. Below the clifftops, far below, herring gulls swooped across the veins of foam on the green water as it swelled and smacked around the rocks. Their cries and yelps rose up the cliff face. The air, hot and balmy, smelling of salt and iodine, felt soft on Sturmer's skin as he lay staring upward into the pink realms of his lids. He heard bees humming, and a faint breeze in the parched stems of grass, and the gulls against the waves below, and the sibilance of rock pipits as they flew from chalk ledge to ledge on the cliffs. From time to time a jackdaw called.

Sturmer was almost asleep, lingering on the border. Strange thoughts seemed normal. The sun on his face made him drowsy. He was enveloped by the sound of the bees, their transparent wings at work in the pink flowers of thrift.

He was thinking about what had been said at the Council. *Reckless to go into the forest, Groden. Reckless and stupid. But they killed Uli, Sturmer. They killed him and I was angry. No plan, nothing clear. Just angry. Yes, we were stupid, we were wrong.* But in his secret face, in the moment's flash of unconcealed triumph in Groden's eye, Sturmer saw that Groden knew. He saw that Groden was not stupid. He saw but he could not fathom the words to fashion an answer to turn the others from believing.

Morfe and Feno and Deak and Parn said the same.

Then they were coming out of the trees, Sturmer. Defending ourselves, only defending ourselves.

—But you killed one of them?

—We had to.

—Then you ran away?

—There was nothing else we could do. If you'd been there you would have seen it.

Groden's face; the circle of believers; the Meeting House closing in.

—You will bring disaster on us all!

—The nomads will call on Tsoaul to avenge the dead man!

Groden talking, reasoning. His hands outspread. Winning them over.

—We must act first and drive them out. For if we don't move quickly it is they who will strike first.

—But we are only farmers, Groden! They are killers!

—We outnumber them . . . if we can take them unawares . . .

In all the shouting was Sturmer's voice.

Now it was all over. Groden had killed one of the nomads. Whether his story was true did not matter . . . nothing mattered, not even that Gauhm had failed to appear to him as he lay here on the clifftop by the Shrine.

Perhaps she did not want to intervene.

He felt no excitement, no expectation. Gauhm was not coming.

Sturmer opened his eyes and raised himself on one elbow, looking at his fingers as they twiddled with a stem of grass. For a long time he gave his thoughts to his family and himself.

At last he brought his legs in to sit cross-legged, and then pushed on the outside edges of his feet, bringing himself in a single smooth motion to a standing position.

He addressed himself to the Shrine, bowing to kiss the edge of the altar slab, and spoke a soft prayer for the village, before setting off along the path and back to Burh.

Happiness had brought a marvelous radiance to Mirin's beauty. Her hair was black, almost blue, the locks wound into plaits which were held by a snood decorated with freshly picked speedwell. On Tagart's head was a garland of white roses woven among brambles. Little Balan, Tagart's son, stood between them, holding hands. He was only three: most of what was being said he could not understand, but he was aware that this was a day of importance, that he himself and his father and mother were important to the tribe.

In front of them, in the sunshine by the water, Cosk was speaking the words of the summer celebration. As he neared the conclusion Sela handed her daughter a bowl of essence of vervain and fenugreek. Mirin drank; Tagart drank; and leaving Balan they waded into the river. While the others watched they merged with the current and let the water wash away the white and ocher pigments from their skin, billowing downstream in a pale cloud.

Tagart took hold of Mirin's hands and looked into her eyes. Some of those on the bank were smiling, aware that Tagart was teasing them, keeping them waiting.

Giving no sign, he slowly kissed his woman, and as they kissed they sank beneath the surface.

An exultant shout went up. It was the signal to begin the feast.

Burh that evening was quiet, in the few hours before dark. There was no communal eating: everyone kept to his own hearth. In Sturmer's house the conversation was sparse and awkward. His children, three girls and a boy, sensed that it was better to say nothing. They ate their beans and oatcakes in silence.

Afterwards they were sent out to the river to clean the pots. Sturmer put his fingertips to his brow.

"I am afraid, Tamis."

"Do you have to go with them?" his wife said.

He nodded.

"Is there no way to stop them?"

"No."

"I know what you should do."

"Send him away?"

"Send him away or kill him. He plans your end. It is only fitting that you should plan his first."

Sturmer smiled ruefully. "He has the Council on his side."

"But Groden is a fool."

"That he is not."

She came and sat beside him. "Only a fool goes into the forest in summer."

"A fool or a schemer."

"What do you mean?"

"He shot his own hound."

"What?"

"Hernou knew it. I could see it in her face. Perhaps Morfe too."

"But why?"

"He wished to start trouble with the forest people. By blaming them he could make a start." He took her hand. "If he succeeds and brings rain I am finished."

"Do the others know about his hound?"

"Would they believe it? They want rain. Groden has promised it."

"You must tell them." She squeezed his arm. "Tell them. You are head man."

He snorted.

The sunset outside made everything blood-red. Pots and discarded tools threw long shadows; the river slid past the jetty, its surface in shade, dimpled by the beaks of the sand martins and swallows as they dipped in flight to drink. Swifts screamed among the barns and over the squat house roofs, chasing each other, climbing to altitudes where the sun was still hot on their wings; the coastline below stretched unwavering into the west, a thin ribbon of beach and cliff separating the sea from the dark shroud of the forest, which spread, faithful to the contours of the land, almost without pause to the very limits of vision.

⸸ 4 ⸸

THE FEAST FIRES HAD NEARLY BURNED OUT, EACH ONE A bed of embers that occasionally popped and sent a mote or a wisp of smoke into the warm night air. The dancing and singing had gone on long after dusk. Zeme was missed at first, a half-serious suggestion made to find her and bring her out of her sulking. Everyone knew she had a crush on Tagart; everyone knew she was jealous of Mirin. But as the celebrations went on the awareness of Zeme's absence receded, even in the minds of her parents, whose other daughter was the proud focus of attention. No one noticed just when the clouds began to roll across the sky to blot out the moon and stars, or when the first low thunder came. For some hours now it had been coming intermittently. The air was humid and close, the darkness almost complete, the hot and sticky night smothering the camp.

The remains of the summer feast lay strewn about: dishes, trampled flowers and garlands, bits of food. For once the rule had been relaxed and the task of clearing up deferred till morning. Any scavengers within ten miles would have been scared off by the music and shouting—at least, that was Cosk's theory. Only the usual guard, one man, had been posted.

Now it was three hours before dawn, and Tagart and Mirin were alone.

A brilliant blink lit up the camp and the humped shapes of the shelters, making black shadow and ice-white of all the colors, jabbing splinters and fragments of light on the leather wall of his shelter. Below him was the pallor of Mirin's face, the vague expanse of her hair. He felt her hands on his shoulder blades, pulling him back to her.

"It was only lightning."

The thunder came then, a double crash, followed by a long rumbling peal.

"The river sang differently," Tagart said. "I thought I heard movement."

"Just a fish."

"Fish?"

"A fish jumping. Nothing more."

Tagart strained his ears, all his senses taut. A wind was rising in the trees. Its hiss mingled with the river currents as rocks broke the surface, the liquid curling its way past twigs and debris, with the flow past stems and stalks, the small ripples against the muddy slope and the tiny beach of the bank nearest the camp.

The press of Mirin's body became more insistent. The bed was filled with her smell. Her mouth yielded, melding with his as her teeth opened. Tagart went further on the familiar exploration that had just begun, that now became more searching as he recognized the rhythm of her movements, the spread of her fingers on his back, her face against his. She spoke the syllables of his name as he kissed her eyes, her ears, her neck and throat.

Again.

She moaned as he broke away.

It was unmistakable. An unnatural sound in the water.

Tagart's shelter was new, built specially, and by chance the one nearest the river. It had no weapons inside, no food; merely a bed and flowers. Now he wished that he had heeded his intuition and left some weapons at the door.

"What is it?" she said.

"Keep quiet."

She tried to pull on his shoulders again. Tagart resisted. His mind was no longer in the shelter. It was outside, imagining the river, the banks, wondering what might be happening. He tried to remember everything as it had been at the end of the feast: the position of the fires, the debris on the ground. He pictured the shelters and their relationship with one another and the trees.

Another peal of thunder, closer than the first. Tagart rolled to one side, crushing scent from the honeysuckle blossoms. Mirin sat up and softly he put his fingers to her lips.

Something was in the river.

It was too late at night for any of the others to be up, except Braul, who had been posted as guard. Guards did not leave their posts. Camp rules were inflexible on that point; a guard was only to leave his post once the others had been awoken, even if his relief did not come.

Tagart raced through his mental catalogue of animals large enough to disturb the water like that, and of animals that might be interested in the camp and its occupants: Tagart reminded himself that there was food lying about. Wolves? Too small. Pigs? No. A bear? There was a brood den some miles southeast, with a mother and two cubs and a nursemaid female; but that was too far away. The he bear? He was probably at large somewhere in this part of the forest, though as yet the tribe had encountered no definite sign of him. Was it the lone male in the river?

Tagart crawled to the entrance and looked out. He saw the feeble glow of the feast fires, and above them the faint distinction between sky and forest. All else was darkness.

If not a bear, then what? A man. Another tribe might have arrived in the region. But they would advance openly and exchange news, share a meal, not come in stealth by night. An outcast? Sometimes offenders were banished from a group. Such men lived the best they could, stealing when it suited them.

A bear, then, or an outcast from some other tribe.

A shape moved across the glow of the nearest fire, too quickly for Tagart to glean any information from the silhouette. He felt his ribs contract with fear. His hands became fists and slowly he revised the disposition of his limbs, ready to move. His heart was pounding and his eyes were wide. He wondered whether to alert Braul, and decided against it. Braul was certainly already aware of the newcomer's presence. To call out might lose them what small advantage they had.

At the crack of a twig some yards off to the right, Tagart jerked his head in that direction, staring hard into the darkness for some scrap of vision. None came. And then another shadow passed in front of the fire, and another, and another. A fourth, a fifth, and shadows were passing in front of all the fires. A wooden bowl was inadvertently kicked. It scraped and slithered into the ashes. Licking flames leaped at once. Tagart saw a reddish glow on legs bound with fur and thongs. An instant later a sheet of lightning lit the sky and the full extent of what was happening in the camp lay revealed.

"Braul!" Tagart shouted, coming out of the shelter unarmed, at a run, cursing the fact that he was naked, cursing everything that had conspired to bring this about.

As the thunder came he reached the nearest man, whose image he had glimpsed in the lightning and retained. He jabbed with straight fingers at where eyes should be. There was a squeal. Tagart gripped a handful of beard and tore it upward and back; he brought his left arm in low, stealing balance by scooping behind the knees. As the man went down Tagart's punch missed aim and plowed up into the solar plexus. He brought his heel up and to the side and rammed it into the screaming face. The jaw broke with a snap like an old branch.

Tagart reached down and armed himself with the fallen mattock, aware of something happening behind. The mattock blade hummed through the air as he spun round, legs flexed. The shock of the blade striking home numbed his hand and forearms, the impact running up the haft from the dead thump of the blade; and there was no time for a scream, or even a gasp: a body in which there would be no more life brought down the ruined head and hit the ground.

On all sides Tagart was reacting to shapes and faces, kicking and lashing out with the mattock, sometimes warding off a blow with his forearm. Any limb that was not his own could be attacked. The farmers, for that they were, were hampered by darkness and confusion. They were clumsy fighters. Frequently Tagart sensed that they had hit one of their own. He heard screaming and smelled the rush of blood, their protests and imprecations in his ears. He had been fighting now for twenty seconds. He marveled that he had not been hit. Again and again he connected with faces, eyes, genitals, kneecaps, in a frenzy to disable as many as he could before the blow that would be his end. The feast fires, disturbed by the throng of men, flared as the embers came to life, outlining at ground level the tangle of arms and legs and waving weapons. Tagart saw the glint of saliva and a pair of terrified eyes, which involuntarily closed just as the mattock blade struck home again, a stone cleaver powered by the whole swing and thrust of his strength; in a vile spray the blade and a section of the handle broke off, spun into the air, were lost. He trod on and seized a digging-stick, a heavy staff wedged into a ring of granite for weight, which, wielded like a sledgehammer, sent down man after man. He became aware of a fresh attack from the side. He raised the point of the staff and hooked it into the oncomer's armpit. Tagart braced, hoisted, and the farmer sailed into the air.

Now the camp was coming alive. Now the men were pouring from their shelters, armed with clubs and spears. Cries of pain and surprise greeted them. Behind Tagart one of the shelters caught light, engulfed by flame from a blazing brand, casting more glow in which he could see. Other shelters were being fired, beside him, by the river, on the far edge near the forest, everywhere. The camp was burning. Tagart saw children running. He saw hair and clothes on fire, small bodies rolling over and over again in the dust.

He saw Balan. It was Balan, falling, and over him a man with a spear. As if casually, as if an afterthought, as if to be rid of an irritation the spear lanced down. In horror Tagart saw his son's last moment of life. And briefly he saw the farmer who had done it: a man as tall and wild as Tagart himself, a man with no beard.

Directly overhead the storm broke with a flaring crackle

of lightning and an instantaneous explosion of thunder so loud that it left a ringing in Tagart's ears. One of the tall beeches across the river had been hit and was on fire.

The beardless man appeared again, behind Tagart this time. He had the advantage. Just in time Tagart dodged the spear thrust: the point buried itself in the ground. In the sudden torrent of sparkling rain Tagart fell backward, rolling into sedges to one side, and snatched at ankles as the other man went past. The other man lost balance and fell. Tagart sprang, landing badly, and in an instant was on his back and the beardless man's hands were at his neck, encircling, strangling, the thumbs pressing into his throat. Tagart was choking. His eyes bulged. There was froth on his lips. The beardless man squeezed harder, his face wet and orange in the flames, his hair dripping rain and hanging forward.

Tagart brought his knee up and into the man's groin; he let go at once but doubled his fists and smashed a blow into Tagart's face. Tagart brought his knee up again, and in agony the other man rolled away. But he was lifting his legs, one across the other, and too late Tagart realized that his neck was between the ankles. Tagart's feet left the ground. With an emptiness in his stomach he saw the camp turn over; and he was coming down in the cold shock of the river, in the mud by the bank.

He watched the other man getting up, coming for him, wiping a hand across his mouth, and for a strange moment Tagart held the cold blue eyes with his own. But from another quarter he glimpsed something coming toward him, a weapon, too quick to see, and then his head was kicked a hundred miles sideways and he saw before him vast streamers of white starbursts, here and there red lights blinking, and his face was in the mud, the taste of it in his mouth. A roaring filled his brain. Long tunnels of pink hoops stretched away, gently descending into pink caverns where he wanted to run and hide. Above him the sky inverted, was sucked into a vortex that followed the tunnels down, leaving the blankness of a glaring white horizon, tinged with red as from behind spots soaked through, staining, hemorrhaging, spreading, sponging up his life as the redness dripped and became a trickle, a flow, a pouring race that rushed along the tunnel walls, carrying him before it. He could no longer breathe. His lungs were clamped flat, going under, arms helpless, borne along and downward at avalanche speed. He opened his eyes and saw only crimson. The crimson darkened and the roar grew louder, many voices in the storm, and in the emptiness beneath him Tagart knew he was going to die. He knew he was going to die even as he struggled in the torrent like a wet insect doomed and drowning, but he was fighting, fighting to the end, swamped by the blackness and engulfed by its pressure as the roaring became louder and louder, a roaring too loud to bear.

The river had carried him a little way. He knew it could not be far, because he could hear voices, and when he looked up he saw faint firelight on the stems and drooping leaves of the sedges of the bank. His face was close to them: his eyes tried to focus, but would not.

He spoke to Mirin. She would not answer. He felt the rain on his body, the river lapping at his skin. He tasted the water and the slime of the bottom. Mirin lay on a bed of flowers. The honeysuckle twined about the white skin of her wrists and ankles, her hair had been spread out on a pillow of ferns, and she was smiling.

The rain was falling steadily, less fiercely than before,

hissing into the fires. Tagart's hands found purchase and he began to drag himself further out of the water and a little way up the bank.

The effort was too great. He saw men going from place to place, turning over corpses with their feet. He saw axes and hammers raised, twitching legs become still, moans silenced. The man with no beard was giving orders. Behind him the shelters burned, and Tagart watched them through the sedges, moving against the glow. It was a long time before he realized that some of the women had been spared. Voices were raised in laughter and jeering. He saw Sela stripped naked and made to kneel.

Tagart tried to raise his head further, staring at what was happening. He was lying face down, his legs in the water. It pained him to keep his head up. The pain spread into his back as he watched them, along his spine and into his legs, becoming excruciating; but he forgot it as he saw Sela thrown sideways, and behind her, being brought forward, he saw Mirin. The beardless man shouted something and there was laughter. He pulled her to the ground and then he was on top of her, thrusting at her. She lay limp as he got up and another took his place.

Tagart watched the sedges. They were orange and black, curved and weaving with each other under the impact of the rain. He could not follow the beauty of their patterns; too many raindrops were falling.

He was drifting now, away from the screams of a voice he thought he knew, away from the shouting and laughter, drifting deeper, toward the center where he could not see them, where he could not hear them, where what they were doing to his wife would not be true.

5

THREE HOURS AFTER FIRST LIGHT, TWO HOURS AFTER crawling from the sedges and onto firm ground, he arrived at a position overlooking the village.

He was familiar with its appearance, in keeping with a general knowledge of the terrain near the camp site, but he lacked the detailed information that only a thorough inspection could provide.

He was at the very edge of the forest, looking down from the top of an escarpment which abutted the village on its east side. Rain-flattened grass clothed the slope, with oak bushes and clumps of blackthorn which would provide good cover for an unseen approach. This, he had already decided, was the way he would come when he wanted to get into the village. At the bottom of the escarpment, where the gradient eased, were a few anthills of varying age. These too would provide cover. Beyond them, a patch of nettles and a thicket of briers and blackberry canes grew up against the structure of the palisade. This was the height of two men, a fence of stout logs buttressed behind with log struts. It enclosed the whole of the village, including several hundred yards of the river; the tops of the logs were sharpened to points. Without equipment it looked impossible to climb.

Tagart shut his eyes. His head ached very badly and the taste of vomit was still in his mouth. The back of his forearm was a mass of congealed blood: he had wound strips of soft leather from elbow to wrist. A dull pain filled his neck and left shoulder. One of his ribs felt as if it might be broken.

Somehow they had spared him. When he awoke he found himself lying in the river, half in the vegetation of its bank. They must have taken him for dead; or, more likely, missed him altogether.

He allowed his face to rest in the wet, musty grass. His clothing was drenched and heavy; the leather glistened and bubbled where it creased as he moved. He groaned and let the ground receive the weight of his body, letting gravity take each muscle. Even though his eyes were tightly shut he could not stop seeing Zeme. They had raped her too. He had found her body by chance, not long after he had dragged himself from the riverbank and left the camp behind. He jumped into the stream and took her up in his arms. He did not know which way to turn with her.

Tagart jerked his head up and opened his eyes. Had he fallen asleep then? Had any time passed? The village looked the same. The rain was keeping them indoors, sheeting across the compound, drumming and splashing on the house roofs. To the southwest, over the sea, occasional bolts and forks of lightning danced. The wind was driving fast paler cloud below the cumulus, gusting and howling and bending the trees behind him.

He pulled his tunic closer to his neck. His hair was soaked and drops of water trickled from the tip of his nose, leaving a salty taste on his lips.

For a long time he lay studying the village. The houses seemed to have been built at random, arranged haphazardly, relying for defense on the palisade. The single thoroughfare was an extension of their path from the shrine on the cliffs. It passed through a gate, now closed, and widened into a rough oval bordered by a huddle of most of the thirty-three dwelling houses. Thirty-three: that meant between a hundred and eighty and two hundred people. The houses were tall, with conical roofs and narrow windows, built of timber and blocks of stone, with pavements to the front where they faced the oval. There were five larger buildings: a barn, bakery, threshing shed, and granary; the fifth was a Meeting House of the type he had seen in some of the more prosperous villages farther east: twice the height of the houses, long and broad, with a peaked roof and a wide doorway with a porch, from which a flight of plank steps led down to the village compound. The walls were of timber, faced with wattle and daub to keep out the weather. The floor was raised from the ground on massive oak piles about chest high. On the right of the Meeting House stood the barn and the bakery; on the left, the threshing shed and granary; behind them flowed the river. Between the granary and the palisade were two circular pits which Tagart took to be silos.

Now and then he heard a snatch of music and chanting, carried faintly on the wind, and it seemed to be coming from the Meeting House. He could see people inside.

The thoroughfare resumed its course between the Meeting House and the threshing shed, ran down to and crossed the river by means of a wooden bridge, built a little way downstream where presumably the bed was more suited to supporting the piers: nearer the village, next to the Meeting House, the path ran beside the riverbank, littered with upturned coracles and piles of nets. There was a landing stage, and a larger coracle tied to it riding the stream.

On the other side of the bridge the path left the palisade by another gate and disappeared westward into the fields. Much of the valley had been dug for cultivation, almost as far as the western slope, and southward a long way toward the sea. A strip of heath remained between the fields and the beach, and more sparsely along the mouth of the river where it widened into a small estuary with a few shingly islets. Northward the land had been cleared for half a mile, mainly on level ground by the river, but also on the north-eastern slope, where a large barley field had been made to catch the sun, or to escape winter floods.

The fields ended; the forest resumed. The line of trees snaked behind the barley field, south to the village and the escarpment, and then downhill, beside the river to the sea. East of the village the forest rose steeply, over the hill and toward the cliffs.

Tagart took his flint knife in hand and began the slow crawl down the escarpment.

At the bottom he broke from cover and with a crouching gait ran the fifteen paces to the palisade. Keeping it close by his righthand side he set off to circle the village.

Whoever had built the palisade had been serious in his intention not to let anyone in. It rose above Tagart, the tree trunks fitted tightly together, shaved at the top to slanting points. The gaps for the most part had been plugged with wedges and slivers of wood, rammed home and plastered with mud and clay. A few chinks remained. Through one of these Tagart had a partial view of the nearest house. He pressed his face to the rough bark. Water was cascading from the roof, splashing against the stone, soaking and making dark the already waterlogged timbers.

He went on until he came to the east gate. This was fitted with a heavy door, opening outwards on three hinges, secured by two great bars. Like the rest of the palisade it was topped by spikes. At ground level there was a gap of a hand's width, slightly more in the middle of the path where the passage of feet had worn a way; and now after some hours of rain the path was turning to mud.

The palisade continued, curving along the south side of the village, down the bank and into the river, the only concession to the water being the wider spacing of the logs; on the other bank it curved to the right and ran beside the river, enclosing a strip of ground ten yards wide. Now the palisade ran arrow-straight for a quarter of a mile, turned back into the river, crossed it, and, following the rise and fall in the ground, looped back to the escarpment and the east gate.

Tagart put his feet into the mass of sedge and yellow cress and went down the bank, let himself into the water. It was deep here, where the current behind the weir of logs had churned up and removed the bottom, and three steps from the bank Tagart was treading water. The river felt warm and soothing on his body, much warmer than the rain. For a while he rested, holding on to one of the logs. From the green and white stains on the palisade it could be seen that the level, although very low, was on the rise.

He dived and the noise of the rain abruptly stopped. Underwater he could see only green; he kicked against the current and felt the bulk of the palisade, slimy with weed. For a second his fingers were where the logs entered the river bed, before he was forced to surface for air. It seemed that the gaps between the logs were the same above and below the water: the wood had rotted hardly at all. He dived again and managed to explore more of the gaps. None was more than a hand's width. After many dives he satisfied himself that there could be no access here. He pulled himself from the water and climbed the far bank.

It was not going to be so easy. He stood shivering in the shelter of the palisade. His arm was bleeding again. He held it up and saw the trickle of blood across his palm, running down the backs of his fingers.

He shook his head angrily and continued along the base of the palisade, still keeping it on his right. Through gaps he could see the river, and beyond it the silos, threshing shed, and granary. To the left of them, a little way ahead, was the bridge, and, in line with it from this angle, the Meeting House. The music had grown more distinct. At one of the windows in the side wall he could clearly see signs of activity within.

A man staggered out onto the porch, his hands across his face, and fell headlong down the steps. Tagart craned his neck, trying to see. A moment later two middle-aged women, both naked, followed him from the doorway. They stooped and seemed to berate the fallen man. He lay face down in the mud, not moving, scarcely even breathing. Presently the women, after discussion, started shaking him by the shoulders, trying to make him get up, without success. The shorter woman went back inside and returned with a third. All three took hold of the man and carried him up the steps.

Still there was no sign of movement elsewhere in the village, no children, and no dogs.

He set off again. The second gate was much like the first, with a narrow space at the bottom—too narrow to get under. Tagart put his eye to the gap between gate and post. He could see no dogs, but something of more interest had caught his attention.

Beside the Meeting House, in a rank, had been laid the corpses from the previous night. There were twenty-six.

Then it struck him that the music inside the Meeting House might be something to do with the corpses, marking their transition from this life to the next. He knew little about the farmers' beliefs, beyond what he had heard in stories at the winter camp, but something of the sort seemed possible, for in the event it seemed their victory last night had not been without cost. Twenty-six. Tagart had not realized it was so many.

The Meeting House was less than a hundred yards away. He was standing at a point in the palisade almost opposite the jetty, from which, on a creaking painter, a large coracle rode the current. It could be of no use to him.

He continued along the base of the palisade, past the Meeting House, the barn and bakery, walking through the rain to the northern corner of the compound, where the palisade turned east and back across the river.

The water was shallower here, but still there was no gap wide enough to admit him. He came up for air again and again.

When he reached his starting point at the bottom of the escarpment he sank to the ground and sat with his head in his hands, overcome by weakness and despair. He felt giddy and ill. The pain in his chest was worse, sharp and stabbing; blood soaked steadily into the bandages on his arm. Every few seconds he fought back an overwhelming urge to vomit, not that anything remained in his stomach.

There were three ways to get past such an obstacle as a palisade. Going through was out of the question: he had no tools, except a knife and his bare hands. Going over involved too great a risk of being seen, and anyway he had no means of climbing. That left going under, which meant a tunnel, and that would take too long; and even if he did manage it he might well emerge in full view of the farmers. The gates? Were they the weak point? Or the river—perhaps he should try again, search more thoroughly.

The ladder-marks: he remembered the ladder-marks.

He stood up and walked past the east gate, making his way toward the river again. With his eye to the top of the palisade, he stopped three hundred yards on. Sure enough, there were the marks left by the harvesters' ladders on the spikes at the top. He found a gap and looked through it to confirm his position, moved four paces west, glanced over his shoulder and dropped to one knee. With his knife he scored out and rolled back a small trapdoor in the turf.

The soil was still relatively dry, black and loamy. He dug with his bare hands, scooping the earth back like a dog. The palisade extended the length of his arm below ground level, no more; his fingers found and felt the bottom of the log where the wood had been shaped by adze to a rough four-sided point. The timber, although treated by scorching, was beginning to rot: decay would be more likely in this part of the palisade. Tagart dug deeper, below the points, resting from time to time to flex his fingers and rub the cakes of dirt from his hands. His fingernails were clogged; his arms were aching, the left forearm crusted with earth and blood, but he was starting to uncover what he had hoped to find: a panel of sticks set vertically, which went down as far as he cared to dig. An hour later he had reached a depth of three feet, not really enough, but it would have to serve. As it was he had displaced a surprisingly large heap of earth which would have to be disposed of when he finished. Sitting at the edge of the hole, he drew back his legs and kicked at the panel of sticks. It caved in at once, releasing a sickly sweet smell of ensilage. Tagart kicked again, and again, compacting the crushed vegetation behind the panel, making a hollow which he enlarged with his hands, punching and pushing at the dirty yellow straw. When he had hollowed out a space twice his size he climbed outside once more and, using his feet, pushed the spoil into the hole. The earth had made the turf muddy: that couldn't be helped. He hoped the rain would wash most of it away and leave the trapdoor all but invisible. He had strengthened the trapdoor with a pair of sticks, so that it lay flat.

With a final glance around he climbed into the hole and pulled the flap of turf after him.

Sturmer abandoned the last vestiges of inhibition and gave himself entirely to the fly agaric. The fire of the fungus at the back of his throat was a flame that filled his brain and made it huge. Unwittingly his tongue slid from his mouth. A string of blackened saliva dribbled to his chest. He was not aware of the girl retching beside him, nor of the other people in the Meeting House. He was alone, swallowing the core of intense heat, fighting along the borders of self-control, tricking himself into ignoring the filthy taste, refusing to acknowledge nausea, making progress to the farther shore.

He reached it and in exultation he soared, borne upward

at tremendous speed: his body shrank to a point and vanished, leaving a tingling spot which glowed briefly and was gone.

He was master of the drug now, riding it, just as the others were riding it.

Occasionally someone screamed, clawing at his face, and fell sideways to lie unconscious on the floor. Others sat with heads hanging between their knees, while some shouted and argued and gesticulated. A few, those who like Sturmer were nearing the peak, sat entranced, rocking from side to side and quietly moaning. The women moved to and fro with bowls and drinking cups, waiting to collect urine from the men.

The fly agaric fungus, a toadstool with white stalk and gills and a scarlet cap, grew in many places around the village, and commonly in the forest where the ground was poor. It appeared suddenly in the middle of high summer after the rains, and went on until the end of the harvest or into autumn. The fungus was a gift from Gauhm. It enabled the bereaved to go part of the way toward the Far Land of the Dead. The drug was sacred. It could only be gathered after special prayer, and was to be prepared only by a priest. First the stalks were discarded and the caps left to dry in the sun, after which they were placed in the Agaric Casket, a beechwood box kept next to the altar in the Meeting House. Its lid and sides were carved with figures of visions achieved under the drug; inside, the shriveled caps were stored in layers of close-fitting trays, one lifting from the other. The trays were replenished each year at harvest.

The mode of using the agaric achieved the greatest possible distance along the road to the Far Land. The women, who were not allowed to eat it, took most of the taste from the caps by chewing them and rolling them between the hands. The pellets so formed were then given to the men to be swallowed immediately.

Ten pellets were enough to kill, and as one of the side effects of consumption was a raging desire to eat more, the women strictly rationed each man's supply; experienced users such as Sturmer could eat fully nine pellets. Younger men were limited to three or four.

The drug seemed to pass quickly through the system, and the urine of the men, though less potent than the pellets, was carefully saved and drunk by the women. Meanwhile the musicians played, drums and flutes and pipes making a dirge. They would not eat the drug till later; they sat cross-legged by the window, their heads and shoulders outlined against the gloomy morning light.

Groden shouted out. Hernou lay beside him. In a while she would be ready to drink again.

In total darkness Tagart groped upward, his fingers feeling for the mat of sticks. Below him his feet found difficulty in getting purchase. The ensilage yielded to his weight, and he knew that if he did not keep moving he would sink to the bottom and suffocate.

His hands closed on the sticks and he pulled himself up. He dug his toes high into the hole he had made and pushed; the combined effort brought his head through the mat and into daylight. Momentarily he hung there resting, looking out across the village.

The silo through which he had burrowed, and the one next to it, had been positioned at the base of the palisade so that the haymakers could drop their loads from ladders instead of hauling them around through the east gate. The silos were largely hidden from the Meeting House by the threshing shed and granary. To the left a patch of waste ground led to the river; to the right and ahead were the walls and precincts of a single dwelling house. Others were nearby, near enough to entail danger of being seen, but then wherever he chose to cross the palisade there would be some risk of that. In all, this was quite a good place from which to approach.

Tagart raised himself up and out, sprinted a few yards to the granary, and to the threshing shed, where he stood breathing heavily for several seconds before, in full view of the Meeting House porch, he ran with everything he had down to the river, launched from his right foot, blurred over the soggy stand of vegetation, and with scarcely a splash plunged into the water.

He reappeared upstream, a few yards nearer the Meeting House, ducked, and swam again. Under the joists of the bridge he came up and clung to the timbers, glad to be out of sight. The water here sounded loud in the hollow space under the bridge; the ripples of his movements echoed back to him. He waded into the shallows on the village side and lay flat on the mud, resting with his eyes shut, listening absently to the current.

A long time passed before Tagart felt able to emerge from the bridge, a long time before he felt safe even to stand up unaided. But at last some of his strength returned; his heartbeat slowed; the pain receded from his chest, neck, and shoulder. He raised himself to a sitting position and noticed that the dizziness was almost gone.

He came out from the bridge. Now he was ready to investigate the village.

* * *

Sturmer did not know how his eyes had become focused on the water falling from the Meeting House porch. Suddenly, he found it interesting. He studied the shapes, the crystals as they fell, the variegation of silver and blue, the exquisitely transparent drops. In them he saw distorted miniatures of the view outside, each one upside-down. He saw the forest on the escarpment, each branch, each tree, each leaf. On each leaf he saw the veins and lobes, the beads of water standing like silver spheres. The spheres were reflecting the forest, the sky, the village waiting below. With slow recognition Sturmer saw the form of a dark young man dressed in nomad's skins, pausing momentarily on the crest and looking down into the village with implacable eyes.

And then the crystal globe exploded in the boards of the porch, and Sturmer found himself searching desperately for another to take its place.

⸸ 6 ⸸

THEY HAD REMOVED ALMOST EVERYTHING OF VALUE from the camp. Fewer than a dozen coils of usable rope remained. All the furs, and all the better skins had gone, as had all the weapons except those stored in a shelter which, partly burnt, had not been properly searched. What food had not been carried away was spoiled and kicked into the mud. Baskets lay smashed, ovens and hearths destroyed. He had managed to find enough food for two or three meals, a pair of pigskin water bags, five bows and seven arrows, a spear, a bundle of lime-bark twine, some tallow, two bags of flints which he emptied into a single pouch, a deerskin, and seven goatskins. That was all. These things, and a heap of indifferent ropes, were all he had to exterminate an entire village.

Despite the pain in his chest he was walking quickly. No direct rain fell under the trees, but the air was damp and water dripped steadily from the branches. A green twilight made a suffusion of the wet bracken and rain-sodden foliage; the acrid smell of disturbed leaf-litter rose from the ground as he made his way uphill.

There was a great deal yet to do. He had already been to see the bears' den, and he had been back to the camp four times so far to salvage what he could and take it the three miles southeast, about a mile east of the village, to the place where he had established his lair: an old yew tree on the slope of the hill, among dense broad-leafed forest. The ground under the yew's spreading branches was dusty and, even after the storm, quite dry. By rearranging and cutting the boughs Tagart had fashioned a hiding place in the space round the trunk. Once inside he was able to close up the screen of branches, and his seclusion was complete.

The bears' den was about a mile to the north. Some days before, one of the best trackers in the tribe had returned with news of the spoor; he and Tagart and another followed the tracks into a part of the forest dominated by oak. One of the larger trees had fallen, and in the root-pit the she bear had burrowed out her den. Brief—and extremely cautious—observation revealed that two cubs were present, and a second, younger female which was acting as a nurse. As expected the male bear was not to be seen, though a few days later crunched mussels were found on the beach which were probably his leavings.

Today the bears were still in residence. Tagart had gone there and heard the cubs' cries. When he and the others had first visited the den the cubs were being suckled; now it looked as if the mother was beginning to wean them.

He was laden with ropes as he began returning to the yew tree once more. This would be the last trip from the camp.

From time to time as he walked he stopped and stood

for several minutes squinting up at the trees. Once in every ten or fifteen stops he left behind a coil of rope; frequently he changed his mind, picked up the rope, and went on. The way they would come along this path had to be carefully anticipated; he could not afford to waste rope. Perhaps he should have taken some from the village that morning after all. Those nets by the riverbank would have been handy . . . he shook his head. That would have cost him his only advantage: the fact that they did not know he was alive.

For the twentieth time he wondered what they had been doing in the Meeting House. He had spied on them through a chink in the wattle, unable to understand what was going on. The men intoxicated and seemingly deranged; the women vomiting and drinking urine; twenty-six corpses in a row outside. While watching he had for a moment entertained the idea of bursting in with his knife. Certainly he could have killed many before he himself was brought down, but not all the men were incapacitated, and it was not unknown for women to fight. Even so, it might have been worth doing, were it not that he had taken a vow. He was going to kill them all.

From the Meeting House he made his departure from the village, going out through the silo as he had come in; from there he had gone straight to the camp to begin work.

The last coil of rope was deposited; he returned to the yew tree. It was the end of the afternoon, toward an early dusk, and he had decided that there might be enough time to try for some deer. At this season the calves were about eight weeks old, large enough to accompany their mothers and the rest of the herd on the evening visits to the drinking place: the shallows a mile downstream from the camp. The shore, muddy and churned, showed a multitude of hoof-slots. Tagart approached upwind, and with his best bow slung across his back climbed into an ivy-hung oak. He chose a bough commanding a view of the muddy area. Sitting astride it he took three arrows, nocked one, and rested the lower end of the bow on his instep.

He composed himself to wait, quite comfortable, motionless. By a trick he disengaged his brain and with his body completely relaxed let time drift over him, trusting his senses to alert him when the deer came.

The river gurgled and splashed; rain was still falling relentlessly. He was aware of the background of happenings on the riverbank, which taken together meant that all was normal, all was well. A water vole came diffidently to the water, and with yellow teeth gnawed at a plant stem held in its hands. The wet made its fur spiky and dark; its eyes, black and shiny as berries, blinked as it paused in its feeding and sniffed for danger with head moving from side to side. No untoward scent registered: the vole went on nibbling. Presently it discarded the last of the stem and slipped into the water, swimming with nose up and feet furiously paddling, its tail streaming behind. Overhanging leaves hid it for a moment; it reappeared with a length of cowbane stem in its mouth, held crosswise like a dog with a stick. The water thrashed: the cowbane bobbed to the surface, and there was a glimpse of the languid white belly of a pike. The ripples merged with the current; the pike lazily finned back into deeper water. The vole did not reappear.

The birds were making an end to their day. Blackbirds chuckled in the undergrowth; a willow warbler called from the base of an alder. A cuckoo flew low over the water, swooping, hawklike, and came to perch, arresting its flight and swaying at the tip of one of the elder bushes lining the river.

As darkness approached the woodland grew quiet. The elder bushes, some with a few white flowers remaining, assumed odd shapes and seemed to expand and contract under Tagart's gaze. The light was failing. Four or five large bats were busy with the insects over the river; from time to time he thought he heard the snap of their jaws. He watched them on their black wings, weaving this way and that, stopping short, going on, in concert with the rain scouring every insect from the air.

Imperceptibly Tagart braced himself and opened his eyes more widely. He was alert again. The herd was coming.

They came forward, one by one appearing between the trees. The leading hind paused by the water as the rest of the herd passed by her: six hinds with calves, four antlered stags, one of which was already stripping its antlers of velvet; and a hummel, a hart without antlers. The hummel was the biggest animal in the herd. Next down was one of the stags, perhaps a ten-pointer, though the light was too bad to be sure.

The muscles on Tagart's arm began to bulge as he slowly drew back the arrow. With his thumbnail resting on the corner of his jawbone, he made allowance for the drop and fixed his eyes on the hummel's flank. He had chosen the surest spot, just behind the foreleg where there was least chance of missing a vital organ. The light was playing tricks. The movement of the deer as they drank seemed jerky, their forms and the foliage round them took on a grainy quality: Tagart readjusted his gaze and with it automatically his aim and his fingers were opening and the supple slap of the bowstring sent the point of the arrow on its intended way.

Before it had arrived he was nocking the next arrow and

taking aim at the ten-point stag. He ignored the hummel, concentrating on the second shot. It flew too high, missed the animals altogether, and he lost sight of it.

The deer were running now, in a frenzy scrambling to turn around and get out of the river. For a moment Tagart thought he had missed the hummel as well, but it was stuck, struggling after the others. They were leaving it behind. The hummel bellowed after them, its head strangely twisted, looking down at the mud. He had hit it in the neck. With growing dismay he wondered whether it could still run, whether he would have to follow it, perhaps for miles before weakness overcame either him or it. The hummel was free of the mud now, still bellowing, charging dementedly forward into an elder bush. It staggered wildly, and charged again, this time into a tree trunk. Its hind legs gave way and writhing it collapsed to the ground.

Tagart joyously came slithering down the oak and ran to the wounded beast. The arrow had been driven further into the neck by its fall; the eyes, showing white, stared open; its breath panted past a lolling tongue. Rich blood started to ooze from the nostrils and mouth.

He worked at speed. With his knife he opened the skin at the anus and along the back of the hind legs. Gripping the cut skin he worked the blade beneath, severing connective tissuc, and one by one allowed the hind legs to slip out to a quarter of their length, as far as their first joints, which he parted with a few skilled strokes. With more flints he cut through the rectum and behind the pizzle, and with the tail free began to roll the skin back along the body, turning the animal this way and that. The skin slipped free of the forelegs: he dragged it over the head, slit under the eyes and behind the lips, and stood clear.

Now, with the skin inside-out, he cut a strip from the

head and tied it very tightly round the neck, below the hole made by the point of the arrow. He turned the skin back, right side out, and went with it to the water, where he allowed a quantity to flow inside. The skin took on the greatest weight of water that he could carry: he slung it over his shoulder and set off uphill.

As he labored up the slope he decided to leave the meat where it was until morning. The bears might find the hummel: he did not care to compete with them in the dark. If anything remained in the morning he would try to get as much of it stored as he could. He did not know yet how long he would have to depend on his hiding place at the yew tree; he needed a larder.

The darkness was almost complete when he arrived with the hummelskin at a coil of rope he had deposited earlier in the day. Using his foot he picked up one end of the coil; spilling only a little water, he tied the rope to the open end of the skin, making use of the remaining bones in the hind legs, and throwing the free end of the rope over a branch just above head height, hoisted the skin and left it dangling. He squatted and held its palm beneath the neck. It seemed to be watertight.

Tagart stood up. As he did so a wave of giddiness came over him. He put a hand out to steady himself against the tree, eyes half closed, jaw tightly clenched, but it was no good: he felt his stomach twisting inside him, being wrung out; he fell against the bark, the spasms coming in agonizing waves. Tagart slid down the trunk to his knees, sick with grief and horror and exhaustion and shock. He was wet and cold, weak with uncontrollable shivering; the thought of food repelled him, but he would have to eat, and get rid of his clothes, soaked and heavy with the rain and the river. He needed comfort urgently: warmth, dry clothes, food. If he did not get them he would be unable to stop the long slide downhill and, as Cosk might say, the forest would have him.

He wiped his mouth, stood up, and turned toward the yew tree. The forest could have him later.

The vigil over the corpses on the Dead Ground began at nightfall. The village square had gone from dust to mud; the rain seemed to be settled now, falling steadily hour after hour. Twilight had come early. Dark figures, some bearing hooded lights on poles, crossed and recrossed the compound, converging on the Meeting House.

Inside was a blaze of light, brightest at the altar, where Sturmer was making ready for the prayers and the token sacrifice to Gauhm. The yellow glow filled the room to the rafters and threw shadows from beams and projections and the moving shapes of those on the floor. No one spoke. The only sounds were of the rain, and the spluttering wicks in the lamps at the altar and in the sconces around the walls. Sturmer stood over the stone slab; the kid struggled in the crook of his arm and lay still.

The Meeting House was full. At this time yesterday there had been a hundred and ninety-six people in the village; now there were a hundred and seventy. The injured numbered forty or fifty, some with only mild bruises, but others with serious wounds or broken limbs, which meant more deaths to come, and permanent cripples among those who survived. These men, like the widows and children of the dead, would be a heavy burden on the village.

It was a harsh price to pay for rain; Groden had been discredited, for a while at least. Sturmer decided not to accuse him of killing his own dog. There was no proof, and an unsubstantiated accusation might lose Sturmer some of the ground he had made.

He reverently placed the bowl of kid's blood on the altar-stone, spread wide his robes and raised his eyes in the chant. The others responded. Groden's bass voice, as feeling and grief-stricken as any in the room, was among them.

7

YEW WOOD MADE THE BEST BOWS, AND THE STRONGEST spears: it was magic, protected by the Sun who gave everything, guarded for the hunters by the Sun's disciple the Moon. To keep animals away the Moon had rendered the shoots and berries poisonous; thus yew trees always remained well filled and dark, a safe place to hide in overnight, as the Sun had intended. The thick branches kept out the rain; the resinous, soothing balm of the leaves lulled and refreshed; and where the shed needles fell they made a soft, dry bed.

Sleep came to Tagart eventually. He had lain awake for a long time, sometimes speaking words aloud, his face hot and puffy with weeping.

When he awoke it was still night. The forest was silent but for the rain. He sipped from one of the water bags, raising with himself and immediately rejecting the question of food; the previous evening he had tried to eat, but gagged and was unable to swallow anything. He felt no more able to eat now. Nevertheless, food remained his priority: he would go and see whether the hummel had been interfered with, cut whatever meat remained and bring it back to the yew where it was dry and the smell of food would less readily escape to bring unwelcome visitors. Possibly he would go to the trouble of finding some flat stones, build a hearth and risk a smokeless fire to cook it, risk a stray wisp being seen in the village. He changed his mind. Raw meat was just as nourishing, if less palatable.

He left the yew tree to relieve himself, came back and dressed in skins which had hardly dried overnight, and he gave his mind to the morning's work. Dawn showed gray above the trees as he set off for the hummel.

A little while later he was back with fifty pounds of venison, sliced into strips and hung from either end of a hazel pole. The hummel had been a big animal, fat and well fed, three times Tagart's weight: he had done well to kill it. A beast like that would have supplied the tribe for two days or more. But now he contented himself with the easy cuts and left the rest for the scavengers. One uncertainty had been resolved in his mind: he would not go hungry.

He finished tying the last strip of meat inside the yew. The rain had slackened slightly, strengthened, and slackened again. Each renewal of gusts dislodged a noisy shower of droplets. The wind had a cold edge; he found himself shivering again as he knelt down to sort through his meager supplies. From them he selected what he felt he would need, packed everything into his pouch and one of the goatskins, and started out.

He went first to the place where he had left the hummel's skin, dangling from a branch.

He was grateful for the fact that it had not leaked. It hung there, a grotesque bulge, the curves of the animal's chest parodied by the swell of water, its flanks and haunches tapered to a creased apex, stretched tight by the weight. The tree to which he had fixed it was just off the farmers' path from the village to their shrine. He had chosen the spot because of a lime tree near the path, a hundred and twenty feet tall, with an unobstructed drop from one of the limbs at a height of ninety feet or so. There were many such trees at various points along the path: what made this one suitable was the way the holly bushes grew below it. Not only did they cover both sides of the path, restricting its width, but there was a particularly stout plant—almost a tree—about twenty feet from the path and directly below the limb with the unobstructed drop.

Tagart set about this plant with his knife. First he stripped the branches from the stem and cut it to waist height, and with a new blade, sharpened the tip to a point. Just below the point he cut out a notch with its upper surface parallel to the ground, so that the holly stem looked like a harpoon with a single barb. From the discarded section of the stem he cut an identical harpoon: the two barbs fitted together, slotting into each other like two hands with bent fingers interlocked. Along the back of the free harpoon he scooped a longitudinal groove, deep enough to take the radius of his rope, which later he would need to bind on with twine, pulling every turn with all his strength, for the lashing would have to support the weight of the hummelskin filled with water.

But for the moment he slipped the bundle of twine into his tunic, selected a piece of tallow, and climbed the tree. He edged out along the limb: the ground was a long way below, his tools, the skins, seemed tiny. If he fell now he would be impaled neatly on the sharpened holly stem.

He fastened a piece of flint to one end of the twine and lowered it gently to the ground. The flint swung backward and forward interminably as he adjusted the position of the twine on the limb. After many attempts he found the point precisely above the holly stem, with the twine hanging still and the flint just touching the tip. He marked the place with his fingernail and let the rest of the twine drop down on the other side.

With his knife he grooved across the mark he had made; when satisfied with its depth he rubbed the groove with tallow, again and again to smother the sticky lime sap and make a practically frictionless surface. The purpose of the twine hanging on either side of the limb was to give a lead with which to pull over the rope. He placed the twine in the groove and descended to the ground.

Alone, without the aid of other hands, the next part of the operation was more difficult. There was too much water in the hummelskin. He emptied part of it out, into two goatskins. With twine and many knots he made the hummel's hind legs fast to the free end of the rope, and cutting it free from its overnight branch he hoisted the skin high into the lime, pulling hand-over-hand until the hind legs reached the groove.

He had judged it quite well: the weight of rope hanging down was a little greater than the weight of the skin; the rope didn't move as Tagart gingerly loosened his grip, and when he took his hands away altogether it merely eased slightly, pulling the skin upward and against the branch.

He pulled the dangling rope straight and held it against the holly stem, and to it lashed the second harpoon. This he fitted into its sister notch on the stem and temporarily bound the two together with a few turns of twine. The rest of the rope, below the second harpoon, amounted to some ten or twelve yards. He began to lead it toward the path.

The dead weight and its release were almost complete: he was ready to start work on the trigger device.

For this he needed two lengths of springy holly, one thrust into the ground at a shallow angle, and the other—which provided the power to work the release—a small sapling stripped and bent over in a loop, its tip shaped to hook into the tip of the first length, in principle like the interlocking barbs on the two harpoons of the release. Pressure on the first length would push it down, allowing the sapling to snap back, jerking with it a length of twine attached to the second harpoon. The two harpoons would then be pulled apart, allowing the hummelskin to fall.

Whoever had applied the pressure to the first length of holly would find the end of the rope—which Tagart was now tying into a noose with a sliding knot—closing about his ankle. The water-filled skin had ninety feet to fall, on to the holly stem, whereupon it would burst. The victim, by now hoisted some sixty or seventy feet into the air, and no longer counterbalanced by the weight of the water, would do the same.

He had to clear two or three branches and sprigs before the trigger cable was completely unobstructed; and he had difficulty with the trigger pedal, for the ground was so dry that it was no easy matter to drive it in. But finally he was satisfied, and he went about with leaves and handfuls of earth to camouflage the noose and the rest of the mechanism. By dragging a small log onto the path he guided the footsteps of his quarry; he roughly guessed at the length of stride, adjusted the position of the log, stood back, made another adjustment, trying to plant the footfall directly onto the trigger pedal, in the center of the hidden noose.

All that remained was to fill the hummelskin with water. This he did by making several trips to the river with his goatskins, climbing into the lime trees and carefully decanting the water into the larger skin. The two harpoons creaked under the weight, but the lashing held firm. Tagart undid the temporary turns of twine holding them together and, with a stick, prized the harpoons apart fraction by fraction until the notches overlapped by no more than a finger's width.

A final inspection, a check that he had left the minimum slack in the trigger cable, that everything was hidden from view, the cut wood disguised with earth, that the noose would not snag at the critical moment; and the trap was ready. Part of the drop of rope was on view, and so was the hummelskin, if anyone cared to look up, but he hoped it would not be noticed against the brown trunk.

The trap had taken a long time and a great deal of effort to make. He had never attempted one of his own before: normally there were others to lend a hand, three or four men to hoist the water-filled skin straight up to the branch and hold it there while the harpoon was lashed.

But, he had done it. He had done it alone, and as he stood looking at it some of his doubts began to dissolve. If he could make one trap successfully, he could make many, and if he could make many he would be well to achieve what he set out to do, which was, notwithstanding how long it took, to secure utterly the total destruction of the village.

He gathered up his belongings and set off for the next

tree. He had hidden the noose so well that he forcibly reminded himself where it was as he passed.

It would not do to tread on the trigger.

Tagart heard the clink of the mattock faintly on the wind and stood quite still, suddenly alert. He had just finished making a ladder, a kind of ramp fifteen feet long covered with brushwood, which he had left hidden at the top of the escarpment. Work had gone well during the day. The rain had stopped early in the afternoon, and now the sky was blue.

It came again. He had not been mistaken.

He was quite close to the fields here. The ground sloped down to the field edge, which he could just see in places where the trees allowed. The barley showed rich brown and gold, lit by a brilliant evening sunshine.

He changed direction, moving swiftly and silently from tree to tree, getting nearer the origin of the sound. His feet were noiseless: by intuition he avoided crackling twigs and beechmast husks, rustling leaves, branches that were dead and would snap if trodded on. He stopped to listen. The mattock clinks came singly, intermittently, as if one man, working none too enthusiastically on his own, were digging the ground, bending, digging again. Tagart moved to the very edge of the woods and looked out across the field. The user of the mattock could not be seen from this angle: the sound originated away to the left, hidden by an elbow of trees. To come upon him Tagart would have to walk across open ground, between the forest and a shallow dip in which men might be waiting.

He was immediately on his guard. It was too easy, too

near, and much too soon after the raid for him to find a man out alone.

Had he been seen the previous day in the village? Was that it? Did the farmers now realize that someone had survived, were they trying to lure him into the open? They would surely know the futility of chasing a nomad through the forest. Their only chance of killing him, of preventing word of the massacre spreading to other tribes, would be to bring him on to open ground and surround him.

Or was he overestimating them, attributing to them powers of cunning which they did not have? They were farmers, men who lived by grubbing the soil and slaughtering captive animals; not hunters, whose living depended on foresight and strategy. Were they capable of such a plan?

He did not know. He was very tired, of that he was certain, and when he tired he knew that judgments could be wrong. Everything in him urged him to go back into the safety of the deep forest, to feed himself and recuperate, to make more preparations before letting the farmers know that all was not to be well for them. He wanted to renew his supply of arrows and flints, establish another hiding place in case the yew were found, replenish his ropes, rig more traps, attend to more of the pitfalls the tribe had dug earlier in the season . . .

But he was only one man, and men were not meant to work in the forest alone. Every hour that passed increased his chances of being injured or falling sick with no one to tend him, or of being overpowered and eaten by some animal larger and stronger than himself. And, however many preparations he made, he knew he would never be fully satisfied, he knew he would always need just one more trap or another quiver of arrows to help even the appalling odds against him.

He turned and went back into the trees, as silent as before, moving in a curve calculated to come out of the woods more or less opposite the laborer and his mattock. As he went he slipped his knife inside his tunic and, forming a makeshift plan, tightened the drawstring at the top of his pouch.

He stood beside fluttering leaves of hazel and whitebeam. At his back was the forest, his world. Before him stretched the alien fields. And there, across the slope, was a stocky man working on his own.

Tagart stepped into the open. The man with the mattock looked up suspiciously.

Tagart set his face in a smile and went on.

"I come in friendship," he said.

PART TWO

1

"IT CANNOT BE TSOAUL," SAID VUDE, A GRANDFATHER with white hair and walnut-brown face and arms, one of the elders in the Council and a supporter of Sturmer. "It cannot be him. How can it when the nomads are all dead?" He turned his eyes again to the stone pointer, and to the mattock thrust by its haft into the ground beside it. The mattock looked like the one Gumis had taken the previous evening, and this was the place where Sturmer had told him to clear stones, but of Gumis himself there was no sign. He had not returned at nightfall, nor had he been seen at daybreak, which had come cloudy and cool, with pearly mists above the river and the rain-soaked fields.

When it was realized in the village that Gumis was truly missing a search party set out: Sturmer, Vude, Domack the Tool-mender, Merth, Tamben, and several others. They had gone first to the top barley field and were mystified to find the stone arrow pointing toward the forest.

“It cannot be Tsoaul,” said Vude for the fourth or fifth time, but his voice lacked conviction.

“See the ground,” said Meed, a small, swarthy man with rounded shoulders and a way of twisting his head sideways as he spoke. “Where is the struggle if Gumis was taken by force?”

Sturmer dropped to his haunches and minutely examined the soil near the arrow. The ground was too rough and stony to show much detail, but Meed’s suggestion seemed logical: if there had been a fight it would show. There was no sign of a fight. Hence Gumis had gone of his own free will. It did not occur to Sturmer that the tracks might have been doctored by an expert hand.

“There was no forcing done here,” he concluded. “We do not know why Gumis should have left his work, but he went in peace.” Sturmer stood up and allowed his gaze to follow the direction of the arrow. “He left this marker to show us where he had gone.”

“Tsoaul enticed him away!”

“Tsoaul made the marker!”

“That cannot be!” said Tamben, a man of twenty-seven, fair-haired and quiet, who had been coerced into taking part in the raid. “The nomads are all dead! How can dead men do his will?”

“Then explain why else he should go! There is no reason.”

“A game. He plays a trick on us to make us fearful.”

“If that is so he has already succeeded,” interjected Merth.

Sturmer bit his top lip. “Gumis does not play tricks; he has no mind for them. He is interested only in food and sleep. He has no time for anything else.”

“Could he have been carried off by some animal?”

"A bear," said Domack.

Sturmer rounded on him. "Did a bear make this marker?" he demanded, trying to keep the mounting panic out of his voice. "Did a bear post the mattock in the ground? Did a bear drag him off and leave no tracks?"

"Then it cannot be Tsoaul," Vude said calmly. "The bears are his servants, just like the nomads. The nomads are all dead; there are no tracks; it wasn't a bear. So Tsoaul was not involved. We are worrying for nothing."

"But Gumis is not here."

"He has been carried away and killed!"

"Tsoaul has acted to avenge the forest people!"

"No! Listen to me! Listen to me!" Sturmer raised high his arms and shouted over the others.

"He may have been taken by traders!"

"Taken to Valdoe and enslaved!"

"Would they have left a marker?" said Meed.

"Pointing in the wrong direction, just to confuse us!"

"Let Sturmer speak!"

Sturmer slowly rubbed his right forearm, moving his left hand up and down, something he did when nervous. He was glad that Groden was not here. That would have made a bad moment impossible.

Sturmer looked from face to face. There was no alternative. He would have to lie. Vude might have already guessed the truth, and one or two others, but he was counting on them to understand, to keep quiet, not to reveal to the others that a spirit need not necessarily work by agency, need not press bears or nomads into his service; that a spirit if outraged could become substantial and real and work directly on the world. Vude had told stories of his youth, of a day when Burh had been farther west, when the villagers witnessed Aih's descent from the sky like a ball of flame, like lightning in a ball no bigger than a man's head. He came into the compound and many of the villagers tried to touch him.

"My reasoning is this," Sturmer said. "First, the nomads are all dead. We made sure of that. Second, there are no tracks to show that Gumis struggled or was dragged away. Third, no animal could have done these things." He gestured at the mattock and at the lines of neatly arranged stones. "Nor," he said, looking directly at Vude, "could a spirit, which can act only by agency."

Vude was about to speak, but closed his mouth and gave an enlightened nod.

Sturmer continued. "It follows that a man made the marker, and it makes no sense to say that man was anyone but Gumis. If it were traders they would just take him. There would be no reason for them to leave a marker, and besides, we would see their tracks. If—and this is only to complete my reasoning—if Gumis was killed by one of us in the village, the murderer would not leave such clues."

The others started to protest. Sturmer cut them short.

"I say that Gumis made the marker. He heard or saw something in the forest, and went after it. To show us where, he left this marker, and to show us that it was not dangerous he left his weapon, the mattock, behind. Now, whatever he was following took him deeper into the trees than he had intended to go. He got lost. He is still lost. Unharmed, but lost. That is all. We must go after him and bring him back." He pointed at the sky. "It's cloudy. After nightfall and in cloud there is no direction in the forest. We'll find him somewhere walking in circles."

"Gumis is not our greatest thinker," said Domack.

The others seized on this explanation. They eagerly agreed, elaborating on Sturmer's theory, recalling past cases of villagers getting lost in the trees. Gumis might have seen a wounded deer and chased it; or he might have heard a strange bird calling and gone to find out what it was. A dozen similar suggestions were made.

"Whatever drew him into the forest, we will not find him by talking," Sturmer said. "We must follow the arrow and see where it leads."

In better humor the villagers set off. "We'll cut blazes on the trees to guide us back," Sturmer announced.

Vude fell in beside him. "You think it is Tsoaul," he said in a low voice.

"I hope I'm wrong."

"Will he act now, in the daytime like this?"

"I cannot say. He might. But what else can we do? We must try to find Gumis. He might just be lost as they believe."

Vude shook his head. "I have never known him to do anything on his own account. He would not follow a deer into the trees, even if it were already cooked and on a plate. And as for following a strange bird call, Gumis divides birds into two kinds: those that can be eaten, and those that cannot."

"I know that," Sturmer said.

"It may not be Tsoaul," Vude said quietly, and just when Sturmer was about to turn in question he added: "It may be Gauhm."

"Gauhm?"

"Groden and the others acted against her wishes. She has been belittled and denied. Twenty-six of the village, her people, are dead. More are dying even now. Do you think she will be pleased?"

Sturmer did not answer. Over his shoulder he called out,

"If we have not found him by noon we'll send back for help."

They reached the edge of the field. A broken whitebeam twig, where the trees began, showed where Gumis had entered the forest. Below it a few bramble leaves had been crushed.

"There," said Domack.

"What is it?"

The Tool-mender reached up and unhooked the talisman from the branch. He weighed it in the palm of his hand, the striped stone smooth against his skin. The talisman had been left dangling on a cord, in plain view at head height. Vude took it. "This is his," he said. "It was made for him by Chal's wife. He wore it always."

"His fortune stone," Tamben said. "I have one of the same." He brought it out of his jerkin and held it up for the others to see.

"Proof he was not taken by force," Sturmer said. "It's another sign to us, like the marker. I expect we'll find others. Come."

They moved forward, filing uphill, through the dense foliage of oak and hazel. It was obvious where someone had passed the night before, a swath of undergrowth crushed and broken down. A few paces on they found a shred of hare's skin, which someone said came from Gumis's cap. The shred, like the talisman before it, was suspended from a branch and clearly was meant to be noticed.

"Make the first blaze," Sturmer said.

They went on.

Even at this short distance from the fields it was easy to see how a man might find himself lost inside the wild tangle of vegetation, the unruly hazel, elder, and honeysuckle bushes pressing and twining from all sides, the brambles snagging at shins and forcing frequent detours which rapidly dulled the sense of direction. Above, the ponderous oaks crowded together, the leaves and branches intermingled and formed a dense barrier to all but the feeblest green light. Pigeons exploded from the treetops as the men pushed and hacked a way forward.

The ground leveled and dipped, rose again, and again began to fall. Still the crushed path led them on. They found more shreds of his cap, hung on branches like the first. More blazes were cut; soon nobody had any sense of north or south. It seemed they were moving away from the village, and generally downhill, but whether inland or toward the sea they could not tell; though as yet they had not crossed a regular pathway, only the narrow, well-defined courses of badger trails.

"Look here," Meed said, pointing to a long tatter of doeskin hanging in the fork of a rowan sapling.

"A piece of his jacket!"

Sturmer took down the strip of leather. "There is nothing to fear," he said as the men crowded round to examine it. The strip passed from hand to hand.

Vude said, "For Gumis to take off his jacket the prey must have been a stag at least."

"Or a beautiful wood-nymph."

"Perhaps it was her singing that lured him away."

"Should we go on, Sturmer?" said Domack with a wink. "Will she thank us if we find them?"

Sturmer smiled. "Let us see what else he has taken off."

Presently, in several places along the way, they came across the rest of his jacket, and then his beaver leggings torn into shreds. Their good humor was beginning to evaporate: the ground was sloping noticeably downward now, and a sinister change was coming over the woodland. The increasing dampness of the ground was reflected by the character of the trees, younger and less massive, oak giving away to oak mixed with birch, and in the undergrowth there was less holly, less hazel, but more elder. They were being drawn down into the valley, toward the river. They were being drawn toward the nomad's camp.

When they found the clogs, lying casually on the ground ten yards apart, Tamben and several others wanted Sturmer to send back to the village for help.

Sturmer refused. He told them again that there was nothing to fear, that they would doubtless find Gumis a little way ahead; probably dead drunk in the undergrowth with a pot of grain liquor stolen from the Meeting House. Privately, Sturmer could see no reason to endanger extra lives. If they were going to be attacked by a spirit better that a few should die than many; not that he seriously felt there was any real risk. The evil had been done the previous night.

For almost half a mile there was no further clue to the way Gumis had come, except for the crushed vegetation and broken twigs. They came to a stream and crossed it.

The stream marked a more profound change in the quality of the forest. The soil here was black. Alders lined the stream. Beyond it the woodland was mainly birch, with stands and thickets of willow. In places the ground seemed to have collapsed and there was standing water: stagnant pools covered by a bronzy scum over which clouds of gnats danced. The bird sounds were different. The ground was strewn with rotting logs, some half in the water; marsh gas was in the air. Sturmer, leading the way, broke through the old dead branches of willow, the noise of it filling the woods.

He stopped dead.

His eyes did not move.

For the moment he forgot the men behind him, forgot his feet slowly sinking into the boggy ground. He forgot everything. There was no past or future, only the present. Only the present in which the forest was a sepia blur, a background to the place ahead, framing it, the place where a man's five-fingered hand had been speared on a stick and the stick thrust upright into the ground, in plain and intended view.

Sturmer forced aside the last of the elder bushes and at the edge of the clearing stood looking out across the nomads' ruined campsite.

Tamben and Merth, despite his orders, had panicked and turned back, leaving only nine men to follow the trail that had been made of the organs of Gumis's body. Draped over branches or merely thrown down, the signs came at closer and closer intervals. Everyone knew they were being drawn toward the camp; those who were not already armed took up heavy branches and held them like clubs.

They had seen the smoke first, curling upward through the trees, a single hazy plume of blue woodsmoke which Sturmer could now see was coming from a cooking fire.

With a harsh chatter three magpies, white and green-black, rose from the riverbank and on short wings fluttered to safety. Simultaneously there was the sound of something falling, crashing through foliage to the ground. Sturmer looked up to see, on the highest branch of a tall oak, the uncertain wavering of a slim, mottled bird of prey as it flexed and unflexed its legs, leaning forward and backward, as if deciding whether to leave or stay. A moment later the kite opened its wings and with a plaintive cry was sailing away, over the treetops.

Sturmer turned his eyes back to the clearing. It seemed different by day, larger and more open than before, the surrounding trees farther away. The river had risen. For most of its length through the clearing it was fringed by vegetation, except on the bank nearest the shelters, which was of bare mud leading straight into the water like a beach.

Sturmer had not seen the final devastation of the camp; sickened, he had left when the last of the hunters was overpowered and clubbed down. He had felt no desire to participate in what Groden had planned for the surviving women. Leave no one alive, that was all he had said.

Little of the shelters remained intact: the skeletons of spars and frames, burnt black like charcoal; charred leather; scorched bedding which had escaped being consumed by flame. Broken baskets and other remnants of human occupation had been kicked here and there.

These things Groden had done. But he had not built the cooking fire.

The smoke issued from the middle of the camp; a small heap of sticks smoldered quietly under a spit with a joint of unidentifiable meat. The smell of it on the breeze was like pork. Seated round it, shoulder to shoulder, with eating bowls in their laps or by their feet, were thirty or forty people. Some held their heads erect, others were bowed to the ground. Their eyes looked dark and hollow, their cheeks sunken, their bodies mutilated and disfigured, the color of decay. They were sitting in a ring round the fire, at a feast. Above them buzzed a multitude of flies.

Domack screamed and ran past Sturmer into the open, brandishing his ax, and the others were running too, yelling and shouting, and Sturmer was among them. One of the feasters fell sideways and lay still. Sturmer raised his mattock and brought it down, opening dead flesh, hacking, slashing. The bodies rolled and yielded to every indignity, every blow, passively accepting, not disapproving, until under the blizzard of axes and clubs and mattocks the dead nomads had been mangled, destroyed, and completely rendered unrecognizable.

But even before they had finished Vude was shouting, pointing into the air and across the river.

On the far bank was the beech tree that had been struck by lightning in the storm. The heat of the strike had boiled the sap within, sundering the trunk from top to bottom; the foliage hung tattered, shriveled and scorched. Many of the boughs had been peeled of bark, giving the tree an odd skewbald appearance.

From one of these boughs a curious shape dangled, like a man but then not, slowly turning in the soft breeze, coming to rest, turning in the other direction. It had no hands, and its chest had been opened from throat to navel and roughly cobbled back with twine. One leg was missing below the knee, and with a rush of comprehension Sturmer knew the nature of the meat on the fire.

Domack climbed into the tree and worked his flint blade through the rope. The dummy thumped to the ground.

He had been skinned. Cleanly and expertly, he had been skinned. To give it bulk the skin had been stuffed with leaves and twigs; as it struck the ground they saw something moving in its chest, crawling and glistening brown. Ants were crawling out. They were boiling over the sides of his chest. An ants' nest had been put inside him. They were already everywhere, all over him, his body, in his nostrils, between the taut lips. The skull had been left in. The features of the face, though shrunken and changed, could be those of no one else.

It was Gumis.

2

NOT LONG AFTER THE FARMERS LEFT, TAKING THE SKIN of their comrade with them, Tagart came down from his vantage in a low branch of a durmast oak and stood surveying the mutilated bodies of his tribe.

He was past anger, for he had ruined it. His trap had worked to perfection, precisely to plan: the men had been open targets, so easy to get in four or five quick shots while they were running amuck among the corpses. Five shots, five dead farmers, and he would be down the tree and vanished into the forest before they had time to react: that was his plan, but he had ruined it, in the most simple, stupid and infuriating way possible. He had dropped his arrows.

It happened when the magpies woke him, for he had drifted off to sleep again despite all his efforts to stay alert. As he awoke he started and knocked the quiver from the branch. It fell, the strap slipping away before he could grasp it. One of the farmers seemed to have heard it, but his attention was drawn by a kite which evidently had dropped in to take a closer look at the camp and its occupants.

Thereafter Tagart had been forced to sit quietly, watching impotently from his tree.

But in a way the trap had not failed utterly: he had managed to frighten them, and he had shown himself that he could draw them out of the village, manipulate them into situations of his own choosing; it was a disappointment that the chief, the beardless man, had not been among the search party—not that Tagart would have killed him. He was reserving that task till last.

Tagart collected his arrows and left the camp behind at once, determined never to go back. The bodies of the tribe meant nothing to him, not even that of Balan: they were mere objects, the spirits within having departed long since, but the place itself held memories and he did not want to see it again.

The rain came and went during the afternoon, in the wake of big piles of cumulus cloud drifting along the coast from the ocean and the west. Toward evening the cloud thinned, became patchy, and occasional shafts of sunshine glanced across the treetops. Smoky white vapor edged the areas of blue which slowly proceeded east.

Tagart emerged from the yew branches and sat cross-legged on the ground, chewing a strip of venison, a water bag at his side. He felt much better for the food and for his afternoon sleep, spent in the cool half-light under the yew. In his mind he was at peace for the first time since the raid, for Mirin was gone and could never come back. Their life together was over. He had been robbed of her touch, her softness. And he had been robbed of his son. But as he ate he filled his voice with peaceful thought, the only way to keep himself calm and level, and consciously, studiously, he kept his mind from the chilling prospect of what he had decided to do next. His arm was healing, the pain in his chest less. His rib, he was sure, had not been broken after all. Strength was returning. He straightened his legs and appraised the muscles, relaxed his calves and felt them loosen completely, then flexed them and they were as hard as wood. He was aware of his body, his sense of speed and balance, and he was glad, glad that he could run as fast as any.

A final strip of meat, a final draft of water, and he chose three blades from his flints, hitched his pouch to his belt, and left the yew behind.

To get downwind of the bears' den he made a long detour, circling back uphill through the oak trees and the thickets of hazel. It took him a long time to cover silently the half mile of final approach to the root-pit where the she bear had given birth to her litter. The hearing of a bear was said to be phenomenal, second only to its sense of smell. In the tribe it was said that a bear could smell fear. If that was so, Tagart told himself as he gingerly moved branches aside, he had doubly good reason for keeping leeward of the den and its mouth.

The den was on a slight gradient, sloping downhill from west to east. It was situated in a glade of large oaks with ground cover of holly, bramble and dog rose. Two hundred paces from the root-pit Tagart halted yet again to listen. He heard nothing of the bears. He went on, halting, going on again, until he reached the place where he had hidden before, with the others of the tribe, that day when they had kept watch on the den and its occupants. He climbed into the tree they had used, stopping when he was near the top, forty feet from the ground.

He looked down. The ground rose from the base of his tree, foreshortened from this angle, sloping up to the den, which was twenty-five or thirty feet below the level of his vision. His view of the entrance was obstructed partly by the uprooted trunk of the oak, partly by intervening vegetation; but he could see well enough to know when one of the bears came in or out.

From within came the faint cries of the cubs. Tagart composed himself to wait.

Bears were the masters of the forest. They hunted anywhere, indifferent to day or night: nothing threatened them, nothing could bring down an adult bear unless it was sick or wounded. Bears in open country were big enough, but those in the forest attained almost unbelievable size through easy living. Females of four or five hundred pounds were commonplace, And in the densest regions lived males which might reach six hundred pounds in the rich months of late summer and autumn. Yet in a run the bears belied their size, and in staying power and resistance to fatigue and pain they were superior to the aurochs which could run for days though mortally wounded.

Their only real enemy was the cold, which they detested, and when winter began to bite they sought out caves and other natural hollows which afforded shelter. It was during competition for these shelters that most fatal encounters between men and bears took place, for, though extremely daring and expert hunting parties—usually spurred by hunger—could exceptionally trap and lance a bear, men were with good reason afraid of the bears and left them severely alone. Trackers of the tribe would find and mark out the breeding sites: and from then on, during the summer's stay, entry to those parts of the forest would be forbidden. Only a madman ventured near a bear's den, and only a man who no longer wished to live went near to or made the merest or most tentative threat to anything that had the remotest connection with their breeding and their young. And inside that hollow under the oak roots were not only two helpless bear cubs, but two fully-grown females, one a nursemaid having all the attributes of the mother except that it was smaller and even faster and would catch hold of and devour Tagart even more quickly, for its jaws were just as strong, its claws as sharp, its devotion to the cubs and fierceness in their defense just as well developed.

He would be killed. He knew he would be killed. It was suicide to remain a moment longer. He would jump down from the tree and run. Run from the she bear, a carnivore, an omnivore, the forest's chosen one, ultimate receiver of all its bounty, its most perfect design for killing: three times his weight, a mountain of brown fur over driving muscle that could power a single lazy slash of her huge front paw to scoop out hearts and lungs and viscera, in her jaws a glistening crowd of sharp white teeth which were there for nothing but ripping flesh, stripping bones, grinding pelvises and shoulders and heads. He prepared to move, to come down the tree and be on his way, to abandon this madness and think of some other plan.

But even before he could release his grip on the branch the mother bear came out. As she emerged from the den she rose up to her full height, and on two legs towered for a moment before dropping to all fours. She looked from side to side, and then, seeming to scent something, took on immediate purpose as she looked straight ahead, directly at him.

Tagart remained absolutely still, praying that what he

had been told by the elders was true, praying that their lore still held. For what he knew of bears had been told him by others. They had told him that a bear could not take his scent from this position; that he would betray himself only by movement, and only then if the movement were pronounced, because a bear's eyes were weak and poorly suited to recognizing shapes alone.

The other female came up out of the hole behind her, a smaller animal, with paler fur, her ears flat against her head. The mother turned to greet her, and then the nursemaid was leaving on the hunt, going past the roots of the fallen oak, trotting south among the holly, along the line of the hill. The outline of her rounded, brown body appeared and reappeared among the trees, merged with the vegetation, and she was gone.

The mother bear irritably shook her head as if to dislodge a fly. She seemed in no hurry to leave, if indeed she were going to: she might have been hunting during the afternoon. Again Tagart heard the mewling of the whelps. The she bear went partly back into the den, and it seemed as if she meant to bring the cubs outside to play in the dusk. But she turned and came out alone, and once more reared up with crinkled nostrils. Something was worrying her.

The sun had gone behind the hill. Deep shade filled the forest. A long way off to the south a nightjar was churring, keeping to one note, changing up, changing down. It too would be hunting soon, wheeling and zigzagging over the bracken, snapping and gaping its wide bill at the moths and dor-beetles as it flew.

The light was deteriorating: Tagart refocused his eyes a little to one side of the she bear so that he could see better. She had dropped down again and was washing, licking her paws with a long pink tongue. He fancied he could almost hear the rough skin rasping against her fur.

The she bear finished her toilet and yawned, revealing for the first time her rows of murderous white teeth.

Without warning, she was leaving. Tagart watched in consternation as she started downhill toward his tree. He had forseen the possibility, but it had all been part of the risk and he had not considered it further. He was considering it now. What if she scented him or his trail? What if she scented him and climbed into the tree? If she made a little spring from the ground and her claws took purchase, and with terrifying rapidity passed branch after branch on her way up the trunk toward him; driving him higher, higher, until there was no height left and she had hold of his legs . . .The wind had not changed: it was blowing steadily from the west, but inside the forest anything was possible, even with a steady west wind. The trees could take a current and break it up, scattering scent in all directions; they could even reverse it. What had been a remote and theoretical problem now took on new significance as the she bear approached. He heard the crush of sticks and undergrowth, and as the distance reduced he made out her eyes, nose, the features of her head; the rolls of fat at her neck; the curve of her claws as her feet, slightly turned in, came padding forward.

The bear was yards from his tree. If she chose to stop and look up she could not fail to see him. His bowels felt loose as he looked down. He clung desperately to the branch, holding his breath, holding himself in, not daring even to think in case she heard.

A moment later her broad back was passing below. She trotted on, downhill through the holly and hazel, each step taking her further below Tagart's level and away from the stream of his scent. He turned and watched her go. She went under the trees, and in a matter of seconds Tagart had lost sight of the bear, of her huge haunches swaying among the undergrowth. She had gone.

Now was the time to get down, to get away. He had been wrong to refuse himself help: he would leave at once and find another nomad group, and with them return in strength to the village to carry out his vow. That is what he should have done from the start; that is what Cosk would have done. Tagart had let his pride take him too far, and as a result he had nearly killed himself for no reason.

With almost no concession to silence he scrambled from branch to lower branch, not caring how badly he might bark his knees or scrape his arms. He paused at the last ten feet and dropped noiselessly on slack knees to the ground.

It was almost dark. The nightjar had stopped singing. Tagart glanced at the fallen oak.

Suddenly he found himself running uphill.

Running uphill, his hand reaching into his pouch to free his knives from their soft wrappings of leather. The yards were behind him: he was standing beside the roots, at the mouth of the den, by the mass of soil and stones that had been dragged up by the tree's fall. Before he could change his mind he was stooping, scrambling down into the fetid warmth of the den, a flint blade in his hand.

The bears had tunneled some way into the earth under the root ball. He could hear the cubs at the end of the tunnel, a few feet ahead. He could see nothing: the only light was a dim grayness from the entrance behind him. The smell of the bears, rich and gamey, almost choked him; the cubs' high-pitched cries reached his ears. His head struck the earthen roof of the tunnel and dislodged a crumble of soil. He reached down and felt warm, coarse fur. He had hold of a cub. It struggled half-heartedly as he lifted it by the loose skin at its neck; but then, realizing that it was not a bear who held it, the cub squirmed strenuously and its cries became louder and more urgent. Tagart felt for it and with his left hand clamped the jaws shut. The cub was still small, and no match for him in strength, but its milk teeth were sharp. The other cub was alert now, snapping at his ankles. He kicked it aside, turned, and, bending double with the cub tucked under his arm, he started along the tunnel to its mouth and freedom.

As he came into the open air he changed his knife from his right hand to his left, and without stopping slashed the blade across the cub's neck. The blood welled, dripped to the holly and the ground. After a moment's resistance the cub went limp in his arms and it was dead.

He ran as he had never run before, away from the den, away from the direction taken by mother and nursemaid, caring nothing now for wind or scent, plunging through the forest and the growing night, exultant, alive, set free. Power, triumph, intoxication possessed him as he ran. In his arms he carried a few pathetic pounds of lifelessness: fat and muscle and unformed bone.

But it was more than a dead bear cub he carried. It was the means to draw out the beardless man, the means to draw him out and kill him.

3

THE DEATH OF GUMIS HAD THROWN A SHADOW OVER THE village. What remained of his body was laid on the Dead Ground; later, it would join those who had died in the raid, buried in the village mound on the western side of the valley. The dead man had no wife and no real family in Burh, and few people whom he had called his friend.

For some reason she did not care to fully understand—she did not admit to a feeling of guilt—Hernou put herself forward as the first watcher in the vigil over his body. She stationed herself beside him, close to the Meeting House, a cape over her shoulders, for the evening was cool. The sun lingered on the hill beyond the palisade, a trembling globe of fire that bulged and became misshapen as the earth drew it down. The underbellies of the few high clouds were lit with orange; the rest of the sky was without feature, a grayish blue turning steadily to violet. Over the forest the first stars of the constellations showed as tiny points.

Hernou felt the breeze stir on her cheek. She clasped her arms about her knees and gently rocked from side to side. Across the compound, lamps were coming on one by one. Normally the evenings saw eating outside, in groups of ten or twenty, but tonight each family kept to itself. Behind her in the Meeting House Hernou heard footsteps and voices, and lights were being lit there too. From its windows a yellow glow came over the Dead Ground and the collapsed and empty corpse, making Gumis one color, a drab brown with deep folds and shadows of black. He was still being discussed inside the Meeting House: his death and its implications were keeping the inner circle of the Council late in session.

Groden was not part of the inner circle, not yet, and he had gone to the house of Morfe to eat. Groden had acquitted himself well in the Council that day, Hernou told herself. How could anyone have forseen that Tsoaul would act without agency to avenge the nomads? For that was the explanation given by Sturmer and Vude for the disappearance and death of Gumis. Knowing that Tsoaul himself was involved, no one in the village but Sturmer harbored any longer even a slight resentment against Groden for the outcome of the raid. The rain had come, as Groden had promised. He could not be blamed for Tsoaul's intervention.

Vude then related a tale of his boyhood, when Aih had appeared in the compound like a ball of flame. The head man, Vude told them, had offered a sacrifice to Gauhm and Aih did not return. If Gauhm could do that, Vude reasoned, could she not do the same with Tsoaul? So during the afternoon Sturmer, the Council, and the whole village made prayer at the small shrine in the Meeting House—they did not dare venture into the forest to attend the shrine on the cliffs—and three lambs and a calf were killed and their blood allowed to run into the ground as an offering to Gauhm, in the hope that she would be able to appease Tsoaul on the villagers' behalf.

Hernou brought the cape further round her shoulders and shivered. With each passing minute fewer people were to be seen. The ground was losing heat. On her right she heard the murmur of the river. From the outskirts of the village came the hard, sharp barking of a dog fox, and with it the shrilling of a blackbird flushed from its roost, somewhere near the east gate.

The lights went out in the Meeting House and Sturmer and the others came down the plank steps.

"Till morning then, Sturmer," came Vude's distinctive voice.

"Till morning."

Hernou glanced to her left. Sturmer was crossing the open ground to the big house nearby.

He stooped and went through the flap of leather at his doorway, and for a brief and painful moment she glimpsed the picture of warmth and cosiness within.

The ladder Tagart had fashioned the previous day was where he had left it, hidden in the undergrowth at the top of the escarpment. It was fifteen feet long, more a ramp than a ladder, covered sparsely with brushwood to keep its weight low. The thing had been heavy and unwieldy enough in daylight, but now it was almost impossible. Tagart was making so much noise dragging it down the escarpment that he was sure he would be heard in the village. He did not really care. Being captured by the farmers would be a hundred times preferable to what would happen to him if he took too long getting the ladder to the bottom of the escarpment.

He tripped on an anthill, lost his footing, and fell for the third time. The ladder came down heavily on his leg. A dog fox was barking nearby; as Tagart fell he disturbed a roosting blackbird from the brier patch. He breathed a curse and struggled to his feet.

There were lights in the village, and food smells on the wind. Tagart hauled the ladder over the anthills. No sound of alarm had yet come from the other side of the palisade. He got under the ladder and raised it, positioning the top against three spikes. The slope was steep—too steep. And would the brushwood stand the load? He did not think so, but there was no time to consider it. He freed the dead cub from where he had tied it, at the end of the ladder so that it dragged along the ground, and, holding it to his chest, climbed the brushwood rungs.

His head came level with the top and he looked into the village. The lights in the Meeting House had now gone out. Lamps flickered elsewhere in several windows of the dwelling houses with their conical roofs. It was too dark to see properly: he could not tell whether there were any people in the compound.

A dog started barking. He dropped the cub over the palisade and climbed over the top, turning round and gripping the spikes, lowering himself as far as he could before letting go and dropping the last six or seven feet to the ground. He landed well, next to the cub.

Taking the cub by a limp hind leg, he dragged its muzzle through the grass as he ran, half-crouching, along the line of the palisade. The houses were on his left, passing him by. Still he saw no one, but more dogs were barking and he expected trouble from them at any moment. He reached the bakery, the last of the buildings before the river, and paused. Beyond the bakery loomed the Meeting House, its walls and stilts and steps silhouetted by lights from the large dwelling house on the far side. This house, Tagart knew, would be that of the chief: that of Sturmer, the beardless man. His eyes glowed. She might be in there at this very moment, Sturmer's woman, the one he had seen at the ceremony. He had seen her well and marked her features as she lay naked, drinking the beardless man's urine from a wooden bowl. He hoped he would be able to restrain himself when the time came to take her into the forest. To kill her too soon would be a tragedy. And he prayed he would not come face to face with Sturmer himself, not yet.

He left the cub by the bakery wall and ran to the river. He slipped into the water, which flowed with sparkles of starlight on green and black and closed over his head without a sound; he dived and wriggled into the slime, came up for breath, dived again, feeling and then not feeling its subtle touch on his skin. Bubbles of methane wallowed up to the surface and broke about his head. He dived three times in all, ridding himself of all trace of scent of bearden and blood, masking his own odor with the sulphurous smell of the mud on the river bottom. Letting the current float him, he drifted past the jetty, past the roof of the Meeting House, black and angular where it shut out the stars, and came to the timbers of the bridge.

He clung to them in the middle of the river, his hair wet and the gritty taste of river mud on his lips. The water flowed about him with small throaty sounds. His eyes were near the surface, below the rise of the banks, which were blacker than the river and sky, tall with vegetation. Above him the bridge was utter darkness. The hollowness underneath it amplified the river noises, and Tagart strained to listen. He wanted to hear what was happening, away from the river, far away on the other side of the village.

With his chin in the water, he waited.

He did not have to wait for long.

The bear came at speed down the escarpment, in her anguish paying no attention to the obstacles in her way: brambles, briers, oak bushes, tussocks, the anthills at the bottom. Without pause she scaled the ramp of brushwood and, merely noticing the eleven-foot drop on the other side of the palisade, gained entry to the village.

She had followed the scent of the cub from the den, each drop of its sweet blood glowing like a marker in the dark. Mingled with the trail she had caught the sickly musk of human feet, and long before the circuitous route began nearing the village she knew that the he cub had been taken by men.

The smell of them was everywhere on the inside of the palisade: their bodies, their animals, their cooking fires and the things they ate. She found the scent of the cub at once, leading beside the palisade toward the smell of water. On her left she was aware of lights, and a throng of barking dogs, and she was aware of the fire she feared, coming from the houses; and as she lumbered toward the river she heard for the first time men's voices raised in alarm.

Hernou stood up as she heard the shouting. Her first reaction was disbelief. The cries of Bear made no sense. The village was bear-proof; everyone knew it. She ran from her vigil place to the corner of the Meeting House, by the steps, where there was a better view. The disturbance was on the far side of the village, by the palisade. Figures of men and dogs were outlined in the light of torches and burning brands. And then she saw the running bulk of the bear as it appeared between two houses, and she knew the inconceivable had happened.

The nightmare of a bear loose in the compound, with nowhere for her to hide, nowhere safe, had come true.

Sturmer, alerted by the shouting, armed himself with a spear and came out of his doorway. Hernou turned her head as the flap raised and lowered, revealing the light inside.

"It's there!" she shouted at him.

"Get inside! Get under cover! I want no one loose!"

She held on to the beams of the Meeting House, numb with fear. The other men, and many of the women too, were appearing at their doorways. Sturmer did not stop to argue with Hernou further. He was yelling orders, trying to organize the villagers, hoping to pin the bear inside a semicircle backing onto the palisade, where it could be held at bay with torches and in time wounded with enough spears to immobilize or even kill it. But the bear had already broken through the line and was running toward the bakery, away from the palisade. Two villagers had been cuffed, another seized and worried in its jaws. The screams of the dying were lost in the confusion of shouting and yelling.

"Force it into the river! Deak, Tamben, Domack! This way! Over here!"

Hernou did not wait to hear any more. She thought of hiding in the Meeting House, but its doorway was wide enough to admit a bear. The nearest safety was Sturmer's house. She ran across to its threshold and pushed aside the entrance flap, scrambling through the porch into the kitchen.

Sturmer had been interrupted at his meal. In front of the hearth were wooden platters, clay spoons and bowls, and cowhorn cups in wooden stands, left half full of food and drink. Hernou passed through the kitchen into the central chamber, and through that into the main room with the tall roof. Here Sturmer's wife Tamis and her four children sat in the rumpled bed of furs and skins, huddling together for protection and comfort. The younger children were crying; the eldest looked up fearfully as Hernou pushed her way into the room.

"Your house was the nearest," Hernou said. "Sturmer told me to hide myself."

Tamis nodded. "Have you seen it? Where is it?"

"By the bakery."

Tamis shut her eyes.

"They can kill it," Hernou said. "I know they can."

"We must pray for our lives. Tsoaul has sent the bear; only Gauhm can save us." She looked with hatred at Hernou, at her gray eyes, her hair, her smooth brown skin, the body that the men still found attractive, watching her deliberate walk as she crossed the compound. Tamis knew that Sturmer had once made love to her—and she knew that Hernou wanted Sturmer back. "You and your Groden have brought this on us. You have brought evil to this village."

"That's not true!"

"Then how did your husband's dog die?"

Even with lights and spears and arrows the villagers had been unable to force the bear into the river, where it would have been hampered by the water and mud. Instead it had stopped by the bakery wall. At its feet they saw it had brought a dead cub with it. Raised up on hind legs, the bear slashed about wildly with its forepaws. In the flickering torchlight it looked brown and shaggy against the wood of the wall.

Groden hit it with yet another arrow in the throat and the bear began a strange, piteous wailing. It stumbled blindly forward and lunged with a wide paw, catching Meed a blow that sent him flying. The bear checked its lunge; lashed out again, missing Morfe by the width of a hand. He did not move, he had armed himself with a felling ax, and in the torchlight his eyes glittered and his teeth showed between his lips.

"The snout!" Sturmer screamed. "Hit the snout!"

Morfe took no notice. He knew what to do.

He had positioned himself for just this blow, and as the bear wagged its head from side to side the axhead came sailing down, and, judged by Morfe's mad, cold, calculating eye, the stone struck its muzzle and it had a muzzle no more.

The bear gave a bellowing squeal and again raised itself up, but it went too far, staggering on its hind legs, and then it was toppling, falling backward, and more arrows and spears were raining into its belly and chest. Its head and shoulders hit the bakery wall and broke through the planking, splintering the wood and leaving fresh white breakmarks. The villagers ran forward and thrust spears into its belly. The legs thrashed, twitched; and lay still.

It was only then that they realized a second bear, bigger than the first, had got into the compound.

No one saw it clamber over the palisade and run along the line of scent. The mother bear was upon them from behind even as Morfe dealt the nursemaid its deathblow.

Left and right the second bear bowled villagers out of the way with swinging forepaws. Skulls, rib cages, pelvises were fractured and crushed. Faces were trodden into the ground by huge hind paws. A woman was taken up in the mother's jaws and her waist almost bitten through before she was flung aside.

Sturmer and Groden were frantically pulling arrows and

spears from the carcass of the first bear as the mother turned on them, scattering weapons and lights, pawing and swiping and striking down man after man. The mother turned to her side, selected Domack's wife, ran her down and with bared jaws grabbed her shoulder; now on hind legs, now on all fours, the bear dragged her along, let her drop, reared up with a roar.

"Get back!" Sturmer screamed as he saw Tamis running across the compound. "Get back! Get back!"

She had left the house when she realized there were two bears to be killed, knowing that everyone would be needed, every hand. She had argued with Hernou, but Hernou had refused to help and had stayed behind.

Hernou could hear the screaming and shouting, the cries of the wounded and dying, the injured and destroyed, and for the first time she began to fear that there might not be enough people left to deal with the bear. It might win. And if it won, it might in its systematic plunder of the village come here and seek her out. She thought of placing Sturmer's children at the entrance, as a decoy, so that if the bear came it would take them and not her. But what if the children served only to attract the bear to this house above all others? Surely it was better for her to wait in the entrance herself, where she could see what was happening. If the bear came, she could run into the bedchamber and escape through the window, while it forced its way into the back of the house and was delayed by the children. That would give her the best chance of making a run for the gate. And if it did not come here first, but went to the other side of the village, she needed to know the best time to escape: she needed to be able to see.

"Stay here quietly," Hernou told the eldest child. "Your mother will be back soon."

Hernou briefly wondered about Groden. He was fighting the bear, she assumed. There was nothing she could do to help him.

She moved aside the flap of leather into the middle chamber, and crawled through it into the kitchen. Here the lamps were still flickering, giving an unsteady light, smoking and giving off the smell of burning fat; but with this smell was the smell of wet leather and mud, and before Hernou could turn and run into the bedchamber there was a rustling on the porch and she was looking into the eyes of a wild-haired and mud-streaked man, a man she had never seen before, not of the village, but dressed in skins like a nomad. His high cheekbones and wide, tall forehead, and the hard line of his chin, gave him under the matted tangle of his hair and beard the semblance of a demon, and Hernou knew she was looking upon the spirit of the nomads in human form: she was looking upon Tsoaul. She was looking upon the Forest God, who had brought down a plague of bears on Burh and would destroy every man and woman and every thing in the village, who was coming for her now because she had incited Groden and it was Groden who had led and engineered the raid on the nomads' camp.

"Cry out and I'll kill you."

She could make no sound, and feebly submitted as he grasped her arm and pulled her toward the entrance. She preceded him, crawling through the porch and into the open air.

In a daze she stood up. The Forest God came behind her, and he too stood up, much taller than she. Across the village the screams were undiminished; Hernou could see lights dancing, the rush of people as the bear changed direction, dark and formless in the night.

The stars were overhead: she felt only the wind from his

fist as Tsoaul struck her. She saw a waterfall of color, and heard a thin, high keening, and then blackness overtook her and she knew nothing more.

Tagart caught her as she fell and hefted her on to his shoulders. She was not heavy, and he ran between the houses of the village, gained the thoroughfare, and in a few moments reached the east gate. He threw down his load and impatiently wrested aside the heavy oaken bars. The shouts and cries far across the village seemed to indicate that the mother bear had been hit—he could not tell how severely. But if she had been mortally wounded and the fighting was coming to an end, there could be no more time to lose.

He swung the gate aside. No one but Sturmer's woman had seen him so far, of that he was certain. In his desire not to reveal his existence he had been almost too cautious, leaving it to the last minute before coming out of the river and crossing the compound to the head man's house, the house of Sturmer, the beardless man, where Tagart hoped and prayed he would find the woman he had seen at the ceremony. And indeed he had almost left it too long. He had almost missed her.

Tagart dropped off the woman's doeskin dress and dropped it on the ground by the gate. There was no time for subtlety: he had to leave a clue, a pointer, something to tell the farmers that she had not merely run away, that they were to follow and try to get her back.

He slung her body around his neck and in the chilly summer night, crisp with the first hint of autumn, started for the forest and the yew tree where he had made his lair.

4

ALREADY THE SUMMER WAS DYING, SPENT AND OVER-blown. The breath of decay blew through the forest, on old leaf mold, on fallen logs and the dead branches of diseased trees; the rains in their wake had brought the first flush of fungi. From their underground threadworks of mycelium they groped upward: shaggy caps, opening like feathered parasols that softened into dribbling slime; autumn morels, white and gray and rust; blushers, which stained cut-red like flesh where they were bored and nibbled by beetles; fairy clubs, tiny white antlers powdered with spores; troops of wood mushrooms, as wide as umbrellas or small gray-white bulbs; stinkhorns that smelled of carrion; wood woolly-foots, yellow stainers, puffballs, earth stars, brackets, champignons, chantarelles; boleti which appeared suddenly among the grass-blades; and the edible grisettes, opening from papery white flasks, just like the others of their tribe which were not edible: fly agaric, red and white-spotted, the fungus gathered by the farmers for their casket; the panther, a poisonous kind; and, on bad ground, the destroying angel: beautiful, a white apparition, with a slimy, shining cap, a poison so virulent that a single specimen in a basket of mushrooms was enough to bring horrible and agonizing death. And there was a fourth kind, more poisonous still, growing under oak trees and beech, coming with the first summer rains, in shape and size like a small blusher, but its cap was a dull and inconspicuous olive-green. It resembled a wood mushroom, and when it was no more than a button could be mistaken for one, but never by the nomads, who knew the death cap and what it would do.

Autumn was in the air. The small birds of the forest had finished their breeding and the tits, nuthatches, and tree-creepers were coming together in groups and family parties that would swell and become roaming bands; the robins and redstarts and thrushes, tailless and molting, skulked in the tangle near the ground; from their eyrie high in the branches of a dead tree, the young goshawks were making their first tentative flights; cuckoos, whose call had not been heard for weeks, were moving south, toward the sea; and the swifts, climbing on their black sickle wings with feeble screams, reveled in the banks of cloud and would soon be leaving late young to starve.

The aurochs, too, were on the move, each bull with his cows. At night their bellowings sounded far through the wooded valleys. Tagart heard them as he lay resting and waiting on his bed of yew needles, in the middle hours of darkness long before dawn. Beside him was the woman, taken from the village earlier that night, now tied at wrists and ankles. To keep her warm Tagart had covered her with skins. He would feed and water her too, to keep her alive.

It was still dark when she regained consciousness. Tagart heard her breathing change, and smiled to himself as she cunningly made her breaths longer as if she had not awoken at all.

"What is your name?" he said.

She did not reply. Tagart knew she had heard him, and he knew that she had understood. They both spoke the same tongue, and although the farmers' dialect was thick and guttual, closer to the language of their ancestors on the mainland across the channel, during thirty generations of slave-raiding and intermarriage the old language of the nomads had been lost.

"Tell me your name, woman."

Still she did not answer. He sensed that her eyes were open in the dark, that she was afraid. The resinous smell of the yew needles filled the air. The woman forgot to regulate her breathing: it came more quickly, and Tagart could almost hear the beat of her heart.

"Tell me your name. I will not hurt you again."

"You . . . you know my name."

Tagart frowned into the dark. The woman's quiet, fear-laden voice came again.

"You killed Gumis as a sign to us, and you sent your servants the bears to avenge the forest people. You have chosen me because of my husband and I know I am to be sacrificed. I am Gauhm's sacrifice to you."

Tagart's frown deepened. "Not if you tell me what I wish to know."

"But you are Tsoaul and know everything."

He widened his eyes with new interest. Tsoaul? Who was Tsoaul? "That is true," he said. "I am Tsoaul. But if you are to be spared I must hear these things from your own lips."

She was silent.

"You must tell me what I wish to know."

"Yes." She almost whispered it. "Yes."

"First. Why do you call me 'Tsoaul'?"

"You . . ." She seemed confused. "You are the Spirit of the Forest . . . that is your name."

"I am known by many names."

"Forgive me."

"Next. Do all the villagers know that I, Tsoaul, have done these things?"

"Yes. They all know it. They are all afraid."

"They know that I caused Gumis to die?"

"Yes."

"And that I sent my servants into your village tonight?"

"They know that also."

"And do they know that it is in my power to destroy the village?"

She said nothing.

"Next. Tell me of the ceremony in the Meeting House."

"I . . . I do not know . . ."

"No harm will come to you. Tell me about the ceremony."

"Which one? There are many ceremonies . . ."

"The morning after the rain returned. Tell me what you were eating in the Meeting House."

She hesitated, anxious to give the right answer, still not quite sure of the question. "We eat from the Agaric Casket to go with our dead to the Far Land."

"To go with their spirits when they die?"

"Yes."

"Tell me what you eat."

"A toadstool, prepared by the priest. He calls it 'agaric.'"

"Explain. What does it look like and where does it grow?"

"It has a white stalk and a red saddle with scales of white. The priest finds it in the woods."

Tagart nodded to himself. The nomads called it by another name, but he knew it well. "How is it prepared?"

The woman described the drying process, how the caps were placed in the casket, where the casket was kept. She told him how many caps could be eaten, and she told him the stories the men had recounted of their visions. She said that whenever the agaric was eaten the musicians played, so that the real world could be found again by its music.

"Who is your priest?"

"He is called Sturmer."

"Sturmer? Your husband?"

"No. My husband's name is Groden." She bit her tongue. Had she offended her listener? Did Tsoaul know that she had once shared Sturmer's bed, could he look into her heart and know secrets?

"What is the name of the man in your village with no beard?"

She hesitated. "Groden."

"And you are called by what name?"

"Hernou."

"Hernou."

"Yes."

"And is your husband head man?"

"No. Sturmer is head man. He is head man and priest too."

"Sturmer is bearded?"

"Yes."

"But Groden is of importance in the village?"

The coldness in the question chilled Hernou and made

her afraid for Groden. But Groden was in the village and Hernou was here in the forest with Tsoaul and now she realized that she put her own life before Groden's and she answered:

"Yes."

Drizzle came from the ocean on a warm wind, bringing back summer to the sea cliffs and the line of endless forest. Heavy clouds rolled in the night above the trees. Cold air worked on the clouds and made them rain; the sea broke muddy and listless along the beach, lifting and dropping lines and fragments of black weed, too feeble to make a roar of the shingle drag, and where the waves sloped on the white rocks below the seven striding cliffs the water swirled endlessly and made no spray. At the mouth of the estuary, on a long shingle spit barely emerging from the sea, black-backed gulls stood in roost and waited for first light. Thirty wing-beats away the river debouched into the tide race: its flow with swollen with rain, winding and meandering through the Burh valley. The valley basin was wide and flat, hemmed in by steep forest to the east, and more gently rising forest to the west. In a past age the river had broken through one of its own meanders, leaving stranded an oxbow lake which had become a calm lagoon. From it rose the voices of wildfowl in the dark: mallard, teal, widgeon, shoveler.

Farther up the valley, lights showed from a village of houses overhung by an escarpment, and sometimes the wailing and cries of grief were taken with the smoke and sent by the wind among the trees.

The bodies of the bears had been dragged into the middle of the compound and set on fire. The smell of burning belched into the rain; meat slowly burnt back from skulls and paws, revealing scorched bone.

It was no recompense. They had killed thirty people. Another twelve were dying; fifteen more were maimed. Fewer than a hundred uninjured people were left, the majority of whom were women and children. Forty-three-able-bodied men remained. Not many wished to respond to Groden's appeal for help. His wife had been taken: her dress had been found near the east gate.

A path led from the east gate, past the escarpment, rising southeastward into the forest. It wound and climbed through the trees; here narrow and closely pressed by undergrowth, there open and wide and passing through woodlands of old beech where the death cap fungus grew. Over a dry gorge the path became a wooden bridge, under which Tagart had hung with his flints and bow-drill in the first hours of loneliness after he had been down to the village and watched them in the Meeting House. Concealed ropes led away into the brambles.

Other ropes lay in readiness elsewhere in the forest, other traps. Deadfalls, dug by the Cosks, had been cleared of debris and restored, the spikes made needle-sharp and coated with wolfsbane. Weights and counterweights waited high above the ground. Snares and loops, nooses and treadles and triggers: one had been fired by a badger, which with the speed of reflexes and impulses running along nerves had leaped clear just as the whip of ropes ripping from the ground signaled the crashing fall of a water-filled skin, straight onto a barb of sharpened holly. The hummelskin exploded in a drenching gush; the water flooded the ground and slowly drained away. The badger caught the taint of human scent on the crumpled skin and ran off the path into the deeper forest, where soon it was unearthing beetles, the incident forgotten.

Gray dawn appeared in the east and the inside of the yew tree became less than black, a gloom in which vagueness could be discerned. Hernou watched the features of the young man taking form, and as she watched her suspicions grew stronger. This was no spirit. Would a spirit ask such questions? Would a spirit be wounded and cut about the arms, bruised and dirty? And would a spirit talk in the accents of a nomad?

In repose, his face seemed almost gentle. He looked a little like Groden, but his expression differed and was more like Sturmer's. His brow was tall and delicate. In the line of his jaw and high cheekbones she saw the nomad face, and in the blackness of his beard and glossy hair, and in the texture of his skin, she saw the old complexion, found only in those village dwellers whose blood was close to the native stock. She noticed his hands. They were scratched and torn, calloused and grimed: strong hands for strangling and punching, gripping weapons.

Hernou was afraid. The nomads were killers. It was the way they lived, by hunting and killing. They thought no more of blood and murder than did the farmers of soil and harvest. The harsh forest life streamlined their tribes and made them strong and ruthless, like the animals they sought for their prey; their discipline, their life, were impossible to understand. For them to swim free in the seasons, not to have precise tasks for each week and day, but to wander the land by whim, thrust the nomads far beyond comprehension. Even after all these generations the farmers still felt themselves to be strangers, foreigners.

Their true home lay across the sea. The only true natives were the nomads.

Across his shoulders, and the top of his chest she saw the form of bones and muscle, rising and falling as he slept. In the crook of an elbow she saw his sinews; his legs were relaxed, the great muscles at ease, and his feet, with their hard soles which never knew clogs, lay to the side. An old white scar ran the length of his calf. At his belt he wore a pouch, and an empty sheath for blades. His garment was a tunic of thick leather, its sleeves held by stitched thongs of seal hide. The tunic was too small: it didn't look as if it had been made for him. Hernou thought of the things Groden had plundered from the nomads' camp. There had been several such tunics among them. Perhaps the one this young man was wearing had been overlooked, just as he himself must have been overlooked by those who Groden said had gone around with axes, making certain. Below the tunic he wore a beechclout of soft doeskin. That too looked as if it had been made for another.

Everything Hernou saw about him, everything she thought, hardened her conviction. This was no spirit.

He awoke with a blink, as if he had felt the touch of her eyes on his face. For a moment he said nothing, and Hernou's heart hammered more violently. She was helpless; she could not move. Her hands were bound behind her back, and her shoulders ached. The nomad had tied her at ankles and wrists and lashed the bonds to the yew trunk.

He sat up and turned to one side, away from her. "Do you want something to eat? Water?"

When she did not reply he stopped busying himself among the provisions and looked back at her face. She nodded.

"If you wish to shit, tell me so. I do not want this place

fouled." He put a rib of venison before her. "Now I will free your hands to eat." He went behind the yew trunk and untied the lashings; she rubbed each wrist in turn, soothing away the chafing and trying to bring back circulation.

"I beg you, free my ankles."

"Why? Do you want to go outside?"

"My ankles hurt."

He considered briefly, and did as she asked. She gratefully massaged her ankles. She was naked under the skins the nomad had provided; the skin covering her shoulder slipped, but she did not trouble to restore it. Hernou looked surreptitiously from under her brow. He was watching.

"Eat," he said.

She diffidently picked up the rank venison. It smelled bad, but out of fear she tried to tear off a piece and chew. The taste made her gag. She felt her gorge rising, and for a moment thought she would be sick. The nomad was already swallowing; he caught her eye and seemed amused. He passed her a water bag. She pulled out the wooden bung, and although the water was musty and stale she drank deeply, for her mouth was dry.

"Rain again," the nomad said, gesturing with his piece of meat at the forest outside, where the water dripped from the trees. "That is good. Good for me, bad for them."

"What does Tsoaul plan?" she said. The beating of her heart filled her head. She was near to panic, hysteria, but she knew she had to say something or it would be too late.

"Don't worry. You will be safe. Do as I say and you will be safe."

The skin covering her shoulder, slipped further, revealing her breasts. She did not take her eyes from his face. The nomad was watching her, no longer chewing, his eyes in shadow. She reached down and slowly took the leather in her fingers and pulled it aside. Her hand opened and let it fall. Inch by inch, she stretched out her arm to touch his hand with her own.

Still he did not move. The water dripped among the foliage outside. She felt her fingertips meet the warm skin of his hand.

He gave his head a dismissive shake and drew his hand away.

His voice came then, heavy with contempt. "Now I understand why they rape children and women who do not love them."

"I—"

"Get dressed. Tie back your hair."

She did as he had ordered; the nomad tied her up again, tighter than before, and between her wrists he tied a longer piece of rope, a halter so that she could be pulled along. He picked up three bows, and from the ground collected a number of things to go into his pouch.

"It is time to leave," he said.

5

THE SEARCH PARTY FILED THROUGH THE EAST GATE, passing over the spot where Hernou's dress had been found, walking in pairs, armed with hammers and axes and bows and spears. In front went Sturmer, beside him Ockom, a tall man dressed in black skins. Morfe and Groden came last. As they left the protection of the palisade those staying behind swung the gate back and dropped the bars into place. Fifteen men had been left to defend the village, too few, against Sturmer's better judgment; but at length he had given in to Groden's persuasion. The village had lost enough people. They had to try to get Hernou back for this if no other reason. The search party was selected and armed, twenty-eight men, and set out at once, barely two hours after dawn.

Few of the men had not lost someone the previous night. Sturmer had been spared: his wife and children were safe, but some men had seen two or even three members of their family killed or maimed.

The path from the east gate—for surely that was the one Tsoaul had meant them to follow, just as he had laid signs to Gumis—was well known by all the villagers. They walked it regularly. It led generally southeast; after skirting the escarpment it rose by a series of swings into the forest. A thousand yards on, at the halfway point, it crossed a dry gorge by means of a cantilever bridge, built to save a long detour. The gorge walls, sheer and white where the chalk was exposed, or rubble-strewn and grown with rough brambles and shrubs, dropped to a fern-filled bottom. Beyond the gorge the path turned south, and then east, coming out by the sward-covered cliffs and the sea, at the Shrine to Gauhm.

The men had come a long way into the woods by now, moving forward cautiously, stopping when Sturmer raised his hand. On either side the rugged trunks of oak and hornbeam were streaked with rain; under the trees the light was bad.

The path turned once again to the left and opened out into a small clearing by the bridge over the gorge. Sturmer signaled a halt.

The gorge, which at one time had carried a stream down to the sea, was part of a long rift which gradually widened and formed the separation between two of the seven chalk cliffs, on the fifth of which stood the Shrine. The rift carried back into the forest for a mile north of the bridge. One of Sturmer's predecessors had built the bridge, thirty feet wide, a long platform of oak logs buttressed into each side of the gorge with oak and beech. Below it the gorge fell away sharply, thirty-five feet deep, its walls partly clad with the roots and twisted branches of stunted shrubs, growing badly in the subsoil. Brambles and tufts of male fern grew among and across the chalk rubble at the bottom.

Sturmer turned to Ockom. "Do you think it's safe to cross?"

The bigger man bit his lip, his eyes, normally wry and humorous, now dull and flat. His brother had been mauled by the bears. Ockom was reckoned the best man in the village for fieldcraft. He knew the different animal tracks, the names of all the trees and plants that had names to know. He said, "There has been no sign of her this far. I see none now. I think it is safe. But send Groden across first—it's his wife we're risking ourselves for."

Sturmer addressed Groden. "We fear an ambush. You cross first."

Groden seemed reluctant, but slowly he ventured out across the clearing and onto the logs of the bridge, testing each step, with both hands gripping the rails. He looked over his shoulder.

"Nothing!"

"Cross to the far side!"

Groden did so, jumping the last three feet onto solid ground. He dropped to his knees and as best he could inspected the timbers of the bridge, stood up, and waved the others on.

They crossed singly, Sturmer going last, standing by the lip of the gorge, vigilant for unusual sounds. There were none. The file reassembled on the far side, and, still watching for tracks, Sturmer and Ockom led off.

Sturmer began to wonder whether they had taken the right direction from the village. They had merely assumed that Hernou had been taken along the Shrine path.

The ground, level for a quarter of a mile, now started sloping down into a shallow dry valley. There had been no evidence of activity anywhere along the path this far: the mud of the path was unmarked by footprints. As the search party descended into the valley Sturmer's doubts deepened. Perhaps Tsoaul had tricked them. Were they going the wrong way? Perhaps Hernou had been taken in an entirely different direction.

He frowned and turned to Ockom. "Do you see tracks?"

Ockom opened his mouth to speak but then Sturmer flinched as in a rush of wind he heard a loud bang and felt a spray of blood on his face. As Ockom's two hands came up Sturmer could see the arrow where it had struck, in the center of the upper lip, smashing through the front teeth and emerging at the back of his neck. Sturmer saw the gray goose quills, and all he could think was that they were not quail feathers, they were not like the fins on the arrow that Groden had shot at his dog Uli . . . they were goose quills, on a polished hazel arrow that had come from among the trees and passed a handsbreadth from Sturmer's face and turned Ockom's head into a screaming mass of flesh and pain and teeth.

The second arrow hit the line of men farther back, thudding into Holmer's kidneys even as Ockom, dead in his black tunic, went down.

The file broke loose in pandemonium. A third arrow slithered across the path and into the undergrowth. It had come from the left, and a little ahead: Sturmer marked the place, and shouted to the others to follow.

They plunged into the forest, branches whipping at their faces, their weapons tangling as they ran. Ahead, Sturmer could see little: oak trunks, the branches above, the bushes of holly and hazel at eye level. There were no silhouettes against the sky, no archers hiding in the trees in the place he had marked.

On his right he heard a shriek and turned in time to see Parn and Coyler, with arms upraised, disappear into the ground, something giving way under their feet. They were out of sight, in a hole in the ground. Sturmer ran to their screams and the edge of the pit. They had fallen on serried wooden spikes, fifteen feet below ground level: Parn face-forward, so that he was partly spread-eagled, partly crushed against the earthen wall of the pit; and Coyler to one side, so that his face was upraised.

"Sturmer!" His features twisted with the new realization of what was happening to his body beneath him. "Sturmer!"

Sturmer had been joined by Boonis and Morfe. "Get them out! The spikes are poisoned! Get them out!"

"We've got no rope!"

"The poison! You can see the poison! Pull them off the spikes!"

It was too late. Coyler's face as he looked upward was a mask. His hands groped for help. His eyes filmed. Already his legs and waist felt dead beneath him. There were faces in the rectangle of light. Faces, and the leaves of trees. Patterns. Waving. Rain coming in. Beside him Parn was on the spikes. Making a tiny sound. The faces in the rectangle would not be able to hear. Coyler shut his eyes.

All but two of the search party were standing helplessly at the edge of the pit. Sturmer barked orders: in the brambles nearby they found a long stout branch. Boonis and Groden lowered it into the pit, and the bodies of the poisoned men were brought out and laid on the ground, among the briers and the wet leaves.

Tamben and Domack, who had run farther into the woods, returned and joined the rest. They had seen and heard nothing of the mysterious bowman.

"It is Tsoaul!" Dopp said. "He will take us all in this vile place!"

"He will deal with us as he has dealt with Gumis!"

"And Ockom!"

"And Coyler and Parn!"

"And the victims of the bears!"

Sturmer shouted angrily for silence. "We must think what to do!"

"We'll be killed!"

"Let's go back to the village and get away while we can!"

"What if Tsoaul drew us here to keep us from the village while he attacks!"

"Let's get back to the village!"

"No!" Groden screamed. "We must go and find Hernou!"

"You bastard! She can protect herself!" Dopp shouted in his face. "You and she brought this down on us—now she must fend the best she can!"

"What did you say?"

"She's a slut, a whore! If she's dead we're well rid of her!"

Before Sturmer could intervene Groden had struck the smaller man in the face: Dopp staggered, and would have fallen into the pit had not Domack and Tamben caught him in time.

"Stop this!" Sturmer shouted. "We must think ahead if we are to survive!"

"The village is cursed!" said Munn. "I am taking my children away! The bears came and killed their mother and sister; Tsoaul shall not have their father too!"

Several of the men seemed to be in agreement with him and were backing away.

"No!" said Sturmer.

"Stay and fight, cowards!" Morfe shouted.

"Scum!" Groden screamed. "Filth! Cowardly filth!"

"I am still Gauhm's chosen one!" Sturmer shouted above all of them. "I am her priest! Any who leave us will have their ground blackened by Gauhm wherever it may be! You must fight for her if not for your own village!"

"We'll take our chances with Gauhm!" Munn said. "She did not mean us to go through this!"

"He's right!"

Morfe jumped forward with his ax. "Leave if you wish, but you must pass me first."

For an instant it looked as if Munn and the others would attack Morfe; but they turned away. Morfe lowered his ax.

"Nothing can be done for these two," Sturmer said, gesturing at Parn and Coyler. "We'll return for them later. Now we must go back to the path."

"But we cannot fight Tsoaul! It is death to fight a spirit!"

"We are defenseless against him!"

"Back to the path."

Sturmer did not know what to do. He considered returning to the village to fetch more men, and some of the women too. Was it wise? He did not know—but he had no other plan. A plan of sorts was better than no plan at all.

They came out on the path a few yards from Ockom's body.

In panic Sturmer turned his head this way and that. A rising terror seized him. He was a fool! A fool! He looked along the path, uphill and down, among the trees. Blandness: mud, rain, leaves, trunks, branches. Just woodland. Nothing else.

"Where is he?" Sturmer shouted desperately. "Where is he? Where's Holmer?"

Holmer, the wounded man, had disappeared.

They found his body in the brambles just beside the path. When they saw what had been done to it there was time for no more words.

They ran.

Even if they had looked, or known how to interpret it, they would have been able to make no sense of the churn of tracks on the path toward the village. Sticky mud sucked at their feet as they ran, obliterating a set of barefoot marks. A stitch was rising in Sturmer's side. Overhead the trees made a smear of gray and green and spidery brown. The faster runners—Morfe and Groden and Boonis—were fifty paces ahead, and even Munn was in front of him, getting farther away. Sturmer realized he was being left behind, dragged back by his age, his years, too many years. Domack overtook him. They were on level ground again. Sturmer reached for the effort to try and keep up, the stitch twisting in his side. He saw Morfe turn a bend and become hidden, then Boonis, Groden, and the others.

Sturmer's toe hit an exposed root and he fell headlong into the mud. He struggled to his knees and to his feet, and with both hands clutched to his side ran on.

He came out of the clearing by the gorge and its bridge. Immediately he saw that the others had stopped, uncertain whether to go on or turn back. On the far side of the bridge, a few yards from the edge of the gorge, stood a slim, dark-haired figure. It was Hernou. She had been bound at ankles and wrists; a tight gag drew back the corners of her mouth. Otherwise, she looked unharmed. She was alive.

"It's a trap!" Sturmer shouted, as he saw Morfe taking the first stupid step onto the bridge, onto the logs above the buttressing.

"We can't go back!" Morfe called out. "We've got to go on and get her safe!"

"No! Come back!"

Morfe ignored him. He continued across the bridge. The others watched as he gained firm ground and turned to them. "See! It's safe! None here but Hernou!" He ran to her to untie her bounds. She was shaking her head furiously.

Sturmer watched in disbelief as Boonis and Tamben went next onto the platform, followed by Emetch and Haukan. Groden ran from the back of the group and shouldered Dopp aside to get onto the bridge. "She's my wife! Let me pass!"

Just as Groden set foot on the bridge he became aware of ropes rising from the ground and tautening on the far side, heavy weights plunging in the trees; and there was a jagged report, a splintering sound, and with a roar the buttressing was coming away from its joints with the platform and the logs were rising and twisting and giving way. The bridge was collapsing.

Groden leaped back. Haukan, the last across, was unable to scramble to safety and Groden saw him falling from the bridge and into the gorge. An oak beam, spinning in the air, caught Haukan with its tip and he was pulped against the rocks.

As he looked up Groden saw Hernou and the four men on the far side; and, from nowhere, from the branches of a tree, from the sky, dropped a white and scarlet creature, an apparition, a god, plumes of white feathers on its elbows and knees and head, taller than a human being, much taller, its face hideously striped with white and scarlet. Tsoaul's teeth showed yellow as softly he hit the ground.

Emetch and Boonis were backing away in terror. Tsoaul suddenly crouched and Groden noticed he was holding a spear, a god's spear with tufts of white feathers. He jabbed it in their direction. Emetch and Boonis turned and ran, across the clearing, to the edge of the gorge, and into space, their legs running in nothing as they fell for a few seconds, shouting as they went, and vanished into the rocks and ferns at the bottom.

Now vicious Tsoaul turned on Tamben. He stood frozen, mute, unable to cry out, unable to react: and in dreamland Tsoaul thrust muscled arms with the spear and Tamben bent his head and saw the blue and cream scalloped blades of its points.

Only Morfe retained presence of mind. On its length of sweat-polished ashwood he swung the head of his felling ax and Tsoaul ducked under its hiss, lunging from below with the bloodied point of his spear, glancing off Morfe's chest; but the power and momentum of Morfe's own ax-swing took him off balance and Tsoaul looped the end of the spear forward and snagged at Morfe's heels: Morfe lost balance and fell.

Tsoaul seemed shorter and more man-like as he dropped to one knee, a knife in his hand. In the blink of an eye he had drawn the blade across the big tendons at the back of Morfe's knees. Morfe had been hamstrung.

"Shoot at it!" Sturmer screamed, remembering for the first time that they were armed with bows. "Shoot!"

But before they could fit notches to their strings the apparition had melted away into the trees, leaving Hernou standing, Tamben dead, and Morfe writhing on the ground.

The bridge had been wrecked, ruined. There was no way to cross. To reach the survivors they would have to detour to the head of the gorge.

"Stinn, Mastall!" Sturmer shrieked at two of the men with bows. "Stay here! If Tsoaul returns, shoot him! The others, come with me!"

They broke into the trees on the right of the path, running uphill and to the east, keeping the gorge beside them on their left, hands up to ward off branches tearing at their faces and necks, and Sturmer, driven on by blind dread, dread of what would happen to Tamis and his children, the village and himself, had lost count of the able men destroyed: Ockom, Gumis, Emetch, Holmer, Parn . . . the victims of the raid . . . Coyler, Boonis, Haukan crushed by the timbers in the gorge . . . the victims of the bears, Tsoaul's bears . . .

At the head of the gorge the soil was leached and poor and it was here that the briers and brambles grew in greatest profusion. Sturmer reached the first of the stout loops of rust-colored stems with their red and green leaves. He did not feel the barbs at his legs; but there was something wrong with his shins and his feet were not working properly and he was falling, crashing with the shock of lost momentum into needles and thorns and prickles. Red appeared everywhere in spots and lines across his forearms and face. He ripped himself free and stood up. Domack was running past him, managing to avoid the briers, skirting the densest patch and left and right things were happening in the trees and Domack was upside-down and being hoisted from the ground at unbelievable speed. Struggling and screaming he was lifted impossibly high into the loftiest boughs of a giant beech: a cluster of bags glimpsed coming down against the light struck a spike and white chalk-rubble spewed forth. Now Sturmer raised his eyes to see Domack seventy feet from the ground, eighty, reaching the height of his rise, hanging motionless, suspended in the forest ceiling: straight and vertical the rope hung to the ground.

It quivered, and Domack began to make his fall.

The ending of his screams left a vacuum. High above the ground the empty counterweights had come to lodge against the branch. They moved once or twice as the weight at the other end of the rope settled itself, and then, were still.

Sturmer struggled free of the brambles. Groden, Feno, Munn and the others started walking forward, not taking their eyes from the place, the one place. The one place ahead.

"There may be more traps!" Sturmer warned them.

He had broken the silence. They passed Domack's body.

"Here!" Deak shouted, ten yards to Sturmer's right. By a tall tangle of briers, between it and three hazel bushes, he had found thin branches laid side by side, covering an eight-foot square loosely disguised with litter.

Groden took a piece of wood and prodded at the covering. It gave way at once, and when they saw the spikes below they cleared the rest of the branches aside. The spikes waited, in uneven ranks and files, their tips soaked and dark, made so by the coating of wolfsbane. Sturmer looked down into the pit. He thought of Parn and Coyler, of Coyler's hands reaching up.

"Fill it in," he wanted to say, but he remembered Hernou and why they had been running, and grimacing turned aside and motioned that the others should follow.

Mastall and Stinn, the men left on guard with bows, had fled. As Sturmer emerged from the trees he saw that Hernou had gone too; and Morfe, previously lying on his face, was now supine with his arms spread wide. With a cry of anguish breaking from him Groden pushed past the rest of the group and ran to his friend's corpse. Groden went down on one knee and lifted the dead shoulders, cradling Morfe's head against his arm. The eyes stared vacantly. There was blood on the teeth. And, around the neck, was the ragged wound where Morfe's throat had been cut.

Something in the grass caught Sturmer's eye. He stooped and rubbed the white-stained blades between his fingers, and, holding his fingertips to his nose, smelled the gritty white paste. He tried to think what the smell could be. And then it came to him.

Chalk.

Fallott grinned, despite the driving rain and the filthy gray mud. Pode and Bico came behind him, leading the team of goats with their wicker panniers, and in the rear the boy Bewry toiled and struggled to keep up. They were walking men, men who could cover a dozen miles a day, or sixty on the Flint Lord's roads that went out like the arms of a spider's web from Valdoe and penetrated far into the coastal strip and the flat country north of the downs. Bewry would have to learn to walk too if he wanted to be a trader.

Fallott turned and caught Bico's eye. They had made Bewry walk behind, where the mud was worst. The seven goats, each with two panniers, were heavily laden with flints and tools: knives, axes, arrowheads, scrapers, and blades of all kinds, already pressure-flaked by the Valdoe craftsmen; and the weight of them made the goats' hoofs sink deeply, turning the trackway to mire.

On their right the trees opened to give a glimpse of gray-green ocean flecked with white. Fallott scanned the expanse of scrubland as by instinct, scarcely seeming to move the eyes in his head.

"Two miles more," Bico said over his shoulder to Bewry, who was hot-faced and near to tears.

"We may go on to Hooe," Fallott said, naming a village twelve miles farther east.

Bewry said nothing. He knew that Fallott was lying. Fallott had been told to go to Burh: he would not dare disobey. Bewry hated Fallott. He hated Pode and Bico too, and he hated the overseers and the soldiers, but most of all he hated the Flint Lord, who had taken him and his sister and murdered their parents and tribe, and whose men had told him his sister would be given to the miners if he did not behave himself on the road with Fallott's team.

Fallott drew up his sheepskin. He was a tall, hard, heavy man with watery blue eyes and lifeless brown hair tied in a topknot. The fingers and thumb of his left hand had been smashed and badly set, and under his clothes a white scar showed where an arrow had punctured one of his lungs, the injury that had ended his day in the Flint Lord's garrison and brought him by way of the armory to take charge of a trading team. He was a veteran of three expeditions to the foreign coast for slave-trading. At that time he had been younger and stronger, but even today he was with good cause shown deference by those in his control. Bewry, a thin child with brown hair and eyes, and an open, small-featured face, was twelve years old. His sister was sixteen and had been showing reluctance to settle with the reality of her new existence; thus the boy had threatened to prove a nuisance. Putting him on Fallott's team had been deliberately done.

The ground rose into a grove of blackthorn. Fallott spoke an order and the pace of the team increased.

Soon they would be arriving in Burh.

✣ 6 ✣

AFTER FINISHING THE MAN HE HAD HAMSTRUNG, TAGART put the woman over his shoulder and made his way north-east through ankle-deep wet leaves, uphill and toward the yew. He covered a wide curve, avoiding a thicket of old hazel where the fallen branches lay in a tangle, festooned with lichens and gray mold: such woodland was impossible to traverse in silence, at least when carrying a load. Instead he kept to the open forest where ground cover was sparse. On the way he collected the rope he had saved from the hummelskin trap—the one that earlier he found had been sprung by a badger during the night—and picked a tree suited to his purpose: an oak, squat, densely foliaged, on one of the thicker slopes, less than two hundred paces from the yew.

He dumped the woman and, taking one end of the rope, grasped a low branch and pulled himself up. He climbed into the middle of the tree, where the trunk forked into five boughs, and fed the rope over a lesser branch a little higher up.

Over the gag, the woman's eyes regarded him fearfully as he climbed down and jumped the last few feet to the ground. He knelt beside her and tied one end of the rope between her ankles, knotting it to the ropes forming her fetter. She began to struggle desperately as without a word he hoisted her into the tree, pulling smoothly arm-over-arm on the rope, scarcely slowing as she came into contact with the great bole, slid past it and ascended to the lesser branch. She hung there, bound and gagged, head downward, in the center of the tree. Her arms, tied behind her back, hung a little away from her body: the weight of them would become a strain that would get worse as each minute passed, within an hour a torture. Tagart was not concerned. He let out a little of the rope and she awkwardly came to rest upside-down in the forking of the boughs; for the second time he climbed up, pulling the free end of rope after him.

"I'll be back later with food and water," he whispered, and hoisted her again so that she hung freely. Upside-down, her eyes and face looked peculiar, as if a mouth should be across her forehead. She made noises of protest under the gag. The skins Tagart had tied to her body hung in loose folds: with a curious delicacy he rearranged them, tucking a flap between her thighs.

He made the rope fast and descended to the ground.

At an easy pace he trotted downhill toward the river. He was still daubed with chalk paste, parts of it dyed scarlet with blackberry juice, and he was going down to the river to wash. That was his immediate task.

But afterward?

He had a hostage, and she could be used in a variety of

ways; and he had taken a useful idea from the details of the ceremony she had so foolishly described; but now his larger plan had run out and he did not know how to proceed. With some surprise he realized that he had not expected to survive this long. He had disposed of more of them than one man acting alone had any right to. The laborer; two shot in the dry valley; three in the gorge; one speared; another with his throat cut. Twenty-six killed in the raid; an unknown number killed and injured by the bears; and perhaps others in the deadfalls, and in the hoist trap at the head of the gorge. Thirty-four certainly dead. The true total was probably double that. But how to proceed? So far he had applied the laws the tribe had taught him, for hunting and luring and waiting. He had observed that the farmers were slow-witted and easily driven to panic. As individuals, few or even none of them were his superior. That was the conclusion he had reached. He was wary of underestimating an adversary; but he was just as wary of underestimating his own powers of observation and deduction. From the things he had clearly seen, from the ludicrous and cowardly way they had reacted to his attacks, he felt safe in discounting any spark of resourcefulness or ingenuity in those who had by virtue solely of their greater numbers massacred his wife, his child, his family, and his tribe.

Again he felt the tide of revulsion and weariness rising in his mind, and furiously he again forced it back. His resolution had not failed him yet—and it would not do so until he had finished. He knew he was pushing himself on, fighting himself on two fronts, refusing to acknowledge any of the new thoughts that threatened to weaken him and make him give up. But with every act of violence, with every man killed he found it harder to maintain that pitch of loathing which had spurred him to go alone into the den of a mother bear. He did not think he would be able to do the same thing again.

He wished he had someone to talk to. He wished he could ask Cosk what to do.

But Cosk was at the camp with the kites and magpies and buzzards.

He reached the river and slipped into the water to wash. Several times he plunged his head beneath the surface to get the chalk from his hair. The river was swollen and he could taste fresh mud in its currents.

The rain. It had been raining for four days. Was it too long?

He stood up, water draining from his body. It might not be. The wind was in the west, and even though the crops had been soaked the ground was still dry and once the flame got hold the wheat would burn. If he fired the fields west of the river, the flames would not be able to spread to the east bank, and the forest and he himself on that side would be safe. In his imagination he saw the western part of the palisade consumed, leaving that side of the village open. He saw the farmers showing themselves, putting out the flames, and he saw himself waiting.

He strode from the river and ran along its bank. There were many preparations to be made.

The fly agaric ceremony came to an end at midnight, leaving the village quiet and sorrowing for ten more men lost. Only seven of their bodies had been brought back: Sturmer had not tried to recover those in the gorge. Mourners with torches sat in vigil over the Dead Ground.

Inside the Meeting House the boy Bewry lay awake and unable to sleep. His mind was alive with the sight of all the corpses and with the stories the farmers had told, of the Forest god and the disaster he had brought. One of the village women, the wife of Groden, was still missing, and Groden and his friends were going to search again tomorrow. They had asked Fallott to help.

"That cannot be done," Fallott said carefully. They had been sitting in the Meeting House, eating the food the villagers had provided on their arrival. It was late morning, raining hard outside. The flints were laid out on the floor for the farmers to make their choice. Bewry was sitting by himself, leaning against the wall, a beaker of water at his knee. He was slowly getting through the gruel of lentils and beans. He could scarcely taste the food: he was just grateful to be still, no longer walking, for his feet were blistered and his whole body ached. He was too young to walk so far.

"That cannot be done," Fallott said. "We must leave at dawn for Valdoe. The team has other walks to make."

"But you are a soldier, Fallott!" said the head man, named Sturmer. "With your help we can fight Tsoaul and get Groden's woman back!"

Fallott corrected him. "I was a soldier. I am a soldier no longer."

"Then leave us Pode or Bico. They know the methods of the Flint Lord and how to fight."

Pode and Bico glanced at each other in amusement, before going on with their gruel.

"Pray to the Earth Mother," Fallott said earnestly. "She will bring you out of trouble."

"No," Groden said. "This time we must fight. I beg you, leave us Pode or Bico."

Fallott held his spoon on one side and carefully considered his words. There were many farmers, and, discounting the boy, only three in the walking team. "They are with me because we need three men," he said. "It's not safe to walk with less; most teams have more."

"Seventy-seven villagers have been killed," Sturmer said. "Another twenty lie maimed or dying in their beds. You have seen them. You have heard them. Now you must help. Were it not for Burh and villages like us Lord Brennis would have no trade. Will he stand by and watch us all murdered? Will he do nothing to stop it?"

"Why should he?" Bico said curiously.

"Because from us he grows wealthy!" Groden shouted.

Bico shrugged. "Keep soldiers like he does to protect yourself from the heathens and the demons. Feed your own barracks. Work hard. Build a fort. Look after yourselves. He has no duty toward you."

"That's enough," Fallott said, and Bico fell immediately silent.

Fallott raised a hand. He spoke placatingly. "You mistake us, Sturmer. We would help if we could, but cannot. Our orders are strict. If we broke them the Flint Lord would be angry."

"Then can you plead for us? Get him to send soldiers?"

Fallott shifted evasively.

"Will you ask the Flint Lord to send soldiers?"

"It is not usual."

"Unheard of," muttered Pode.

"My wife is still with Tsoaul," Groden said, near to despair.

"And mine lies outside with her face bitten through," Stinn said, and all those who had been bereaved began to plead with Fallott for his intercession.

Again Fallott held up his hand. "You say you have seen Tsoaul himself."

"He came from the trees. It was Tsoaul."

"Then you will need many soldiers, half an army."

"Will you ask, Fallott?"

Fallott hesitated. "I will," he said.

"It is enough," Sturmer said. "We know you, Fallott."

"Depend on me. When the soldiers come I will take charge. We will sweep the forest clean."

Soon afterward the fly agaric ceremony had commenced. Now the Meeting House was empty of villagers, and Bewry was lying awake. He could hear Bico snorting in his sleep, and the drone of Pode's snoring. The light from the watchers' torches danced on the ceiling and made flickering patterns; Fallott's body was a huddle, his sheepskin pulled up to his ear.

Bewry did not know how much time had elapsed when Fallott sat upright and rose to his feet.

"Two hours to first light," he announced, kicking Pode and Bico awake.

Bewry stood up himself to avoid being kicked.

"Better not piss on their Dead Ground," Fallott told him. "Do it by the steps." He turned to the two men, who were sitting up and complaining. "Bico, go and get the head man up. Pode, you make sure we eat a good breakfast. We've a fifty-mile walk today. Bewry, see to the goats."

Fallott, rubbing his hands, went to the nearest window and inspected the sky. Stars remained unblinking behind wisps of thin moving cloud. "Rain this morning before Whitehawk," he said, as Pode and Bico went out of the doorway and down the steps, with Bewry coming respectfully behind.

* * *

Tagart struggled through the silo, groping for the covering of sticks. His fingers found them just as he felt his body being sucked into the ensilage, and he drew himself up and into the fresh windy night, pausing with his head and shoulders above ground while he checked the village.

Torches burned beside the Meeting House, and in their light he saw the mourners sitting by what he knew would be bodies. The rest of the village was in darkness.

As before he heaved himself out of the silo, ran to the granary, the threshing shed, and down to the river, where he leaped from the bank and into the water. He swam underwater for three strokes, took breath, and crossed to the far bank to make his way upstream and past the bridge.

In his pouch, wrapped in a square of tallowed skin, were the pieces of death cap fungus which he had prepared during the preceding day. He had found the toadstools growing in many places between the river and the yew, and in the beechwoods near the gorge, in ones and twos and small groups. With meticulous care not to put his fingers to his mouth or eyes or any part of his skin which was not whole, he collected every cap he could find, numbering three hundred and six. In the valley north of the yew he gathered twigs and bents and shavings and in a three-sided oven of flat stones built a hot, smokeless fire which he buried in pebbles. On the bed of pebbles he gently heated the fungus, taking off each cap as it shriveled and dried. They were small, smaller than fly agaric caps would be, but they looked sun-dried and in his memory they matched closely enough the caps described to him by Hernou—closely enough to pass without suspicion. By nightfall he had finished. At dusk he fed and watered Hernou—whom he had allowed to sit on the ground during the afternoon—and hung her again in the tree for the night. He slept then, for his normal term: the next day he would need all his alertness and strength.

Two hours before dawn he had come down the escarpment to the village, and now he was inside the compound, wading through the shallows by the river bank.

The Meeting House showed as an angled bulk against the compound with its scattered houses contained by the spike-topped palisade. On the right hand side of the Meeting House he saw the seated mourners, their torches thrust into the ground in front of them. He waded farther upstream. He knew he would have to get inside the Meeting House silently, find the Agaric Casket, exchange the caps, and get out again without alarming the mourners. That was counting on the fact that the Meeting House would be empty; otherwise, he would have to wait his chance, or even give up the idea altogether.

Making small ripples he swam to the village-side bank and stealthly climbed into the sedges. The rear wall of the Meeting House was directly opposite, thirty feet away. Tagart shook the water from his limbs, squeezed his hair and beard, and one by one took off his garments and wrung them dry before replacing them. He came further up the bank. The sedges rustled as he left them and darted to the Meeting House wall. For a long time he leaned against the wattle, listening. No unusual sounds came. He put his ear to the wall and could hear nothing from inside. The building appeared to be empty. He edged to the corner, away from the Dead Ground, and gingerly put his head round. Nothing. The barn and bakery were in full view, as were nine or ten houses; but it was dark and moonless and if he were observed he would be no more than a faintness against the river behind. The only danger came from the mourners' torches. The glow among the network of piles and crossbars beneath the Meeting House floor would show the movement of his legs. If he was going to be seen from the bakery side, that would be the cause.

The risk had to be taken. Pressed against the wall, he worked his way along to the first sizable gap in the wattle, wide enough to see inside. He looked. The interior was much as he remembered it: the wooden floor, the altar, the windows and walls, the doorway at the far end through which he could glimpse more of the village.

The room was empty.

He made his way to the first window. The ledge was eight feet above the ground: he jumped and grasped the timber of the frame, hanging for a moment as he listened for a reaction. None came. Gradually he pulled himself level with the ledge and climbed over. He landed soundlessly on the smooth boards of the floor; his feet left slight damp stains as he crossed to the altar. In the uncertain light of the mourners' torches he found the Agaric Casket Hernou had spoken of, a cubic beechwood box the width of his forearm, furnished with a lid that opened with a soft gasp as he swung it on its hinges. The casket had been superbly made. It was airtight, the back, lid, front and sides carved into panels of stars, clouds, comets, mythical beasts, the deities of Earth, Forest, Sky and Sea, the sun and wind, and the fly agaric toadstool himself, growing under birch trees by the gates of the road taken by the dead to paradise. Ten trays inside fitted one upon the other, each scrupulously polished and fashioned.

The top three trays were empty. Tagart removed the other seven and tipped the fly agaric caps into a heap on the floor, replacing them with the caps from his pouch. He did not have quite enough: he made up the deficiency in the bottom trays with fly agaric caps, and put the rest of the trays back into place. He shut the lid and positioned the box as he had found it, and scooped up the fly agaric from the floor to pack into his pouch. A few crumbs he scattered by blowing this way and that on the floor.

There was a noise at the doorway.

Someone was coming up the steps.

Tagart stared terrified past the altar and into the darkness at the end of the room. Thoughts flooded his mind. He could not attack, for the mourners outside were too close and he would be heard. He could not jump out of the window and run: it would take far too long to burrow into the silo, or if he ran to the path, too long to get the gates open. He could not fight them all. And he could not hide here in the Meeting House, for whoever was coming up the steps would already have seen him.

It was all over.

He stood up and turned and saw that it was worse than he had thought. There were two of them, at the top of the steps, men outlined in the doorway, coming inside.

It was all over. They would kill him.

The two men came farther into the room. Tagart stood quite still, oddly peaceful now that he knew it was coming to an end at last. He did not care. In his heart life had no value and he did not care.

"Good day to you," one of the men said.

Tagart croaked.

He started walking toward them.

The man on the left caught him by the arm and Tagart tensed.

"Have you seen Fallott, friend?"

"No," Tagart brought himself to say.

The two men seemed to lose interest in him. He edged past them to the door. From the corner of his eye he saw one kneel and begin tidying a pile of bedding by the wall.

Tagart hesitated in the doorway, in full and heady view of the whole village, and casually he was descending the flight of plank steps, the mourners' torches behind him and to the right. He reached the ground without challenge, still forcing himself to go slowly, turned left and sauntered toward the bakery and darkness. Shortly he turned left again, strolled by the side of the Meeting House, and retraced his steps to the river.

The water was his friend. It was warm and buoyant and smelled of the forest. Its broad surface curled and gurgled and carried him past the bridge, past the lights of the mourners, and to the bank beside the threshing shed.

Moments later he was in the silo and pushing open the trapdoor of turf.

A small bundle lay next to the trapdoor: his bowstrings and fire-making kit. He took it up, with his quiver and bows, and ran beside the palisade back to the river, which he swam with his arm high in the air holding the bundle clear, gripping the bows and quiver with it, making deep strokes with his free hand and frog-kicking at each threat that he might go under and risk getting his tinder damp. It was not easy, and he came to the western bank a long way down from the village. A moorhen squawked as he crashed a passage through the flags and sedges.

Tagart gained solid ground and stood facing the fresh west wind. Ahead, the low shape of the hills. Behind, the river and the forest, the trees heavy with summer coming almost to the water. To his left, the widening mouth of the estuary. To his right, acre upon acre of wheat and barley.

He turned his face to the northwest and set off across the fields.

Sturmer preceded the trading team across the bridge and opened the gate for them. Daylight was just showing above the forest behind the village; the air felt chilly and smelled damp from the river.

Most of the farmers were out of their beds and had come to see the trading team leave.

"Have you all you want of our wares?" Fallott said routinely as he let the goats pass him by.

"We have."

"Good."

Sturmer stepped forward. "You'll not forget us, Fallott?"

The larger man slapped him on the back. "My word is on it. Lord Brennis will be your savior if I am worth anything at Valdoe." He glanced at Pode and Bewry, chivvying the goats through the gate and on to the road. The animals' panniers were loaded with grain, skins, cuts of meat: mutton, goat, pork, and the stringy beef of the semi-wild cattle that served the village as milk beasts. "We must be gone," Fallott said.

Sturmer stood back.

"Come on there, Bico!" Fallott called out. To Sturmer he said "In a few days, then."

"In a few days."

The gate swung shut and the flint-sellers heard the oak beams being dropped into place. Fallott quickened his step and caught up with the end of the team, where Pode was prodding the trailing goat with an elder switch.

"Lord Brennis their savior," Pode said with a grin.

"Did you want to be held there by force?"

"True enough, Fallott. There was nothing else to tell them."

"They were desperate."

"What if the Forest God comes down and kills them all?"

"We strike Burh from our list of walks," Fallott said drily, and Pode gave a short, harsh laugh as his leader moved to the front of the team. "Bewry go behind."

Resentfully Bewry dropped back. The path was still bad, very muddy, and today the team had to cover the whole distance to Valdoe by nightfall. The goats' hoofs churned the track, making small deep holes which immediately filled with water. Already Bewry was struggling to keep up, his night's rest counting for little.

On either side was the expanse of the farmers' arable; in the dawn light the barley looked bracken-brown, paler and darker where the storms had beaten it flat. The path led through the fields for half a mile from the village, and at their edge wound through a spinney of maple and oak. Beyond the spinney spread a gentle incline of short grass kept neat by the villagers with flint sickles. Ordered lines of small chalk boulders marked out a large rectangle, in the center of which was the village burial mound: six feet high, fifty feet long, twenty wide, looking like a black upturned barge. The farmers kept it free of weeds; at its base were posies of chamomile and red campion, laid for the newly dead. Here the trading team had seen fresh earth the previous day: the graves of those killed in the attack on the nomads' camp.

For protection and other purposes on the road, the flint-sellers went armed. Fallott wore an ax in his belt, and in his pouch ready to hand was a slingshot and a supply of pebbles which he could propel with speed and accuracy over a distance of forty yards. Also in his pouch he kept a set of bolas, three fistsized stones sewn into leather coverings connected by long thin straps. This when thrown at a fleeing deer would wrap itself round the animal's legs, entangling it and bringing it down.

The team came out of the spinney.

The man was walking along the top of the burial mound. Bico saw him first. He was dressed in skins, without shoes, a tall and powerful figure moving with noticeable fluidity and grace, unarmed, a quiver of arrows and two unstrung bows leaning against the base of the mound.

The man looked up suddenly, as if he had been disturbed in deep thought.

Fallott had seen him too and was already unfurling his bolas. He moved clear of Bico and began to swing the leather-covered spheres, feeding out the straps as he did so.

"You there! Wait!"

The man leaped from the mound and scooped up his quiver and bows and started running.

The trebled thong of the bolas hummed loudly as Fallott worked power and momentum into the swing: the balls blurred into a perfect circle, precisely horizontal.

Fallott was waiting.

At first the fugitive had put the mound between himself and the team, but as he climbed the slope he came out of cover and his legs were revealed. He was eighty paces away when Fallott let fly.

Unerringly the balos snapped out of orbit and raced after the running man, whirred over the mound, and before he had taken another five steps the balls were spinning past each other in opposite directions and the straps were winding themselves again and again round his knees. With a shout of dismay he flung his arms wide. The quiver and bows were thrown into the air; he left them behind, falling heavily, sliding on his face to a tangled halt in the dew-wet grass.

Before he had even a chance to sit up Fallott was standing over him with his ax. The man looked round, took in Fallott's form, and turned his eyes to the ground.

Bico joined his leader.

"A bonus for us," Fallott said. "How much do you think he'll fetch?"

"A walk saved or two days with the whores for each of us," said Bico with enthusiasm. He cautiously circled the prostrate figure. "He looks well fed. Too well fed to be a farmer. Do you think he's one of them?"

Fallott shook his head. "I know them all by sight. This is a stranger, a nomad I think. A wild man." He prodded Tagart with a foot. "You. Where are you from?"

"I am from Highdole," Tagart answered. "I have journeyed to see my friends at Burh."

"Alone?" Bico said to Fallott. Fallott smiled.

"And is this how you pay respect to their dead? Walking along the barrow?"

Tagart said nothing.

"Let's go back to the village then, and see if they know your face."

Tagart looked round again and held Fallott's eye. "They will tell you I am their friend. Untie my legs and we can go."

Bico was frowning with recognition. He squatted and took hold of Tagart's hair, wrenching his head back to see his face. "I know him," he said to Fallott. "Pode and I saw him. We saw him this morning in the Meeting House."

"Of course," Tagart said evenly. "I slept at Burh last

night. I am the guest of Sturmer. I am here for a week to help with harvest."

"What is your name?" Fallott said.

Tagart did not hesitate. "Meker."

"You say you come from Birdbrow."

"Highdole."

"What is the name of your head man?"

"Foss."

Fallott laughed. "A good try, my friend. You forget we are a walking team. I know them all." His expression changed and he jerked his head at the goats. To Bico he said: "We're wasting time. Cut a yoke from that spinney. We must be on our way."

PART THREE

⚘ 1 ⚘

TAGART'S WRISTS WERE TIED ABOVE A STOUT OAK branch across his shoulders, his ankles fettered with a short length of rope. He could walk, but no more, and if he did try to escape he would not be able to get far before the oak branch snagged and barred his way. As extra insurance Bico fixed a sliding noose round his neck, and, at the end of this halter, Tagart began the long walk to Valdoe.

Their progress was slow. Fallott found the delay irksome. On many occasions Tagart stumbled and fell into the mud, only to be kicked and again dragged to his feet. Before long there was no part of him that was not spattered with gray slime. His shoulders were burning centers of pain; all sensation had gone from his hands and forearms, and where Fallott's kicks had struck his kidneys he felt a dull, hard ache. From time to time the boy Bewry wiped his face and gave him sips of water. The boy did not speak, but in his eyes he was sorry for Tagart and Tagart's mind began to work.

"Come on, Bewry!" Bico shouted.

The team followed the road, up the western side of the valley away from Burh, and along the slope of the chalk hills which, half a mile to their left, became white cliffs above a shingled bay. Spectacular cloud formations were building up in the west: purple, black, lead-gray, green; cold, sudden showers came and went, the rain making clean streams across Tagart's skin.

They descended into a wide, flat valley filled with an expanse of reeds, broken up by wind-ruffled lagoons and meres over which flights of wildfowl made straggling chevrons. A black, oily path led through the reeds, between the walls of rustling stems. It came out on a rough grass marsh where the sky was reflected in ribbons of water. On the far side the spread of a gray river crawled toward the sea. A line of posts stood across its width; weed-hung rope looped from top to top. Fallott and Pode went out on the shingle by the water's edge and righted some of the punts that had been left there beyond the tide's reach.

After the crossing they turned south, in the shelter of brambleclad cliffs of crumbling chalk, and by a steep path climbed the headland where wizened shrubs bent before the salt spray.

As the team emerged from the lee of the headland the sea wind struck them. Below, beyond the cliffs, white crests showed against green swell, in irregular patches deep blue where cloud shadows were passing. Puffins whirred overhead. Terns, delicate gray and white, patrolled offshore, plunging for sand-eels; a pair of black jaegers, heavy and sinister, selected one and chased it, relentless, twisting and turning, along the surface, gaining altitude until they were high specks against the sky: at last the tern could take no more and disgorged the contents of its crop. The jaegers dropped back, and with easy, tumbling flight caught the fish-mash as it fell.

The road along the cliffs was firm and the team made better progress, and in an hour they had covered more than four miles. Soon afterward, three hours after leaving Burh, Fallott ordered the first rest stop. The panniers were taken off the goats, which grazed quietly on the clifftop turf; Fallott, Bico and Pode took out the ale and bread given them in Burh, and at Bewry's suggestion the slave's wrists were temporarily untied from the yoke.

Tagart fell back on the grass and shut his eyes. He heard the voices of his captors, talking as they ate. One of them laughed, the sound of it swept away on the wind. Bewry said something. There was an indifferent reply; a few moments later Tagart became aware that the boy was shaking his shoulder.

"Some food," Bewry said.

Tagart sat up and accepted the proffered bread. It was unfamiliar to him. He sniffed at it, tasted a corner, bit off a mouthful.

"These men," Tagart said in a low voice. "You do not wish to walk with them."

"I have no choice. I am a slave. At least I am too young for the flint workings." Bewry glanced over his shoulder. The three were taking no notice. "That is where they're taking you, to the mines."

Tagart nodded.

"What tribe are you?"

"The Cosks," Tagart said.

"I am of the Guelen. Guel was my father's brother. We

were on the beach at Lepe, by the big island. Then they came with dogs and spears. They chased us into the salt marshes. Some of us drowned. I got stuck in the mud with my sister and my parents and some others. The soldiers killed many of us there, on the saltings. They killed my mother and father. Guel was killed too, and the rest of the tribe killed or taken for slaves and sent away. They took me and my sister Segle. If I do not do as they wish, Segle will be put into the whores' place where the miners go."

Tagart looked into the boy's open face. "How old is she?"

"Sixteen."

Tagart had never heard such despair in a child's voice.

"She is the niece of a chieftain," Bewry said. "And they make her serve swill to the miner slaves."

Sixteen. Two years younger than Mirin. "I can help you," Tagart said. Bewry looked up. "I will get your sister out of Valdoe if you help me to escape."

Bewry's eyes widened.

"We are not meant to be slaves," Tagart said.

"What are you whispering there?" Fallott shouted. "Give the slave a drink and get away from him!"

The rest stop lasted five minutes more. Even as Bico came to pull Tagart to his feet, Tagart was toying with the idea of jumping over the cliffs. It would be better than Valdoe. There was no real chance of escape: Fallott was a very different man from Sturmer or Groden. The only chance, if chance it was, lay perhaps with Bewry.

They did not stop at Whitehawk fort, one of the Valdoe outliers. It passed them to the north, its forbidding black palisade topped by ramparts where Tagart glimpsed the movement of men. Fallott kept to the cliff road. He was forcing the pace, making up for lost time, and as a concession to this Tagart's wrists were fastened below, not above, the yoke. Soon Whitehawk was far behind.

Six miles on, at the approach to Thundersbarrow fort, the road swung inland, northwest and into the hills. The chalk track climbed at a grueling rate up the lower slopes of Thundersbarrow. Rain was blowing off the sea as they came within sight of the fortifications; Tagart felt his stomach fill with sick fear as the faces of the guards by the gate became discernible.

Fallott was recognized and the team admitted for fresh pack-animals and a meal. Tagart had never been inside a fort before. Compared with the Trundle, this was nothing; but he stared despite himself and the yoke, marveling at the timbers of the palisade, the earthworks, the buildings, the horn and leather armor of the soldiers.

"More Valdoe meat?" one of the guards said as Fallott came through the gate.

"Fallott has a talent for it," said another with a grin.

"Serve as I did on the slave runs and you will learn it too," Fallott answered. He crossed the inner compound to the door of the mess room, looked around once, and went inside.

Pode and the guard exchanged glances. "He does not like delay," Pode said.

"Or anything else."

Pode smiled agreement. "Food for the boy and slave," he said. "Keep them apart."

The team did not remain long. Less than an hour later they were on the move.

To their left, seemingly tilted toward them, spread the expanse of gray sea. The track, glaring white against dark-green scrub, dipped and rose with the land, past a small village on the hill next to Thundersbarrow where the farmers paused to gaze at the prisoner as the team went by.

The few huts of the village dwindled; ahead and below, a mile away, wound the course of a lead-colored river. At its mouth it became lost in the waters of a glittering estuary, protected from the breakers by a long fawn shingle-bank mottled green with seablite. Westward along the coast rolled marshland as far as the eye could see, with scattered lagoons, salt creeks, and mile upon mile of reeds, the plumes in mass making the horizon purplish-brown. The line of hills rose again from the river a mile or so inland, running slightly away from the coast. Parts of it were covered by forest, parts by old farmland turned to scrub; but with each mile nearer Valdoe more of the landscape came under cultivation.

Fallott led the team down into the valley and across a flooded field. The water came to their knees; they splashed and waded through the shallows, the grass green at their feet. Strands of haycolored seaweed drifted on slight currents, and under the water they could see drowned thistles and clumps of burnt ragwort.

The river was too wide and too frequently crossed to depend on punts. The Flint Lord had built landing stages on either bank, and a ferry station to house the men who worked the raft. The ferry station, with stone walls and a plank door, stood on raised ground between the river and the flooded field. Beyond it the river slopped and slapped against the logs of the raft as it rode its moorings. The sun showed behind the clouds and lit up the hills on the far side, then the flooded land at their base, the river, the ferry station; and the sunlight moved on toward Thundersbarrow.

"More rain coming," Pode observed.

Fallott merely grunted and climbed the steps to the

threshold. Before he had a chance to knock, the door was pulled back and a tall, red-haired man appeared. He was dressed in armor like the soldiers Tagart had seen earlier. With a glance at the other members of the walking team he said something over his shoulder and two more men came out, both dressed in soldiers' clothes, with oxhide greaves and vambraces, helmets and cuirasses of thick leather, and mail made of linked ovals of deer-horn. On their feet they wore thick-soled boots in pattern like the fur-lined walking boots issued to the team. Their belts, studded with bone, carried sheaths to take knives, and axes with sockets cushioned by cartilage; in addition they carried spears fitted with elliptical tangs of the very finest ground and polished flint.

The red-haired man smiled at Fallott. "You have found us more work," he said, a reference to Tagart.

"I would like to stay and talk, Gane, and even drink your filthy ale, but as it is we shall not be making Valdoe by nightfall."

Gane, the red-haired soldier, shrugged and walked along the duckboards to the landing stage, followed by his assistants. "Bring the beasts on first!" he called out.

While Bico and Pode helped Fallott usher the goats on the raft, Bewry stood next to Tagart, pretending to keep guard. Tagart, weak with exhaustion, watched the farce of loading the seven animals onto the raft, no expression on his face.

"I will help you," Bewry said.

Tagart slowly turned.

"I will help you escape. If you promise to free my sister, I will help." Bewry looked at Fallott. His back was to them. "Do you promise?"

"Very well."

"Tell me what I must do," Bewry said.

Tagart struggled to think. His mind refused to respond. He could think of nothing but the raft, the goats, the drab river and the silvery light in the droplets of spray. He saw the wicker panniers filled with provender, the goats' backs, Bico striking them with his elder switch. Gane had grasped one animal by the head and was dragging it bodily from the landing stage on the raft.

"At the next rest stop," Bewry said, "shall I help you then?"

"Yes. Help me then."

"If he lets me take your yoke off I'll steal a flint from the panniers and give it to you with the bread. You can cut your fetter and run."

Tagart nodded wearily.

Bewry bit his lower lip. "You must run hard, and if they catch you say you had the flint in your clothes. My sister is in the slave quarters, by the gate. She serves in the kitchen there."

"Yes."

"You will want to know what she looks like."

"Yes."

"She is beautiful. Her hair is dark brown, to here." Bewry indicated the nape of his neck. "Her eyes are brown. She has a soft voice. She wears a deerskin tunic with a circle on the back."

"And her name is Segle," Tagart remembered.

"Everyone knows her."

Again Tagart nodded.

"You promise to help her?" Bewry insisted.

"I promise."

"Fallott will thrash me if he finds I helped you escape."

"We will be careful."

The last goat was aboard; Gane's assistants went to the mooring lines and untied them. Pode shouted to Bewry, telling him to bring the slave. Tagart preceded Bewry along the duckboards and onto the undulating deck of the raft. For a few seconds the men were busy shoving off, Gane and the two others bending poles against the bank, while Fallott, Pode and Bico drew in the mooring lines and made sure of the goats. Bewry examined Tagart's face anxiously, beginning to doubt whether he could be trusted.

Tagart noticed and looked into the child's eyes. "I keep my word," he said quietly

The next stop came eight miles farther west.

From the valley they had climbed to the ridge of the hills and followed it, through scrubby woodland where the wind groaned and made dead branches squeak, and onward to the fields of the open settlement by Cissbury fort. A flock of sheep with wooden bells scattered in their path, and the shepherd with a hand to his brim acknowledged Fallott's nod. Dogs barked as the team went by; one ran out and snapped at Tagart's ankles until Pode growled and struck it with a stick. They went on, skirting Blackpatch Hill and the small flint mines at Findon, and, leaving the fields, entered a belt of oak forest.

The road became a leafy ride, the grass still lush under the trees despite the summer's drought. A mile into the wood the ride opened into a glade, hemmed in by piles of bracken, shaded by the quiet branches, and here, beside an old fallen oak tiered and clustered with brackets of brown fungus, Fallott decided to halt for rest.

He and Pode unpacked the last of the route-victuals, while Bico went into the bracken to relieve himself. Fallott instructed Bewry to give food and water to the slave.

The sun had gone behind cloud; the air was gray. Early afternoon in the wood was silent, with no birds' song. Hoverflies, striped yellow and black, hung momentarily like little wasps in front of Tagart's face before darting away to investigate something else.

He was sitting alone, a little way apart, leaning on the fallen trunk. His wrists had been untied and the yoke left lying on the grass nearby.

He stared at the ground. The whole of his body was a mass of tiredness. The yoke had seemed to drain all feeling from his hands and arms, and as he sat there he slowly clenched and unclenched his fists until a trace of sensation returned. Where he had stumbled his feet were raw; criss-cross lines showed where brambles had torn at his legs. Dull bruises covered his thighs and body, bruises from being punched and kicked or from falling helpless to the ground, unable to put out his arms to shield himself. His left eye had turned red and puffy; he could no longer see from it. Dried blood was crusted in his beard and top lip below and to the side of one nostril.

Tagart looked up and into the network of leaves and light above. He was thinking of Burh, wondering how soon he would be able to get back there and finish what he had set out to do.

"Take it," Bewry hissed. "Quick before they see." He was pressing something cold into Tagart's palm. "Take it."

Tagart turned and came face to face with Bewry, and he remembered what they had arranged earlier. He was to cut through the fetter. Bewry was going to help him escape.

"Take it."

"Yes," Tagart said. His fingers tried to close on the flint. It slipped from his grasp.

"It's on the ground," Bewry whispered. "I cannot reach it yet. Fallott will see."

"I'm sorry. My hands are slow. I'm tired . . ."

"Drink."

"Those bastards have done for me."

Bewry had positioned himself between Fallott and Tagart so that nothing suspicious could be seen. He raised the water bag to Tagart's lips. From time to time Fallott glanced in their direction: Bewry and the slave had been whispering at the first rest stop and it seemed prudent to watch them, not that there was any serious danger of trouble.

"The flint is by your leg," Bewry said as he corked the water and broke off a piece of bread.

"I know."

"Can you reach it unseen?"

"If I reach it I will still not be able to use it. I have no strength to cut my fetter." Tagart put his hands to his face. "Leave it till later."

Bewry looked over his shoulder. It was a mistake. Fallott noticed and with a frown got to his feet. "What are you doing there?"

"The slave is eating bread." As he spoke, Bewry sneaked his hand to the ground, and changing his mind did not palm the flint but pushed it under Tagart's thigh.

Bewry's manner made Fallott narrow his eyes. "Show me your hands."

"Just bread, Fallott."

Fallott's gaze revealed no feelings as he saw the opened hands. It went to Bewry's face, to the ground, to the slave's bent head. "Move aside that water bag."

"I was giving the slave bread as you ordered," Bewry said as he lifted the bag. There was nothing under it.

"You. Slave. What were you whispering?"

The slave mumbled.

"What was that?"

"He was giving me food."

Fallott glanced round. He had an audience: Pode was watching; Bico had returned from the bracken and had found himself a piece of bread.

"I asked you what you were whispering, nomad."

"He was giving me food. He asked if I wanted more. I said I did."

Fallott was unconvinced, but he didn't know why. He was on the point of turning away when Bewry said, far too quickly, "The slave is exhausted, Fallott. Leave him alone."

"And why should I do that?"

"If he dies he'll be worth nothing to you when we get to Valdoe." There was a tremor in his voice.

"What has the slave been saying to you? What do you care if he lives or dies?"

"Nothing. I care nothing."

Fallott's frown deepened. "You care nothing, but you whisper to him at every stop."

"At the ferry station too," Bico called out.

Bewry shook his head. "He's said nothing to me, Fallott. Nothing at all."

Fallott could see the boy was terrified. He wanted to know why.

"What are you hiding there?"

"Nothing. Nothing, Fallott. I'm hiding nothing."

With the sole of his boot Fallott thrust against Tagart's shoulder and pushed him aside.

His eyes fell on the flint.

He bent and picked it up. "Nothing, you say. A sharp

nothing from our panniers. Is this why we haul a slave across the country, so you can cut him free with a knife stolen from your masters?"

"It was my plan," Tagart said weakly. "I made him bring it."

For an instant Fallott contemptuously studied the slave before turning back to Bewry.

"No," Bewry said, backing away as Fallott advanced.

"Nothing, you little heathen. Nothing, you say."

Now Pode had risen, worried for the first time that Fallott was losing his temper.

"Get to your feet!" Fallott shouted at Bewry.

"It's nothing, Fallott," Pode said. "Forget it. Forget it and we'll be on our way."

"Get to your feet!"

The boy put his hands against the fallen tree. He could back away no further. With his eyes fixed on Fallott's face he seemed to shrink against the bark, as if he would melt into the wood itself.

Fallott drew back his hand.

"No!" Bico cried out. "Don't hit him!"

The Brennis Gehans had made the beginnings of Valdoe over a hundred years before. The flint mines, discovered at first and tentatively worked by local people, lay on the southern slope of a commanding hill, its summit six hundred and seventy feet above sea level. The presence of the flint mines, the configuration of the landscape—not least the proximity of a system of salt-marshes and creeks and natural harbors—and the high quality of the local forest, had all persuaded the first Lord Brennis that Valdoe would make a suitable base for his operations in the island country. He was not the first colonist: for eight hundred years ships had been coming from the German homelands, and most of the coastal farmers shared his ancestry; but the Gehans were something new.

On his arrival the hill had been in the possession of a group of natives, brigands who lived by raiding the villages in the region and pressing their inhabitants into labor in the mines. The brigands had built for themselves a kind of fort, leveling part of the summit.

The Gehan force swiftly overwhelmed the hill fort and dealt with its occupants. Slaves were seized from the surrounding countryside and the building of the Trundle began. This was to be the heart of Valdoe, an impregnable fortress. Further leveling of the summit took place, forming a plateau of roughly oval shape, some fourteen acres in extent. A ditch nine feet deep was dug around the circumference, and inside the ditch was erected a burnt oak palisade twenty feet high, with elevated guard towers at intervals of sixty or seventy yards. Two gates, at southwest and northeast, gave ingress and egress. A second ditch and palisade, with a single heavily fortified gate, enclosed three acres in the center of the main enclosure, and here Brennis Gehan First (the first Gehan who ruled over the island country) established his residence and the barrack to house his personal guard.

The main barracks were built in the outer enclosure, in two sections, one by each of the gatehouses. Other buildings and structures, including dwellings for craftsmen and overseers, storehouses, animal sheds, an armory, two brothels, reservoirs for ten thousand gallons, dewponds, hawk mews, kennels, and a prison, were set out close inside the main palisade, leaving an open space and parade ground by the inner palisade. Quarters for slaves and miners were erected outside the defenses.

Meanwhile the hill itself was cleared of whatever timber remained, and strip-fields dug on the lower slopes. Roads to Eartham in the east, Bow Hill in the west, and Apuldram Harbor in the south, were pushed through to form the basis of a road system.

Soon the investment of time and effort began to pay. A stream of trading vessels from the homelands docked at Apuldram, where a quay and worksheds were under construction. Ships from the home yards were paid for with exported flint of the best grade, manned with soldiers, and sent on slaving sorties to the Normandy coast, for local labor could no longer supply the ambitious programs of road-building and mining. Freemen at home, dazzled by the tales of wealth and plenty, eagerly applied to the Gehans for permission to make the sea crossing, and within five years the slopes of Valdoe Hill supported the largest single community the island country had ever seen: there were soldiers, farmers, and friendly natives too, derived from those tribes which over the years had intermixed and provided petty traders, itinerant workmen wandering from village to village and harvest to harvest. At the age of forty-two the first Lord Brennis returned home, leaving his nephew in charge.

The initial impetus did not continue. The second Lord Brennis had failed to inherit his uncle's particular talents, and the rate at which Valdoe annexed new tracts of land became slower. A policy of exterminating the native nomad stock was allowed to fall into decline, and in consequence their numbers again built up in the densely wooded region north of the downs. Domination of the coastal villages was relaxed. The secondary forts at Butser, Harting, Whitehawk and elsewhere became weaker and in some cases were abandoned altogether, as were the small mines at Findon and Cissbury and Raven Hill.

It was not until the advent of the fourth Lord Brennis that the Gehan attitude was reasserted. Now the mines were vastly extended, the secondary forts refurbished. The number of slaves was doubled, then trebled and quadrupled. Military and naval strengths were stepped up. French and Cornish raiders, who in the past had made heavy depredations among the slow-minded farmers of the coast, now met a different reception as their ships were seized and their crews taken prisoner and enslaved. During this period certain coastal villages, such as Burh, were becoming more settled, and the fourth Flint Lord tried a system of direct extortion rather than troubling with trade, but soon this was given up: it was easier and more productive to control the slaves at Valdoe than the scattered population along the coast. Plunder and pillage were in future reserved for the settlements across the sea. To enforce the revised discipline tough new recruits were brought from the homelands and trained, and with their help the boundaries of the Valdoe empire began once more to expand.

Now the fourth Lord Brennis was dead. His son remained. At the age of twenty-nine, he had been in command for six years, in control of all the soldiers, the ships, the craftsmen and overseers, the slaves and miners, and in control of the Trundle, the unassailable fortress built by his ancestors on the top of Valdoe Hill.

⚴ 2 ⚴

THE NEXT DAY TAGART WAS PUT INTO THE MINES. HE WAS given no chance to recover from his journey, for on their arrival long after midnight Fallott informed Bewry's overseer that it was Tagart who had struck and broken the neck of the boy, and the other slaves heard the news.

The fertility of the mines—the richness and extent of their flint seams—was influenced by Gauhm just as the fertility of her fields; effigies of the Earth Spirit in chalk, together with chalk phalli, were enshrined at the entance to each shaft, and in alcoves underground. Ladders went down from the surface to the galleries, leading off from the shafts at various levels and in various directions, up to seventy feet below ground. The slaves worked by the light of oil lamps, roughly hollowed in small lumps of chalk. To remove flint from the rock face, they were issued with picks made from the antlers of red deer. The points of the picks were hammered into the chalk and the flint-bearing rock levered out and broken up, the rubble being pushed back with shovels made from cattle shoulder blades lashed to a handle. The shafts and galleries, from two to six feet high, were shored up with oak planks and props; these frequently failed and collapses were common. When this happened no real attempt was made to rescue the trapped men, for they had been claimed by Gauhm and were regarded as her right, an offering, payment for the flints extracted from the soil. The dead were only slaves, easily replaced—especially if not too many had been lost. A simple shrine would be made at the entrance to the fallen tunnel, to remind Gauhm of the sacrifice that had been made.

Throughout the mines a system of ropes and leather bags brought the newly dug celts to the surface, where they were sorted by specialists, ready for transmission to the knappers' and blademakers' workshops inside the Trundle. Here the raw flints, first split along lines of natural weakness to make two or more implements from each, were shaped by simple chipping, or, for axes and tools of a better and consequently more expensive grade, the flints were subjected to pressure-flaking: a highly skilled technique in which the pressure of a hand-held stone, applied at precisely the right spot, forced away flakes of flint to leave a sharp and durable cutting edge. The blades were then ground down by rubbing on a slab of wetted sandstone. In this way an ax-head could be produced that was capable of felling a hundred trees before it dulled, and with which one man could clear fifty square yards of birch forest in under an hour.

Tagart did not see Segle, Bewry's sister, until work finished that night. She was serving food in the slaves' quarters, in the refectory, passing bowls of porridge from the ladlers to the man at the head of each bench. An inclined head, a pointed finger, and Tagart was brought to her attention.

Tagart was on the verge of collapse, from lack of sleep, exhaustion, and from the punishment he had received on the walk and since his arrival. During the day, in the mines, he had been kicked and shoved and deprived of his lunch bowl. He'd had no sleep: word quickly reached the sleeping quarters that he was responsible for Bewry's death; supervision there was less rigid than in the mines, and he soon learned that the overseers were prepared to ignore peccadilloes which if noticed and acted on might incite the majority of slaves to more general trouble. They had done nothing while he was being beaten up.

During the day he could barely summon the strength to move; his partner, the man allotted to work beside him in the gallery, had been compelled to push Tagart up the ladders in order to get out himself.

Together with the rest of the day-shift, some ninety men in all, they had been marched from the flint workings to the slave quarters, a collection of leather tents and canopies enclosed by a tall wooden cage in the shadow of the southwest gatehouse. The quarters were partitioned into refectory and sleeping areas, the sleeping area enclosed by an inner cage with a roof of tattered skins on a grid of poles. The refectory, next to the kitchens, was formed by four large canopies over eight long wooden tables flanked by benches. It had just been vacated by the outgoing night shift: the dirty bowls cluttered the tables.

Tagart's partner, Boak, was a heavily built, doleful man with black eyes, wide lips and nostrils, and an overlarge square chin showing under a sparse black beard. He was handing dirty bowls to Tagart, who in turn handed them to the next man, up the table to kitchen-slaves who took them to the ladlers. The long wooden ladles dipped again and again into the smoke-blackened clay caldrons, emptied their steaming contents into the bowls, and other slaves, including the girl, distributed the filled bowls among the tables.

"That's the sister of the boy you say you did not kill," Boak said.

Tagart looked up. He saw the circle on the back of her tunic, just as Bewry had described. She turned from the caldrons with two bowls. In broad cast of feature she resembled her brother; but where Bewry had been ordinary, she was delicate, and even now, begrimed and oppressed by her existence, Tagart could see that in the forest, clean and free, she would be very beautiful.

"Pretty for a kitchen-slave," Boak said. "It won't be long before they move her to more important work."

"More important?"

Boak smiled, showing yellow teeth in a weary face that had seen too many people degraded and destroyed.

"She is not yet ready," Tagart said.

"Tell that to the brothel Trundleman."

"What is a brothel?"

Boak explained. "Blene has an eye on her," he said.

"Blene?"

"You saw him today. In the lynx jacket. He wants her out of the kitchens; come Crale Day he'll have the first taste. When he's finished she'll go into the Trundle, for the soldiers I expect."

With his baton the nearest overseer warned the two men to stop talking.

Tagart was seated third from the end of the table. The dirty bowls were cleared; full ones were being given out.

Gradually each man was served. When Tagart's turn came, he saw that the bowls were being brought by the girl.

She paused at the head of the table, and for a moment stared with hatred at Tagart, a bowl in each hand, steam curling upward. She gave one bowl to the first man, who passed it to the second, who passed it to Tagart. He slid it in front of Boak, whose meal it was.

Segle stood holding the second bowl, the one destined for Tagart. All eyes were turned. The overseers watched. Everyone in the refectory knew who Tagart was, knew what Fallott had told the supervisor.

Segle drew her arm back and with all her strength threw the bowl at Tagart's face.

The boiling gruel seared his face and neck; the bowl struck his temple and clattered to the table. He sat unmoving.

There was a murmur from the slaves. Tagart gripped the edge of the table, eyes downcast; three of the overseers stepped forward, and the murmur ceased.

The meal resumed in silence. Boak shared his gruel with Tagart, giving most of it away. At first Tagart protested when Boak offered him his bowl; but Boak from the corner of his eye noticed the overseer and by a quick lowering of his head warned Tagart to be quiet.

After the gruel the kitchen-slaves came round with water bags and baskets of the coarse brown bread baked in the camp ovens. Segle came to the table once more and Tagart seized his chance. When she put down the baskets he lunged across the two men beside him and took hold of her wrist; she tried to pull away as if his touch were poison.

"Listen to me," he said, as at arm's length she struggled to free herself. "Your brother died for you. Before Fallott killed him I made Bewry a promise." Tagart noticed the overseer stepping forward, pulling his baton from his belt. "I promised I would get you out."

"Hands off," the overseer said, prodding the back of Tagart's neck. "In two weeks she'll be promoted. You can have all you want then—if you wait your turn."

Tagart released her. Segle drew away, nursing her wrist.

"What were you saying to her?" Boak whispered.

Tagart ignored the question. "Why are they waiting two weeks? What happens then?"

"In two weeks is Crale Day."

"Crale Day?"

"The first day of Harvest. High Summer comes to an end. Crale Day is a feast. We're given ale, food fit for a human being, and a visit to the Trundle. I told you she was too pretty for the kitchens."

When the meal was over the miners were herded into the sleeping cage, moving in single file through the wicket while the overseers watched and counted heads. In the brownish light of the oil lamps Tagart shuffled behind Boak. He passed the overseer by the wicket.

"Sleep well, nomad."

Inside the cage the smell of sweat and excrement was stifling, despite the fact that it had just been sluiced down and besomed by other slaves, cleaning up after the night shift. Tagart, knowing that he could expect a repetition of his previous night's treatment, tried to find a position close by the wooden bars in one corner.

"Stay with me," Boak urged him, stepping over those who had already staked places on the floor.

They sat down in the corner, Tagart with his back to the bars.

The enclosure was full; the overseers shut and secured the gate, and the miners were locked in until mid-morning when the nightshift would return to take their place. For a while longer the glimmer of the lamps lingered on the dull leather awnings, the bars of the cage, the limbs and bodies and heads of those within, and then the overseers withdrew, taking the lamps with them.

Boak formed his words distinctly, so that all could hear.

"Any who strikes Tagart will have to strike me too. He's had enough."

"He killed Segle's brother," came a voice on their left.

"For that we have an overseer's word," Boak retorted. "Tagart says he didn't do it. I choose to believe him."

"And if we do not?"

"Then you are insulting me and I must act accordingly."

The others objected, but did nothing to approach. Tagart remained unharmed.

"I am grateful to you," he said to Boak.

"Don't be. Like it or not I have been burdened with you as partner. If the roof falls in tomorrow I depend on you to pull me out." He spoke more quietly. "Whether you killed Bewry or not, I don't care. My only interest is in a partner who is strong and well."

"That I can understand. But for my sake I will tell you again: Fallott killed the boy. He hit him in a fit of rage and broke his neck. Fallott blames me for it because a slave's word here is worthless."

"I have only heard of this Fallott," Boak said, "but as he leads a team you may even be telling the truth. That's how I came to be here myself—a walking team caught me. They took me from the fields while no one saw."

"How long have you been here?"

"A long time. I cannot remember. Some have been here all their lives."

"Do you ever think of escape?"

"Of course."

"Have you tried?"

"It's impossible. You will learn."

"Has it been done?"

"Only in rumor," Boak said. "Once a man was brought back who they said got away. A nomad, like you. They made us watch what they did to him. If you'd seen it you would not be asking these questions."

Tagart lowered his voice still further, in case they were overheard. "You've given up all hope, then."

Boak did not answer at once. "Life is sweet," he said at last. "Even for a worm."

"But not at Valdoe."

"Even at Valdoe."

"No."

"You'll find out."

"I would rather be dead."

"You are young and know nothing."

"I know that I must get out."

"Those men in armor today, did you think they were shadows?"

"Not shadows. But not gods. They are men, mere men. Cut a soldier's throat and he will bleed to death like anyone else."

"That is what the other nomad thought, the one they brought back."

In the morning the slaves were counted out of the cage, fed and taken downhill to the mines. The older men, or those who had found favor with the guards, were given light work such as rubble-clearing, hauling up the leather bags of flints, fetching and carrying water and food. Others were formed into details to replenish the heaps of struts and planks used for shoring and shuttering below ground. The rest of the slaves were counted down the ladders and sent into the galleries.

Tagart and Boak and two more descended the creaking ladders to one of the deep seams off a minor shaft. The first man down carried a light, a small flame in a chalk lamp which served to do no more than throw confusing shadows. His partner carried a bundle of fifteen or twenty deer-horn picks. Boak wore a leather pouch with supplies of lamp fat, hammers, and a water bag, while Tagart drew down the ropes which would be used to bring out the flints. As they went deeper the air became cooler. The chalk, brown and dirty white, came off on their clothes and knees; in other places the walls of the shaft were unstable and had been shuttered with planks. They passed the entries to several galleries before reaching the one they had been told to work.

It was low and constricted, narrowing from the entrance, turning slightly from side to side as it followed the flint seams. At its end, twelve feet from the shaft, there was not even room to move on hands and knees, nor was there enough room for a light, and Boak was compelled to work blind. He levered out the chalk blocks with his pick and with his fingers, passing them back to Tagart farther down the tunnel. Tagart passed them back to the third man, who broke up the blocks and pushed the rubble aside. The flints went into the leather bags, which when full were dragged out of the gallery by slaves on the surface. The fourth man went up the shaft with the bags to bring them back; while they were being filled he fanned a panel of laminated reed-leaves stuck with glue, in an attempt to bring fresh air to the gallery mouth. But it had little effect. With the lamps lit, and four men working in a restricted space, the air in the gallery rapidly became foul. Sweat ran unceasingly into Tagart's eyes; the chalk dust clogged his nose and mouth and turned his hair and beard white. Every few minutes the four men changed places so that none should have to spend too long at the end of the gallery. Boak took the brunt of Tagart's work.

The hours fell into a numb, deadening routine. The leather bags came and went. Faintly through intervening rock Tagart could hear other picks at work. At long intervals an overseer climbed down the shaft to supervise progress.

Halfway through the shift a wooden gong sounded at the top of the shaft: the signal to break for food. An old man brought them bread, and bowls of boiled meat or beans and lentils. The same gong sounded at the end of the day when the shift was over and the miners were marched up the grassy slope of the hill, past piles of timber and white rubble, to the canopies and poles of the slaves' quarters.

Bewry was dead; Segle knew that her term in the kitchens would soon be coming to an end. Luckily Blene, the mines Trundleman, had no direct authority over her, but she had seen him watching her as she worked, and now that Bewry was gone and they no longer needed a lever to make him compliant, there could be no reason to deny Blene's request much longer.

It made no difference to her, not now. Her life, the tribe's honor, had finished. They had finished at that moment under the cliffs at Lepe when the soldiers appeared.

She remembered the look of the sea, green waves blending to gray in the strait, foam crashing on the shingle as the tribe wandered the tideline. In pairs and threes oyster-catchers, black and white, piped from their red beaks and fought the wind in the troughs, flying just off the beach. Over the drab expanse of saltings and samphire to the west she remembered the wild cries of the curlews and godwits; the distant noise of the gullery where the Guelen had spent a week living on eggs; and she remembered the smell of the marshes, of brine and rotting weed, the air somehow making your skin more smooth, and when you licked the back of your hand it tasted of the sea. And she remembered another sound, urgent and dangerous, emerging from the roar of surf: hounds.

The soldiers had outmaneuvered them, coming from the east along the shoreline. Others were appearing against the sky on the clifftops. There was nowhere to run but into the mud.

Segle emptied another bag of oats into the caldron. Now Bewry too. She was past tears; she thought of his small body lying somewhere in the bracken and a little more of the light went from her eyes.

At first she had believed the story, that the nomad had killed him, but now she was not sure. She did not know. Boak, she had heard, had defended him last night. Did that mean anything? And what had he said to her about a promise? She could think now of nothing but the strength of his grip on her wrist. His words had escaped her. But his eyes had not, nor had the sound of his voice. In them she had recognized her own kind.

"More beans here!"

Segle pushed the hair from her brow and went to obey.

* * *

"So from what you have told me," Tagart said, "there can be no escape from the cage, nor from here. That means we must wait our chance and break from the bathing party."

It was the fifth day: Tagart and Boak were working alone in a minor gallery at the bottom of the main shaft. Tagart had recovered much of his strength. The cuts and bruises sustained on his walk had almost healed, his eye had opened, and regular food and sleep were bringing back tone and balance to his muscles and limbs. Work underground was arduous and unpleasant, but he was young. The output of the other slaves was well within his capacity, and he saw no reason to extend himself. For long periods when lightly supervised he and Boak sat and rested, taking up their picks and hammers when they heard the creak of rungs which meant an overseer was descending. The overseer in charge of the main shaft, named Stobas, was a broad-faced man with pale blue eyes and straight black hair, shoulder-length, tied into a pigtail. Like all the overseers, he was himself a former slave who knew no other existence but Valdoe.

"He's coming," Tagart said, and crawled into the end of the gallery, where he began to hammer conscientiously at the chalk.

Stobas appeared at the mouth of the gallery, swinging himself off the ladder and into the tunnel. He carried a lamp with him, and in his belt a blackthorn cudgel fitted with a wrist-strap.

"Work is slow here," he said. "You're slacking."

"The seam is harder at this end, master," Tagart said.

Stobas briefly examined the rock face. He scratched it with his thumbnail, wiped the chalk off with his index finger. "More bags or you'll both be beaten," he said tersely, returning to the ladder.

"Yes, master," Boak said.

Stobas paused. "Didn't you hear the gong? End of shift. Get above ground."

At the top of the shaft, in a wide cavern, the ladders became a permanent staircase of worn and chalk-stained planking which led up into a sloping tunnel with daylight at its end. Tagart and Boak emerged with eyes squinting against a red sunset.

"Full count!" another overseer cried out as Stobas stood surveying the ragged ranks of slaves, three deep, thirty yards long.

"To quarters!"

The men wearily turned and started up the hill, closely guarded by the overseers and the squad of soldiers sent from the Trundle at times of shift change. Other soldiers kept watch during the day and night at each exit from the mines, armed with spear slings and bolas; and, following a mass breakout some years before, the watch on the slaves' quarters had been reinforced. A system of head-counting at shift change, meal times, and on entering and leaving the sleeping cage reduced still further the opportunities for undetected escape. Similar vigilance attended the details formed for timber cutting, water haulage, and the like, or when, twice a month, small groups of slaves were taken down to the river to wash and have the lice removed from their bodies. If a slave did manage to escape, his chance of remaining free was almost nil. Teams of tracker dogs with their handlers could be dispatched from the Trundle within minutes.

The men of the night shift were counted out and passed down the hill to the flint workings; Tagart and the others were counted into the refectory and in silence sat down to their meal.

Bewry's sister was there. On several occasions over the past four days Tagart had met her eyes; but since the incident on the first evening they had not spoken, for by chance he and Boak had always been seated well away from the caldrons. But tonight, as they had been the last in line, they were put at the end of the table nearest the big clay hearth. Segle moved to and fro; Tagart watched her, and with a pang realized what he had not admitted to himself before—that she reminded him in her movements and attitudes of Mirin.

"What is it, my friend?" Boak said.

Tagart shook his head.

Warily Boak kept an eye on the overseers. "What's troubling you?"

Tagart could not tell him: he did not know how to put his feelings and longings into words. How could he explain what his life had been; how could he describe what they had taken away?

"I do not take to captivity," Tagart said at last.

"Then you are serious about escape? Or was that just talk?"

"You said you'd changed your mind today. If you want to come with me, I plan to break from the bathing party."

"We'll never do it. They bring the dogs down to the river."

The overseer passed behind them. Tagart continued handing dirty bowls to the serving-slaves; Segle was two tables away, not near him. He looked at her and she half turned, and Tagart knew that she was aware of him as he was of her.

"You've never been in a bathing party," Boak hissed. "I know what to expect. There must be another way."

"How did the other man do it? The nomad."

"No one knows."

"Then it must be the bathing party. When are we due to go?"

"The day after tomorrow." Boak sneaked a glance over his shoulder at the overseers: their attention was elsewhere. "It's too dangerous," he whispered to Tagart. "Even if we get away, where can we go? Where can we hide?"

"In the forest. No one can catch me there. If you come with me you will be safe too."

Boak bit his cheek.

Tagart shrugged to himself. He needed Boak, or at least, he needed someone who knew the routine. But once on the loose Boak might well prove a nuisance. "Decide tomorrow," Tagart said.

Boak nudged him to silence. An overseer had come to stand by the caldrons, idly watching the ladlers at work. Now the freshly filled bowls were being given out. A gray-haired woman had been serving Tagart's table; Segle spoke a few words to her.

Deliberately Segle came over. Her presence beside Tagart was almost tangible, and even before she opened her mouth and spoke he sensed something shared, wordless, a sensation he had only known once before. But her face was hardened by determination and as she slid the bowls onto the table she spilled a little of their contents and he saw that her hands were trembling.

She looked straight into his eyes. "Did you kill my brother?"

Tagart slowly shook his head.

"Then was it Fallott?"

"Would I kill a future hunter, one of my own?"

Her expression softened and Tagart knew that he had been believed, that she now regretted her first feelings; he felt an urge to touch her hand with his own and make contact, physically to confirm what had passed between them in looks, but Segle was already moving away, back to the caldrons.

3

THE FOLLOWING MORNING DAWNED WINDY AND GRAY; spots of rain began to fall as Tagart and Boak stood in line, waiting to be ordered underground.

Blene, the Trundleman in charge of coordinating the mines, a man of forty, unapproachable and fastidious, appeared from the Trundle and at his leisure made his way downhill. His black hair was cropped very short, close to his scalp, and twice a day he scraped off his beard with a flint razor and seaweed mucilage as soap. His eyes, pale gray, missed nothing: no detail of the mines was beneath his attention. Today he had discarded his lynx jacket in favor of a sealskin cape fixed at the throat with a cherry-wood clasp.

He arrived. "Six more for the west workings," he said crisply. "Take them from the main shaft."

With jerks of his finger Stobas indicated the six slaves who were to be reallocated. He chose carefully. If productivity in his section fell he would lose privileges, but if he gave Blene men who were obviously old or infirm he would incur the Trundleman's disfavor. He picked one old man, a youth with scarcely a beard, two brothers who were well known as reliable workers, and, smiling inwardly, Stobas indicated Tagart and Boak. At his command all six joined the remainder of the day shift for the west workings. This was an old part of the mine, nearly exhausted now, providing flints that were only barely superior to those that could be picked up off the ground anywhere along the downs; the shafts had gone as deep, the galleries as far, as the flint seams and the difficulties of ventilation allowed. Blene was anxious to complete work there and make a start on new excavations farther down the hill.

"Have you decided on escape?" Tagart said to Boak as they waited. "Are you with me?"

The other man looked at the ground, unwilling to meet his eye. "The bathing party is tomorrow," he said.

"What of it?"

"Tomorrow is too soon."

"Not for me."

"We must prepare. Let's go tomorrow just to look."

"No."

"Why?"

"I must get out."

"Leave it another half month till the next bathing party. We can do it then."

Tagart was adamant. He refused.

"But why?"

"Crale Day."

Further conversation was impossible; Tagart and Boak were teamed with the old man, Maphen, and a dark, quiet foreigner named Chorn, issued with lamps and picks and a water bag, and sent down the ladders to a wide gallery thirty feet below the surface. For much of its length its walls and roof were boarded and supported with oak planks and struts. Broken picks littered the floor. Maphen set lamps in crevices and alcoves, and Chorn started work on the rock face even before the rest of the shift had finished climbing down past the gallery mouth. Tagart and Boak exchanged glances; Boak wagged his head in mock amazement.

At a lower level men were shouting orders and responses. Boak explained that the gallery below theirs was being closed: the six extra slaves had been needed to help reinforce the shuttering, retrieve the ropes and bags, and dismantle the ladders.

"You still have to answer me yes or no," Tagart said, shoveling rubble back. The work was beginning to make him sweat. Chorn, the foreigner, hacked at the chalk as if he bore it a grudge. "You must tell me if you are coming."

"I know," Boak felt himself standing on the edge of a precipice. But realizing it, he already knew he was falling.

"What have you decided?"

"Let it be tomorrow."

"And are you with me?"

"Yes."

The attempt was doomed, Boak knew it as well as he knew his own name, but he no longer cared. He had been affected by what Tagart had been saying day after day. At first he had refused to listen. Boak knew the boy's words for what they were, facile and immature; he knew the hard reality. A slave at Valdoe could not get away. They would both be caught. But he also knew that even if they were seized in the first instant of escape, even if they were, like the nomad who had tried it, tortured and put to death as an example, even then he would have made an attempt, a gesture, futile perhaps, but he would have been free for a few seconds, no longer in bondage, no longer in the service of those who had made themselves his masters. He would have shaken them, brought a moment of uneasiness to the Lord of Valdoe, a man he had never seen, a man who despised him as a slave. It would be worth it for that alone.

The first gong sounded. Work in the gallery ceased. Stew was brought down the shaft in leather satchels and given to the miners in the wooden bowls left in each gallery for the purpose.

"Stew good," Chorn said. He was sitting with his back to the shuttering, picking fragments of meat from the bowl, raising his fingers to his open mouth, head tilted back.

"Make you work faster," Tagart told him.

"Ya." Chorn nodded. He noticed Maphen. "Old man," he said. "You don't eat. I eat for you."

Maphen waved his words away. He was tired. The lamps were sputtering. He shut his eyes and rested his head against the boards.

Tagart finished his stew. It left an oily taste in his mouth. "Pass me the water," he asked Chorn.

Chorn did not understand.

"The water. Give me the water."

Comprehension came across his face. "You want water."

As he handed Tagart the leather bag there was a low, barely perceptible vibration, a kind of distant groan, in the strutted roof above them. The boards at Maphen's back moved slightly. Tiny streams of dust showered down. Then from a much deeper level a loud, dull booming rose up the shaft and was followed by a series of percussive cracks as if structural beams were breaking. Behind Tagart the boards rattled and jolted and two of the lamps tumbled from their alcoves.

"Get out!" Boak screamed. "Get out!"

But even before they could scramble to their feet the ceiling props were no longer vertical and in the moment before the last lamp went out Tagart saw broken boards collapsing and the shape of boulders and dust and slabs of chalk falling in a solid roar, burying Maphen and Chorn in ton after ton of crushing pressure, catching Boak as he struggled toward the mouth of the gallery, and Tagart himself was being buried, struck by the fall, pounded across the shoulders and back, on his head, his legs, pinned to the floor by the intolerable weight of rock above him. He was unable to breathe, unable to move, utterly caught, his face being forced with increasing insistence downward. A little longer and he knew his cheekbones would fail. They would give way under the unbelievable weight and his skull would be pushed in from behind. But the ground had not yet stopped moving: it was still shifting, grinding, settling, filling in from above and at random the vacancy of galleries and shafts tunneled out below.

He lost consciousness. The voices woke him.

At first he had tried to accommodate them in his dreams, but the voices resisted, growing louder, intruding, annoying him: he wanted only to be left in peace. The voices made him frown. He was made to listen as his warm landscape dissolved and he became suspended in blackness and cold.

"Is anyone left alive?"

"Knock if you can hear us!"

Silence.

"You slaves, dig there and see how far in it reaches. There may be a pocket."

He heard rocks being pulled aside, dull and hollow.

"Is anyone in there?"

"It is Gauhm's will."

Tagart remembered what had happened.

The voices were not far away, three feet at most. Tagart raised his head and found it free. He could move his arms also. He felt them. They were not broken. He put his fingers to his face and discovered blood.

"Gauhm has taken them in this gallery too. Back to your labor."

The blood was in his beard; he traced it back to his nostrils and the warm ooze was slippery on his fingertips. From his nose he ran a finger along his teeth. One at the front was broken. The rest were intact. He probed them with his tongue. The taste of more blood. His hands were shaking.

"How many lost in all, master?"

"Overseer?"

"Seven below and four here, Trundleman Blene."

Pain sliced into Tagart's chest at each intake of breath. The bruising felt as if it extended down both his sides and into his buttocks.

"Eleven men lost in all, then."

"It might have been worse, Trundleman."

"Shall we make the shrine here, Trundleman?"

"Below. Make it below where more were lost."

A long time later Tagart realized the voices had gone away. Vaguely he could make out the sounds of activity at different levels, and when he heard the gong it was not long before the ladders creaked close by and he knew the day-shift men were going above ground.

There were varying weights on his lower back and legs. His feet seemed to be splayed at an odd angle and he hoped they were all right. He was trembling, shivering with the cold, yet there were chilly points of sweat on his forehead. With care he began turning his back, putting more weight on his right side. Lumps of chalk rolled off him. He turned completely and realized he was no longer trapped: his legs, like his body, were bruised but otherwise undamaged, and all he had to do to free himself completely was pull them out from beneath the pile of rubble.

Boak's voice, feeble and hoarse, came from the darkness behind him. "Tagart? Tagart?"

"Boak?"

"I can't move."

Tagart reached up and his fingertips sculptured the outlines of the crossed struts that had fallen against each other in the cave-in and spared him the force of the final collapse; the floor of the gallery had shifted sideways and down, forming a small chamber where he and Boak were left alive.

Boak was in pain. He said, "I'm cold."

"Keep still." On hands and knees Tagart crawled toward Boak's voice. His hands lit on the water bag: he felt it, the leather, the bung, the strap, acknowledging what it was. "Are you thirsty?"

Boak groaned. Tagart reached him and quickly found his face. There was something slimy over it. Boak was lying on his back, breathing quickly. He coughed. Tagart felt his jaw, his nose, behind his head. Much of his scalp had been torn off. Lower down, at the nape, Tagart touched something hard, wet, and strange, gritty with dust, the place where his neck was broken and his spine exposed.

"What are you doing to my feet?"

Tagart held the water bag to Boak's lips. He kept knocking the spout against Boak's teeth: for he was trembling very badly. A trickle came out. Some of it found its way into Boak's mouth. He retched and coughed and Tagart took the water away.

The rocks under which Boak had been buried were too heavy to shift. For the moment Tagart had been able to clear Boak's mouth and nose so that he could breathe more freely. That was all. He knew that Boak was already finished. Even if they were rescued, even if Boak were given the best treatment with comfrey and splints, he would never survive. A broken arm might be cured, with luck; perhaps even a broken shin. But not a broken neck.

"I'm cold," Boak said. "I'm cold. I want to be in the sunshine."

Tagart sat rocking from side to side with eyes closed. His chest hurt. He hugged himself, trying to ease the pain of bruising.

"Boak?" he whispered.

No answer came. Boak was dead.

Tagart crawled to the other end of the chamber, to the place where he had heard the voices, and put his cheek to the rocks. Sounds of picks and hammers reached him, faintly, from another level. He moved his face from side to side, listening, watching, and tried to catch a glimmer of light. There was none.

Tentatively he explored the pile of rubble in front of him, desperate not to make a sound. It was composed mainly of small fragments of chalk. distinguishable by its greasy texture, some larger chunks, and a few flints. Here and there he felt broken planks and spars, and the shapes of wooden pegs and rope, and leather bindings that had burst from their brackets.

Piece by piece, he moved the rubble behind him.

The major obstacle was a pitprop, wedged at an angle across the blockage. Even if he could have managed it, removal of the prop would have brought down the rest of the gallery about him and summoned help—the last thing he wanted. He was forced to work around the prop. The necessity for silence slowed his digging still further, but the blockage was less than four feet thick and his progress toward the other side was sure.

He had actually pierced the blockage, made a hole large enough to put his arm through and feel air, when the gong sounded and he thought he had missed his chance.

But instead of the night-shift men coming up the ladders, he heard the descent of the meal slaves with their bags of stew. And in spite of everything he grinned with delight. At last fortune was beginning to go with him again.

He continued to pick at the rubble, making the hole wider, wide enought to get through, and then he put some larger lumps back to fill the gap and settled down to wait and to examine himself properly, to take stock.

He had not suffered any internal injury, of that he was fairly sure; but the pain and bruising in his chest was very bad and spreading further, into other regions, especially down his left side. The trembling in his hands had scarcely improved. But his limbs were intact, especially his legs, for which he was glad: whether or not he had received a concussion, he could still run, and for the moment he could think. There in the complete darkness of the collapsed gallery his thoughts ran clear and cold, uncluttered in a way he had never known before. He felt he could see into the future, if he wanted. He knew what was going to happen. It was no mistake that events had fallen in the way they had.

For him it had all been a lesson. The forest, impersonal, indifferent to him in his time of need, now promised to take him back. He saw the pattern. He saw the end, his release from the acrid loneliness that had been with him since Balan died.

He waited, as if he were waiting for deer, exploring his thoughts. The water bottle lay at his side. No mistake. Fifty miles to Burh. He could not risk using the Valdoe roads. A forest route, then. Twenty miles a day, his usual speed, might be too much for him in his present state. Fifteen, then. Allow three days. Four at most. He would have to feed himself on the way. Burh in four days. Four back to Valdoe. That left two spare days before Crale Day.

It could be done. He could get the girl out somehow.

He gave his mind to luring the head man from the village. Among the trees, he wanted him among the trees. Easy.

Everything easy, falling into place . . .

How to deal with Valdoe afterward, how to bring Segle out, as he had promised her brother by the ferry station with the clouds blowing over Thundersbarrow and the spokes of sunlight across the river, giving the weight of his honor; and, because he was the one chosen to be left, the weight of the tribe's honor, given to a small boy struck dead that day because he loved his sister more than his own life.

Valdoe would not be so easy, not so easy as the village, but in his delirium Tagart knew he could do it too.

* * *

At the second gong Tagart was ready. He pulled the lumps of chalk from the gap, and, before the first slave had started up the shaft, he was squeezing through the hole and into what was left of the gallery. He lay there momentarily, overcome by the excruciating pain in his chest, forcing himself by an act of sheer will to do what he had planned next.

The ladders were creaking with the weight of men passing upward by the time he had finished it, the painstaking task of filling the hole in. He waited his chance in the darkness near the gallery mouth, and, the water bag thrust inside his tunic, he swung himself onto the ladder and joined the exodus.

A rainstorm was blowing above ground. The guards and soldiers wore glistening sheepskin capes and shouted to each other against the howl of wind. Tagart was the sixth or seventh miner to emerge blinking in the morning light; he turned with a comment to the man behind him.

"I hope they plan something better for us than the mid-shift meal."

"At least we can drink with it." The other man nodded at the rain, pelting the ground, driving in sheets across the face of the hill, obscuring and then revealing the shape of the fortress at the summit.

All the miners were filthy, grimy with chalk: Tagart's appearance excited no interest or comment, for he had cleaned most of the blood from his face and beard. He moved forward, covertly glancing at the piles of timber newly removed from the west workings. The others, twenty-seven in all, came behind.

Tagart traded remarks with his new-found friend, establishing himself, he hoped, as a member of the night shift.

"Quiet there!"

More men were appearing at the entrance of the other shafts, while the soldiers watched and the overseers shouted orders, mashaling the slaves into a rank. The soldiers and overseers looked cold and wet. Some of them had been standing in the open all night, and would get no shelter until this shift was safely behind bars.

Tagart heard Stobas's voice issuing instructions. The rain blew in curtains across the workings, streaking chalk on the miners' faces, plastering hair to heads. Tagart felt his clothes increasing in weight.

The line of men was moving too fast, too far away from the pile of timber Tagart had chosen; he stopped and pretended to see something in the grass before shuffling on. The man with whom he had spoken went ahead.

"All up!" shouted the overseer from the west workings, and one by one the others reported the same.

"All up!"

"All up!"

Tagart felt a flood of gratitude. The weather was doing it for him. The weather.

From the back of the rank he glimpsed the overseers standing tall, moving their hands edge-on, counting off slaves in threes. The first had finished his count and was frowning slightly. He started to count again.

On either side of Tagart the slaves were looking straight forward. One was a thin, spare man who looked like a farmer, the other a shorter man who could have been a foreigner like Chorn. Neither seemed to have noticed him particularly. Like the others, like the guards, they were keen to get the count finished and hurry back to the buildings for shelter.

The back of the rank was being observed by at least three soldiers. From the rank to the pile of wood he thought it twelve or fifteen paces, too many to cover undetected with the soldiers watching, even in this rain.

A hundred or so heavy struts made up the pile of wood, laid parallel to the line of the rank. Just beyond it lay other piles of wood, and a series of white chalk spoil heaps discolored by topsoil, leading downhill and away from the fort. The ramparts were nearly a mile off. In this weather there was no danger of being seen from the Trundle.

"One over!" the first overseer shouted, and for a moment all heads turned.

It was enough. Tagart, backing gingerly at first, cleared the rank and ran to the pile of wood. He glanced behind. Everyone, mildly curious, was listening to Stobas ask how ninety-three could come out when only ninety-two had gone down.

Everyone except one man, the farmer who had been standing next to Tagart.

Tagart met his eye.

The farmer smiled, glanced sideways at the soldiers, and turned back with every sign of renewed interest to watch the dispute between overseers.

"One over!" the second overseer shouted.

"Check count!" Stobas ordered. "Rank form into pairs!"

But Tagart had already found a place to hide in the middle of the pile. He crawled through a triangular gap, constricting his chest again, pushing with the heels of his hands on the rain-soaked timbers. The pain of working himself past the struts threatened to make him cry out. But his chest was through and he dragged himself further inside, into a space lower down. Vision fuzzed by pain, he forced himself into it, and, just as the rank re-formed and the soldiers again began their supervision, his feet and then his toes slid through the triangular entrance to his hiding place and disappeared from view.

4

THE OAK TREE IN WHICH TAGART HAD HUNG THE WOMAN grew on the slope above his yew tree, less than two hundred paces east, but it was not until some while after his return that he was able to focus his mind on his hostage and what he had done with her.

His journey had taken five days, the first spent in hiding under the heap of struts. The worst moment came after the completion of the check count. Stobas became suspicious, and considered sending a man to the Trundle to advise Blene; but for the weather, and the fact that the check count gave, after all, the right total, a search might have been ordered, and perhaps the dogs brought down. Tagart tried to draw himself further into the pile of timber. He was hungry and very tired, suffering the symptoms of shock, and mild concussion, and the pain of the bruises on his body was turning steadily worse. Later in the day more timber was flung on the heap and Tagart feared that he might not be able to get out. But at nightfall, when the shifts had long since changed and the soldiers were least expecting anything unusual, he silently crawled out and hobbled into the darkness unobserved.

That night he made only five miles, stopping in the early hours to rest and await the morning. Any exertion made the discomfort worse. His sleep, a few minutes together, was colored by nightmares that seemed to persist in his waking thoughts. The same dream repeated itself. Segle was with him in some unfamiliar place, a lake in a clearing. He knew they were safe, a great distance from Valdoe; they were beside the water, drowsy in the afternoon sun. Tagart had shot a wildcat and they were roasting it over a bed of embers. Beside the lake stood the brown stems and umbels of chervil and keck. Creamy blossoms of hemp agrimony billowed pink across the water, in line with the course left by the passage of their bodies through the weed. They had been swimming, out through the frogbit and into the center of the lake where from a deep spring the water welled limpid and cold. The girl was naked, her hair wet and lying close, revealing the shape of her brow; but as he looked into her eyes her face became a grinning skull. He ran to the water's edge and knew what he would find. She was floating just beneath the surface, white and swollen.

There were other dreams, all involving the girl. Frequently he shouted himself awake and sat up, shivering and trembling. At last he got to his feet. The strength had gone from his legs. He found it hard to keep moving, even from tree to tree: he was bone tired. Full daylight was coming on. He ate a few berries, felt slightly better for them, and in the dry leaves below the bushes discovered a hedgehog, curled up and asleep. As he had no knife or hand-axe he urinated on the animal to make it uncurl and killed it by pinching the snout. With a broken pebble he did his best to skin it, and ate it raw. A little later he came across a wood pigeon's nest in the ivy against an oak and gulped down the contents of both eggs.

He was traveling northeast, into the deep forest behind Eartham Hill, keeping well away from the coast and the danger of open ground. The sky cleared gradually and by the time he reached the first of the great rivers there was intermittent sunshine. The sun stayed with him on most of the following days, days of slow progress and weariness. Increasingly he found it hard to think straight, to remember details; his thoughts were sluggish, and his body refused to respond properly. The second day was the worst. After that he began to improve; he was able to cover more ground. On the third day he came across the remains of a temporary camp, vacated less than a week earlier by a tribe whose bark-cut signs he identified as the work of the Jays—people he knew. Not for the first time he considered seeking help. But he had no time to spare. The Jays had gone northwest and might be days ahead, and he was on his way to Burh.

On the fourth night, under a gibbous moon that made the marshes silver and black, he came out of the forest and used one of the punts to cross the wide river in the reeds, the last great river before Burh. And on the fifth day, at mid-morning, he found himself once more in sight of the village.

He had been absent for twelve days. Outwardly, there had been little change. From the escarpment he saw people in the compound and on the steps of the Meeting House; work had resumed in the fields, which now were markedly greener. After a while had made out the beardless man,

Groden, working with several others, cutting hay from a field by the river. Tagart wondered if his hole in the silo, his entry and exit, had been discovered.

He could not find the yew tree straight away. It had been concealed and camouflaged too well, and his memory deceived him: the tree was more to the north than he remembered, and it looked different in shape. But even if he had been unable to know the place at all, his attention would have been drawn by the carrion flies and the smell of putrefaction. The strips of venison had turned. A fox had taken many of them. The rest were crawling with maggots. Tagart carried the strips beyond the yew and flung them far into the undergrowth.

He checked over what was left of his stores. A few flints, three bows lacking strings, an arrow, short lengths of twine and rope, two water bags, and the bottle he had brought with him from the mines. He would need to arm himself before going back for Segle. The village: they would have weapons down there; and he would have to have clothes and clogs to get inside Valdoe. Those too could be found in the village.

Yes, he knew the way it was all going to unfold.

He shut his eyes and covered his face. His hands were still trembling: they had not stopped, not completely, since the cave-in. He felt as if he were burning his reserves at a profligate rate, fighting alternate waves of chill and heat. Still his thoughts were not normal. There were blank spots, areas of impenetrable and hazy memory, moments of lucidity followed by a kind of delirium in which his mind raced extravagantly, inconclusively. The toll of the past weeks was catching up with him. Physically the bruising on his body had begun to heal: yellow, green, purple. He undid his tunic and examined himself again.

He told himself that he had been in low states in the past, and he had suffered bruising. He had been hurt before. This was nothing new. The exhaustion and fever, the delirious thoughts, these were nothing new. He tried to console himself.

But in his condition he had no defense against mistakes.

He pushed the thought aside, fastened his tunic, stood up, and went outside to find food.

Only in the late evening, after he had slept, did Tagart remember there was something else in his camp that he still had to investigate. He found the oak tree after a short search, and climbed into it.

Hernou was still there. Hanging upside-down, the blood had drained into her head and the upper part of her body. From the contortion of her features he gleaned an idea of the circumstances of her death. In her throes the rope had been worn almost to its last fiber wherever it rubbed on bark. Tagart undid the gag. Her face seemed barely recognizable. She had been dead about eight days.

He cut the body down.

He was trying to think. How could he have forgotten?

How could he have forgotten such a thing?

No answer came. He put her over his shoulders, and, remembering what he had planned to do, gasped and struggled with her weight on his way toward the escarpment.

Sturmer paused in his work and stood upright, pulling back his shoulder blades and stretching his spine. Stooping no longer agreed with him so well. In his right hand he held a sickle, a yard of blackthorn with a steam-curved end in which were set half a dozen flint chips to form a cutting edge. With it he had been swinging gradually along the river bank, cutting down the tall bromes and meadow grasses for winter silage, in line with thirty others. Between them they had cleared most of the river field since daybreak. Now, at mid-afternoon, women and children, and those who could no longer do full work, came behind collecting the cut grasses into sheaves ready to be bundled and dragged back to the village. The old men, supervised by Vude, trimmed the hay-sheaves to size, ready for packing in the barn.

This task would not normally have fallen to the old men; but the population of the village had been almost halved, with the worst losses among the young, those whom Burh could least afford to be without. The crippled and maimed numbered more than twenty, and they, like the orphans and widows, would have to be fed.

Most of the surviving young men wanted to leave. They were afraid that Tsoaul had not yet finished. Fallott had failed to come with help, and for that Sturmer had been partly blamed; but he had reasoned with them, and begged them to wait. Since the new moon the forest had been quiet. The trouble was over. Tsoaul had taken Hernou and would not be back. Why allow themselves to be driven out? Why throw away years of work for nothing? Why face the danger and hardship of founding a new village when their true home was here in Burh?

The Council decision on the matter had been inconclusive. The older men felt that Hernou had been taken because it was she who had been to blame for the killing of the nomads, and only right that she should be sacrificed for the common good. They said she had plotted to attack the nomads, blinding Groden and those around her with her beauty, an evil and poisonous influence. Now that her influence had gone, there could be no more risk; and even Groden had given up hope of finding her. The younger men argued differently. The only reason, they said, that no one had been abducted since Hernou's disappearance was that no one had left the village, except in parties of a dozen or more, and no one at all had ventured into the trees. Tsoaul was still in the forest, waiting his chance.

Sturmer had been unable to convince them. In deference to the elders, and for that reason alone, the young men had reluctantly agreed to stay.

Now their fears had been eclipsed by the urgent need to make a harvest. The prospect seemed bad. Even though there were only half as many bellies to fill, there would not be enough food to last the winter. The drought had persisted too long. The barley crop was all but ruined; the wheat down by three-quarters; the millet by half; and the oats had failed completely, the panicles stunted, crumbling to dust when rubbed between the fingers. To save feed, all but a few of the animals would have to be slaughtered. Some could be sustained on the rougher ensilage that usually was not even harvested, which included the bromes and meadow grasses.

Sturmer returned to his cutting. The line of men moved steadily forward, in a rhythm with the swish of sickles and the soporific chuckle of the river as it went to the sea. Behind them the slain grasses lay strewn across the field.

The women had not been gathering for long when Sturmer heard his name called out from the village. He looked up. Vude, white-bearded, his bald head hatless, was hurrying toward him along the river path.

"Sturmer!"

"What is it?"

He went forward to meet the old man. They came face to face, twenty yards ahead of the line, and Vude bent and leaned on his knees, breathing with difficulty. He turned his face. "You must come, Sturmer. They're in the barn. They haven't seen it yet."

"Seen what?"

"Come quickly."

Vude led him back to the village, through the east gate. On the far side of the compound they saw the women, on ladders leaning against the palisade, dropping bundles of hay to the old men waiting below. Another group of old men trimmed and shaped the sheaves, while a third carried them into the barn and packed them crosswise and lengthwise, making a solid rick.

"This way," Vude said, branching left from the thoroughfare and leading Sturmer between the houses.

At the base of the palisade he stopped. "I came to see how much of the trimmings we could save. I took off the covers. Look."

A tunnel had been burrowed through one of the silos. Its cover, a mat of interwoven sticks, showed holes and signs of damage.

"The tunnel is large enough for a man," Sturmer observed.

"It joins up with a trapdoor in the turf on the other side. I thought you alone ought to know."

"So you have guessed the truth too."

"Not before now."

"I told Groden to make sure none remained alive," Sturmer said.

"You should have seen to it yourself."

"I think it was only one."

Vude nodded. "Any more and the ambush would have been different."

"That is how I reasoned it."

"Do you think he's still up there, in the forest?"

Sturmer squinted up at the escarpment behind them. "There's been no trace of him for a fortnight. He must be ill, or dead. If he'd gone for help it would all have been over for us a week ago."

Vude agreed. The nomads could signal each other, by magic, over great distances. One survivor of the massacre, if he had sought them, could have brought many to attack the village.

"You did well to tell me first," Sturmer said. With his sickle he rearranged the silo to hide the tunnel. "I must have your silence, Vude. If the others hear of this, the young men will prevail in the Council."

"But suppose the nomad is still alive? Suppose he has gone for help?"

"He hasn't."

"I trust you, Sturmer. I believe what you say. But the young men . . . they're saying you're not what you were. They say you're too old. Groden . . ."

"Groden is disgraced," Sturmer said curtly, standing up.

Vude let the comment pass.

"If you doubt me," Sturmer said, "tell the others. Tell them an army of nomads is coming and Sturmer is too stupid to admit it. Tell them and kill the village yourself."

"All I say is that you must take care."

"I shall."

"Then you have my silence, head man."

Tagart shifted sideways, throwing the woman's body from his shoulders. She rolled a little way down the escarpment and came to rest, arms and legs at strange angles, her face bloated and stretched, as tight as a drum. Tagart came after and shoved her with his heel. She turned over, twice, three times, and came to rest again.

The village lay in shadow; from up here the last wash of sunset could be seen. The moon, almost full, rode in the sky among the trees. Already its shine outdid the dusk: he could see it on the roofs and palisade, and on the curves of the forest across the valley, where the evening star burned steadily in the west. A heron flapped its way inland, like a pale gray wraith following the reflections and rushes of the river, neck curled back, legs outstretched behind, still dripping the water of the estuary. Over the village it uttered a single harsh cry.

Tagart rolled the corpse most of the way down the escarpment, stopping well short of the palisade for fear of alarming the dogs.

He dragged the body upright and manhandled it over to an oak bush, resting it against the drought-scorched, prematurely brown leaves. It slid rustling to the ground. He hoisted it again, positioning it another way, and another, until it remained, spread-eagled, in full view.

With many pauses to catch his breath, he turned and climbed back to the forest.

5

BY EARLY AFTERNOON THE NEXT DAY STURMER KNEW that to save himself and the village only one course of action remained. His special knowledge, shared with no one but Vude, made the decision easier to take, for it promised him the recapture of the support he had been losing throughout the day in Council. But the courage he needed did not come easily and in the floating unreality of the Meeting House he almost left it too long. His announcement that he alone would go into the forest and fight Tsoaul, drew gasps of disbelief, amazement, and then admiration.

The hours of the day had begun rapidly. His bed was still warm when he heard the news; and then Deak and Feno brought the corpse into the compound and he saw it for himself. The thing laid in the dirt before him had at one time been Hernou. It had housed her spirit, long since fled. He himself had, many years before, slept with it, made love to it, even once thought it might mother his children and be his wife. In those gaping orbits, eyes had sparkled. Tsoaul, the young men were already saying, had finished with her and flung her back: an omen, a sign of hostility renewed. In the early half-light, made chill by mists from the river and fields, Groden came at a run from his house and thrust his way among the villagers gathering around the body. He broke through the inner circle and stood transfixed, staring at what had been his woman.

His face twisted; he took a step back. His mouth seemed to fill, and he turned away.

An abomination sprawled there, a body with no soul. Without prayer, without the necessary repose on the Dead Ground, her spirit had been driven out, forced to wait too long alone in a disembodied state. Her soul had been lost forever to the demons and the wilderness. They could not give her a place in the burial mound. She had become part of Tsaoul's works, like the bodies of the bears.

But they did not burn her. At Sturmer's order, with Groden's acquiescence, she was taken to the beach and left for the ebb tide to carry out beyond the river mouth and on to the shoals, where the surf would pound her to fragments.

They returned to the Meeting House and sat in session all day. Every aspect of the omen was discussed. It meant further violence, further deaths. It meant plague and murder and terror. Tsoaul had not finished with them. There could be no mistaking his intent. In the voting and arguing the young men now held firm majority. All those with families wanted to pack their belongings and leave; and many of the old men were changing their minds and voting to join them. Vude stood out against the many.

"Where will you go? And what of those you leave behind? The old, the sick, the orphaned?"

"They can come with us or starve!"

"It's all the same to us!"

"We've seen enough of crippling and killing!"

"Time to leave while some of us can!"

"To go is to stay alive!"

"No!" Vude shouted. "To go is to be defeated!"

"Easy for you to say, old man!"

"Where were you in the fighting, old man?"

"Listen to Vude!" Groden said, and Sturmer for the moment could not understand what was happening. "Listen to him! He's right! Where will you go? No other village can take you. You will have to start anew. And how long will it take to build another Burh? Five years? Ten? How many will die before you can finish a new palisade? How many will the wolves come for? How many the bears? Do you think Tsoaul's hand can't reach wherever you go? This is our home! Our lives have gone into these fields! Nothing, not even a spirit, must be allowed to drive us away!" He turned on Sturmer. "This fool denies the truth! He refuses to face it! He still tries to tell us Tsoaul has gone! Well Tsoaul threw back my woman and any man who says not is no longer fit to lead us!" He thrust an arm toward the forest. "Tsoaul is there! He's there but we can fight him and we can win. We can win and we can stay!"

"I'll fight," Feno said.

"And I," Deak said.

"Who else will show himself a man?"

But before anyone had a chance to reply, Sturmer rose and told the Council what he meant to do.

* * *

High above the village, well into the forest, Sturmer thought he heard something.

He listened, turning his head, holding his breathing.

The random sounds of the forest at night came to him: the squeak of dead branch on dead branch, a low hiss of breeze.

He cupped his hands to his mouth and shouted again.

By day or by night, he'd had to make the choice. He knew the nomad was ill and alone, no match for a fit man. But in the forest a nomad would have all the advantages of woodcraft and silence. Night among the trees held many fears, imaginary as well as real, but Sturmer had witnessed the nomad's skill at shooting, and only darkness would rob him of it. To kill him Sturmer's best hope would be to come at him face to face and attack with a spear; and a hope was all it could be, even though one man, sick and alone, made a very different adversary from the Spirit of the Forest. So Sturmer had chosen night. He waited and listened on the path, sick with fear.

The promise of a return triumphant, boasting that he had personally slain Tsoaul, now shrank in importance in his eyes. Again he wondered whether to go back to the village and disclose what he and Vude had found, to take a group of the better fighters with him. But then he would never be able to flush the nomad out. He had to go on his own, to entice the nomad from cover and into a position where he could be seen and attacked. If he were to disclose what he knew his advantage over Groden would be reduced still further: and how much longer then would Sturmer be head of Burh, even if there were a Burh left to be head of? Self-preservation, more than bravery, or any desire to spare the village, kept Sturmer standing there.

"Come out! Come out! I am your friend! I mean you no harm!"

Far off to the left he heard the sound again, the rustling that had made him stop and listen before.

He put one foot off the path.

"Show yourself!"

The branches swayed a little in the breeze; the multitudes of leaves gently moved and returned, moved again. The wind had freshened. Sturmer looked up. Behind the sparse, high cloud, moving like fish scales across the sky, he saw the faint disc of the moon.

"I wish only to talk! Come out!"

No answer came. Sturmer stepped back onto the path and took a few paces along it, toward the gorge and its ruined bridge. The clearing there would be a good place to wait; he had already decided as much. The danger of traps in the clearing would be less than under the trees, for on the day of the ambush the nomad himself had walked freely to and fro across the clearing and presumably would not have rigged it since.

The cloud thinned and the moon appeared briefly, misty at its edges, casting a faint bluish light down the length of the path.

For less than a second, in less time than it took an eye to blink, Sturmer glimpsed someone moving ahead, glimpsed the movement of limbs, sensed rather than saw a sunken face in shadow; and the hazel branches by the path had opened and swallowed the figure up. He barely heard the scrape of leather on bark, circling him to the left; but it was as loud to him as any sound could be.

"I wish only to talk!"

The nomad had halted.

"Show yourself! I mean no harm! Come out and we can talk!"

The soft crush of a foot on dry leaves reached him, and hesitantly, another. He caught the judder of bramble hooks across leather, the tiny snap of a twig. And he realized the nomad was moving away, leaving him.

"Come back!"

But it was no use. The nomad obviously suspected trickery, or else was too timid to show himself. Sturmer listened closely and heard another twig break, deeper into the trees.

He looked up and down the path, not sure whether to follow. Was he himself being lured on? Was he being led into a pitfall or a hoist-trap? Or was the nomad merely afraid?

The spear he carried bore a short shaft, so that it would be less likely to catch in undergrowth. He slid it into his belt and stepped off the path. As he put down each foot Sturmer made a conscious effort to avoid breaking dead wood, felt with his hands for sprigs and branches which might whip back. The woods here, hazel under oak and hornbeam, lay deeply littered with dead leaves and he could not prevent them from rustling, seeming to him to be making much more noise than his quarry. He stopped to listen. A little way ahead he caught a faint scratching, and then it was as if the nomad had stopped to listen too.

"I must talk to you! I mean you no harm! I can help you! Answer me if you hear!"

The given reply came as a loud snap of old wood. The nomad was going on. Sturmer followed. They were climbing slightly, across the side of a slope.

Behind them the cloud went past the moon's face, becoming patchy, showing deep-black fields and ribbons of clear sky with stars. When these crossed the moon its circle stood sharp and flooded the trees with light, sliced to checkers and lozenges and black shadows by the leaves and branches, and Sturmer was able to see that he was being led into a grove of older hazel. He waited for the moon to be covered, and went on. Something like confidence began to encourage him; he could hear the nomad plainly now, breaking a way forward. They were entering the grove. In places the rotten hazel sticks lay this way and that, some caught up in the living bushes, others on the ground, half buried in the leaves. Lichen, pale in the weak moonlight, festooned the sticks and bushes.

Sturmer took his spear from his belt as he heard the nomad stumble. He quickened his step, no longer caring how much noise he made, snapping off projecting stubs, treading on dry branch after branch. He was gaining on the nomad, whose progress seemed to be slowing, growing weaker, the attempt of a sick man to get away unheard.

After three paces more Sturmer realized that the grove had fallen silent. The other man had stopped.

Gripping his spear with both hands, he warily turned from side to side. In the stillness following the crashing trail of the preceding minutes, he strained hard for a sound of movement or life.

Sturmer bent and listened, a frown on his face. He could hear nothing. Nothing at all.

The moon sailed from the clouds and illuminated the hazel grove. He stared at the place where he thought the nomad might be. Perhaps the nomad had fallen; perhaps he was injured, wounded, even dying.

Sturmer opened his mouth to call out, but another thought checked him. He looked around. He had allowed himself to be drawn into the middle of the hazel grove, a natural sounding box strewn with dead branches and obstacles, from which, whether he chose it or not, he could not hope to extricate himself without revealing his exact whereabouts with every step he took. The nomad had stopped making a noise; but had he stopped moving? Could he pass quietly where a farmer could not?

Suddenly Sturmer felt oppressed by the trees, isolated, confined in a place where he neither belonged nor had any right to be. He was a trespasser here. A hostility seemed to come at him from the forest itself, as if it somehow knew that he lived by the ax, cutting fields and clearings where green had reigned, the village an intrusion, the palisade and all the stolen timber, the trees uprooted and shorn of their branches a crime, an act of sacrilege.

Behind him, where no sound should have been, a spray of leaves rustled as if deliberately shaken. He whirled round to see its source, but cloud once more obscured the moon and the grove darkened.

He began to back away, his hands shaking and his mouth dry. He trod on a stick and broke it, turned, and with his forearm held high he plunged through the grove. A forked branch snatched at his spear. He let it go, too frightened to stop.

He ran straight into it. The force of the blow knocked him off his feet and flung him sideways, and he was landing hard and badly, smashing through dead wood, slithering into the carpet of leaves and rotting sticks. His fingers stretched out and the violence of his fall drove them into the ground. Dazzling numbness flared into pain in his neck and shoulder and jaw where the club had struck him.

He looked and against the sky saw the shape of his killer with arms raised, club held high for the finishing stroke.

* * *

Tagart's eyes opened at the scream. He had been almost asleep when he had heard it, a little way off to the southwest, a man's scream ended abruptly as if by death.

He lay there listening, wondering if he had imagined it. His condition had improved a good deal in the day and a night since putting the woman's body out on the escarpment. But he was still not right; for long periods he had lain motionless under the yew, his mind invaded by irrational plans of revenge and strategy. More than once he had determined to set fire to the village, or to build a dam and divert the river, or to lie in wait forever if need be and shoot the farmers one by one. But when the delirium receded he remembered Segle and Valdoe and he was unable to think of anything but getting back to her. At dusk he had checked the village again. He knew that he must wait for the music to come from the Meeting House, the music: he kept that in his mind, centrally, and even when he could not remember why he was waiting for the music he knew that it was important and he could not make a move before it came.

At nightfall he had returned to the shelter of the yew to sleep, to recover more of his strength; and then, some hours afterward, had come the scream.

He sat up and pushed himself to his feet.

Broad white moonlight bathed the forest outside the yew tree. Tatters of cloud drifted overhead; away from the moon's glare a rich haze of stars filled the sky. Tagart looked up and found the constellation of the Giant, a bowman with arm outstretched and one foot crushing the head of the Snake. The third star of the Snake's tail, between the Ladle and the Bear, marked due north. Taking his bearings, he set off to the southwest, downhill, frequently breaking the run of his progress with the heel of his hand against a branch or trunk, not daring to risk a fall by going too fast.

Groden untied the end of the twine from the bush and wound it around his hand, making a neat hank which he pushed into his pouch. The trick had worked well, just as he had intended. And now Sturmer had atoned for Hernou's death: for it had been Sturmer's fault that the bears had found a way into the village, Sturmer's fault that Morfe had been killed, Sturmer's fault that the village was dying and all the families planning to move away. But Groden had long ago suspected him of worse than just poor leadership. His opposition to further clearance of the forest and his unwillingness to fight back at the nomads who infested the trees and made spells against the village and its crops: all had made Groden suspicious, adding to his fears about Sturmer's secretiveness and his pretense of introducing new methods and crops. Over the months a pattern had begun to make itself clear, and in the days before the raid, while the sun steadily baked the fields to rock, the truth emerged. Sturmer, for months or even years, had been in league with Tsoaul. And when, in Council that afternoon, Sturmer had offered to go into the forest and fight its Spirit, Groden suddenly knew he had to stop him before he had a chance to make a new pact with Tsoaul and finish the village altogether.

His suspicion had been completely vindicated as he followed Sturmer from the village and heard him calling, trying to lure his evil master from the trees. Groden's last doubt evaporated: he went to the hazel grove and put into effect the plan he had made, to draw Sturmer there, and with the twine to deceive him and throw him off guard.

Now it had succeeded. He pulled Sturmer's body through the thicket and toward the path. He did not trouble to retrieve the broken branch he had used as a club. He had no further need of it. The corrupt head man had been disposed of. With his going the canker that had rotted the village would go too, and Tsoaul would once again shrink away before their axes. When Burh became strong again, with time to heal the damage Sturmer had done, Groden would tell them the truth. But for now such revelations could serve no purpose; they might even prove dangerous, for Sturmer had so warped their minds that they could not see. For the moment Groden decided to pretend that Sturmer had fallen in battle with Tsoaul. After the change of leadership he would take a fighting party and go deep into the forest to challenge Tsoaul, and the matter would be resolved. He knew that Tsoaul would be afraid to come forward: Gauhm's power was too great. With her help, and the people of the village, Groden would work to make Burh new again.

He reached the path and put the body over his shoulders.

Tagart kept his distance, following Groden, the beardless man, down the path to the village. In the moonlight Tagart saw that he carried a corpse: the owner of the scream. He had not imagined it.

Tagart badly wanted to attack, to kill the beardless man, but he hung back, slowing when Groden slowed, forcing himself on when Groden went faster, not sure what to do. He wished he were armed.

They were getting near the village. Tagart had left it too late, even had he wanted to make a move; but his curiosity had been aroused and it impelled him to follow.

Groden turned off the path, to the right, and through the stand of oaks which gave onto the top of the escarpment. He passed among the black trunks and the moonlight, bearing the weight of the body easily, one of its arms hanging loosely and swinging as he walked. Tagart left the path and in utter silence passed over the twigs and brambles.

At the edge of the escarpment Groden let himself down and onto the steepness of the slope, taking it sideways, faltering a little now. Halfway down he stopped and let the body fall from his shoulders, just as Tagart had let Hernou fall; Tagart drew back into the shadows in case Groden were to look up.

When Tagart stepped forward again the body had been leaned against an oak bush, and Groden was crossing the escarpment, descending as he went, making for the east gate. At the bottom he merged with the total shadow of the palisade, and Tagart lost sight of him.

The gate opened slightly and effortlessly, as if it had been left unlocked for his return, and Groden slipped into the compound. Tagart did not hear the two wooden locking bars being eased into place, but he saw the gate drawn shut and a few moments later Groden's figure on the village thoroughfare, walking toward the cluster of houses.

6

STURMER'S BODY LAY, COVERED WITH FLOWERS, ON THE Dead Ground. His common clothes of pigskin and beaver had been removed and consigned to the altar flame, and in their place he had been dressed in a chief's grave-robe of ermine, the hood drawn up and showing only the oval of his face with beard and mustache and eyebrows shorn. Beside him lay everything he had owned, everything that would go with him into the burial mound. His wife Tamis knelt weeping at his feet. Their four children, also dressed in white, stood nearby and watched. The youngest did not understand.

The villagers climbed the steps of the Meeting House one by one. Nobody had yet challenged Groden's sudden promotion to prospective leadership of the Council, for at the meeting that morning, held to discuss the finding of Sturmer's body, no other suitable candidate had emerged. The new head man would have to be formally chosen tomorrow, by Council vote, or by trial and contest of strength and wisdom if Groden were challenged; but today they mourned Sturmer. He would be buried at sunset, after they had tasted the agaric and joined him on the road to the Far Land.

As they passed into the Meeting House they left their clothing by the steps, a mark of purification, and naked crossed the floorboards to take up their positions in the circle of village hierarchy. By the altar sat Groden, at his right Vude, the oldest man on the Council, friend of Sturmer the priest, in whose hands now rested the health and spiritual guidance of the village until a new head man should be chosen. Beside Vude, in their order from high to low, sat the members of the inner Council, on their right the other Council men, followed by the wealthiest of the ordinary villagers, decreasing in power and importance as the circle curved around toward the altar; and on Groden's left squatted the lowliest man in the village.

The women came forward and took their places behind the men, ready for their part in the ceremony, each holding a wooden bowl or drinking vessel.

Vude arose, his hands under the Agaric Casket, and turning toward the Dead Ground inclined his head and reverently slid the casket onto the front of the altar, in line with the small flame flickering there, which represented Sturmer's soul.

"We take this hour the gift," he said, and waited for the congregation to speak the words of response.

"The gift of the Earth Mother."

"On eagles' wings we go with our loved one."

"Borne in peace along the road of the dead."

"We see the gates of the Far Land and the journey safely done."

"We turn back."

"And in sadness and in joy come home again."

The musicians took up their instruments and on pipes, tamtams and flutes opened the dirge. Vude went on reciting the phrases of the Agaric Chant, and as he did so pulled back the lid of the casket and removed the trays. The first three were empty; he put them aside and handed the caps from the fourth to the woman behind him and to his left, who passed them around the circle. The chant finished: the women put the caps on their tongues. Vude lowered himself to the floor and sat cross-legged.

When the women had fashioned the caps into pellets, rolling them between their palms, squashing the fungus in their mouths to take away the taste and rolling it again, the men reached behind and took the pellets with their fingers, opened their mouths wide and thrust the pellets to the backs of their throats, and swallowed.

Chal's wife came to the altar and spoke quietly into Vude's ear. "Something's wrong, Vude. The taste is not the same. It tastes like . . . like pepperwort. Usually it burns like fire and makes us sick."

None of the women were showing any sign of nausea. Vude glanced at Groden, who opened his hands slightly, able to offer no explanation.

"The caps must be old and weak," Vude decided. "How long have they been in the casket?"

"I cannot say," Groden said. "Did Sturmer replenish the whole casket every autumn, or just the empty trays?"

Vude did not know.

"What is it?" Feno said from across the circle. "The pellets aren't working."

Others spoke up to say that the fungus tasted different, that it was having no effect.

"Then let us eat more," Vude said, and gave out more caps, from each of the trays. He himself tasted a cap from the bottom tray. At once the fierce burning flared in his mouth and he spat the fragment out. "This one has not lost its power," he said, holding it up for all to see. He turned to the girl behind him. "Chew this for me, child." To the others he said, "Taste the caps until you find those with strength."

But although they found many caps which still seemed potent, most had lost their vigor and there were not enough good caps to make a ceremony. As Chal's wife had said, the stale caps tasted peculiar, peppery, and the men as well as the women ate several of each, hoping without success to produce some of the effects of fresh fly agaric, even in a diminished form.

Not long afterward they came out into the compound and, taking their clothes from the pile by the steps, walked slowly to their houses to prepare for the funeral of their chief.

Across the river, in the sunshine, blue cornflowers and scarlet poppies made color in the drab fields extending to the edge of the valley. Rooks flapped in the haze above the ground, pitching unhurriedly here and there in small groups to dig at the soil and turn over clods; from the estuary came a faint skirling of terns, and the piping cries of the wading birds as the tide went out and the rich gray mud flats appeared. A warm sea wind blew across the village, carrying before it a few husks and wisps of barley, gently knocking a loose plank on the bakery roof.

The west gate opened. Tamis and her three daughters, keeping near the palisade, stooped and picked bunches of chamomile, which together with red campion would make their simple wreath for Sturmer.

Tamis had decided to leave the village, with the sick who could walk, the children, and the animals. The others had been persuaded by Groden to wait, to remain behind while he challenged Tsoaul anew. And when Groden triumphed the animals would come back, and the children, and even the sick; but not Tamis. She meant to take her children back to her home village, where her mother was still alive and the children could be raised in peace and safety. In time the grief of Sturmer's death might recede; until then she would go on in her numb state, stunned, doing what was best for her family. As was the custom, she had not taken part in the fly agaric ceremony, and she had chosen to stay outside on the Dead Ground with the body of her husband.

Just before sunset his funeral began.

Vude led the villagers over the bridge, through the west gate, and along the narrow, dusty path across the barley field. Groden came at the rear. Six men carried Sturmer's body, on white leather straps passed beneath his ermine grave-robe.

At the spinney on the far side the path curved between the trees and Tamis looked over her shoulder for a last glimpse of Burh. She would not be seeing it again. Chal and Hombeck were to escort her that evening after the funeral on the nine-mile walk to Highdole, where her mother lived.

The procession left the spinney and halted on the close sward of the burial ground, outside the line of chalk stones containing the earthen barrow where for many years the dead of the village had been interred. This evening a chief was to join the ancestors. Part of the barrow at its head had been freshly dug away, ready to receive him.

Vude spoke the incantation. In the long shadows of sunset, and then the gray light of darkening dusk, the corpse in its robe and the dead man's possessions were covered with earth and filled in, to begin by their decay to dust and fragments the slow return to the place from which they had come.

Over the escarpment the moon appeared above the trees.

Tagart stared into the space below the yew branches and tried to remember: how many days? How many days had he been here waiting his chance? How many days before the Crale Festival and Segle was taken from the kitchens and put into the Trundle?

His thoughts swirled. He would need weapons, concealed weapons, and clothes from the village. And if he wore clogs and looked enough like a farmer he could use the coast road and pass the forts unchallenged to reach Valdoe in a single day. In darkness, with ropes and grappling hooks, he would make himself find a way to scale the ramparts and get inside; and somehow he would find Segle and bring her to the gates and they would be free: free to run into the marshes and reed beds along the coast and hide where the Valdoe dogs could never find a scent. And after that, when he had kept his promise to Bewry, he would ask Segle to stay with him and travel northwest, away from the coast and the farmers and the acres of land by the sea they had befouled and lain waste. And together they would search for the Waterfall people, his old blood tribe among whom his father had been born.

He sat up. Tomorrow. He must attack tomorrow. He was well enough; he had recovered much strength. His bruising was better. He could walk, and he could run, and he tried to tell himself that his thoughts had cleared and that he was planning lucidly again for the first time in days.

But with the fever of ideas in his mind it was a long time before he closed his eyes and allowed sleep to come.

Before dawn he had settled on a scheme to finish the village. By appearing on the escarpment he would draw them after him, south through the forest and down to the beach. There, in the corner of land between the estuary and the sea, he would trap them while the forest burned and the wind spread the flames east and south. At high tide there could be no escape under the cliffs, nor along the beach of the estuary, where the scrub grew close on the shore. Those who could not swim would be burnt alive; and of the others, many would drown in the tide race out by the shoals. But he would have a coracle waiting, and if any of the farmers tried to swim toward land he would chase them and club them in the water with the paddle.

This was his plan. To enact it he needed a coracle. He knew there would be coracles at the village, some left outside the palisade.

The moon had set when he arrived. He skirted the village to the south and came to the river. Two coracles had been left upturned on the bank; he holed one by thrusting his heel through it, and launched the other. At once the current tugged at the painter. He walked beside the bank, letting the river carry the coracle along, easing it round clumps of sedge, and led it down-stream into the tidal reach. Jumping over channels and runlets, or walking ankle-deep in mud, he brought the willow and leather craft to the edge of the estuary, where the broad water of the river merged rippling with the sea. Here he dragged the coracle onto a narrow strip of shingle and left it hidden by the bushes.

From the shore Tagart turned back into the forest and climbed uphill, reaching the edge of the gorge and following it past the wreckage of the bridge and onto the path. East of the village, a quarter of a mile behind the escarpment, he knelt and nurtured the first fire, knocking flint against flint until the sparks ignited dry grass stems. Carefully he held them to thicker dry stems, blowing gently, to brown bracken, to thin twigs broken into lengths, and blew to make the flame dance. Bitter white smoke curled: the twigs burned. He put them against a small cone of dry sticks, and when they had caught he brought larger branches and heaps of bracken until the pile burned orange and strong. Ash and glowing charcoal began to fall into its heart. The encircling ground slowly grew hot; the grasses and twigs withdrew in a scorched circle, elongating on the leeward side, and suddenly the neighboring bracken was alight.

He waited until silver rectangles appeared on the end of a charred branch, lifted it from the fire and checked that it went on burning alone. Taking this brand he laid a trail of fire southeast, coming after half a mile to the hazel thicket, which he fired in three places before throwing the burning brand into its center.

For a moment he watched the shimmering farther up the slope, behind the trees, his eyes smarting and his face gray with dust and ash. The fire had not yet taken off, even though the wind had picked up and he felt a push of heat on his face.

He lingered there, overcome by fascination for the flame, seized by a desire to see it all burning, the sky on fire, the wall of flame racing through the forest and destroying everything in its path. All his life he had been ruled by fear of flame, scrupulously dousing camp fires, obeying the elders, never allowing flame to get out of hand. But now he was watching it develop its full glory, growing and feeding, demanding and consuming, towering into the sky and across the land. It carried for him a lesson of vitality, power, singleness of mind; and it reminded him that the village waited below, ready for his arrival.

Along the ridge of the forest columns of pale smoke stood in similar and parallel shapes against the sky. They seemed to be truncated, the white pillars cut off sharp where the rising sun shone on them and made the smoke invisible. The forest was burning.

Vude waited no longer. No more could be done. There was no cure. As priest, doctor, he had remained till now, going from house to house, trying to make them comfortable. He had wanted to bring himself to kill them, to end their misery, but he could not.

In the early hours the first terrible herald of death cap poisoning had announced itself, arriving without warning, taking with sudden and violent abdominal cramps all those who had tasted the peppery caps at the agaric ceremony. One by one the symptoms visited each house, coming again and again as if the stomach were being wrenched to a hard knot and released, only to be racked more tightly and viciously than before. No one escaped, save the wounded and the crippled in their beds, and the women who had been tending them, and Vude, who by chance had not eaten any of the strange caps.

Now the victims lay past vomiting, weak with watery bowels, cold sweat on their bodies. Some had crawled into the compound trying to find moisture to slake their thirst.

Vude knew they would be like this for two days, growing steadily weaker, until the pain abated and they were able to rest for a few hours before the cramps and the sickness returned with a venom that would make the first attacks seem mild. Disintegration of the vital organs, and seizure of the limbs, would lead into a period of madness and repulsive visions, relieved at last by coma, collapse, and finally death. Those who had eaten several caps might suffer for three days; those who had tasted only one might last for ten.

Vude, his spare clothes and belongings on his back, hesitated by the bridge. He was the last to leave the village who could.

He saw Feno crawl from the doorway of the threshing shed, his face twisted and alien, the eyes sunken, streaks of filth in his beard and hair. Feno opened his mouth to cry out but made no sound. His lips and tongue were the color of sand. His head fell forward and he stretched out one arm, the fingers clenching and unclenching in the dust.

Vude turned and went out by the west gate.

7

TAGART COULD SEE NO MOVEMENT IN THE VILLAGE. HE came farther out on the escarpment and shouted at them again, hoarsely, sick and gray and tired. Sweat lined the dust on his forehead and around his eyes. His clothing, crusted and dirty, bore gashes which revealed grimy skin and, below his tunic, the ugly bruises on his left side. His hair and beard were matted and tangled, and his teeth, when he drew back his lips to shout, showed yellow and broken. But his eyes, though rimmed red and stinging from the smoke, shone clear.

"Bastards! Bastards! Come out!"

He half ran, half jumped, a dozen yards down the slope and shouted again.

From the compound came no response. He ran stumbling to the bottom of the escarpment, through the anthills, through the nettles, and with his right hand fending along the rough bark of the palisade logs, arrived at the east gate.

It would not open. They had tried to lock themselves in. He struck it with his fists, shook it until the latches and hinges rattled, and turned away. With the fields on his left he ran beside the palisade, down the bank and into the river.

The west gate swung freely, he flung it open and entered the village.

It was deserted. They had gone.

Only then did he see the man writhing on the ground, face down in the dirt by the threshing shed door; and he saw that there were others, here and across the compound. He crossed the bridge and with a fork-tipped pole taken from a stack leaning against the threshing shed, cautiously prodded at the man lying there. A bearded face, tormented and disfigured, lifted to look at him, pleading without words, begging for release.

Tagart frowned and went further into the village, unable to understand what had happened. The others in the compound were the same, women as well as men, all seemingly poisoned. It made no sense.

Inside the houses he found more victims of the poisoning, sprawled on the floor or in reeking bedding, groaning or silent, but all with the same look in their eyes, the same twisted faces. In the second house, in a cramped chamber noisy with blowflies, he found, as well as a poisoned man, two women with sheepskins drawn over their bodies. The stench of gangrene made him cover his nose and mouth. He lifted a corner of one of the sheepskins. Part of the womans's body was not there. He realized she was watching him; he let the skin fall and staggered outside into the morning sunshine.

Arming himself with an ax from the porch, he went from house to house, searching for the beardless man.

He found him by an upturned water butt, behind a house on the far side of the compound. Groden moved feebly in protest as Tagart's shadow fell across his eyes. He groaned and Tagart heard the voice again, the voice he had heard in the rainstorm by the burning shelters. He thought of Mirin, her face beneath his own, soft in the honeysuckle scent of his shelter; and then her face in the mud and slime on the riverbank, the story of her agony in her eyes, what they had done to her, what they had singly and together made her endure. He thought of the lightning and the ranks of men coming into the camp. And he thought of Balan, his death, and he remembered the man who had done it, a man with no beard.

And in glimpses and fragments Tagart remembered Hernou's voice in the darkness of the yew, and he saw again the preparation of death cap he had made, and then he knew the nature of their poisoning and how it had come about.

He took Groden by the ankles and dragged him onto open ground, and left him there. It was enough. He could do no worse to Groden. To torture him now, as Tagart had intended, to hasten his death, would be a crime against Balan and his mother and the tribe of hunters Tagart had once loved.

In a house nearby he discovered a leather sack with an osier carrying-frame to fit the shoulders and back, fastened with straps and wooden toggles. Into it he bundled a selection of clothes to make him look like a farmer: clogs, jacket, leggings, a badgerskin toque, wristbands. From a kitchen he chose food for two days, to save him the time of catching his own. Discarding his flints, which were blunted and virtually useless, he took the best he could find from the farmers' supplies, and put them in the sack, together with baling twine, a length of rope, and a grappling hook made from fire-hardened blackthorn. Across the top of the pack he laid a pair of short axes with new blades. He carried the sack into the sunshine and beside it laid a full water bag.

Tagart crossed to the Meeting House, an unlighted torch of bundled kindling in his hand. At the far end stood the altar as he had remembered it. A flame burned there, a wick held in a bowl ground from the stone and filled with oil.

8

BEHIND THE ESCARPMENT AND DOWN TO THE SEA THE smoke made a mountain, black and white and gray. The roar of crackling and exploding branches, fanned by the wind, merged with and engulfed the crash of falling trees, their trunks and skeletons showing black among the flames. As the fire moved on to fresh forest, boiling sap whined and hissed; green leaves scorched and curled and passed through brown autumn to become traceries of veins that glowed and burned instantly to nothing. In its path the fire left black ground: cleansed, purified, ready for new growth.

On the far side of the barley field, by the spinney of maple and oak, Tagart paused and looked back.

For the gangrened and dying, the wounded and the mauled, for those he had not dragged from their houses and into the open, the end would be swift. He had set fire to the village.

It was achieved. Against even his own expectations, it was achieved. Tagart had overcome all obstacles and discharged his duty to the tribe. He had reached his goal, using only the forest to help him; it animals, its plants, the weapons it provided. With these and with his own strength and singleness he had realized his ends. From within himself he had drawn on reserves that perhaps not even Cosk had possessed. And now the village was finished. He personally had destroyed it. One by one and in groups he had executed its inhabitants and swept away their houses and the things they had made. In a matter of months no trace of them would remain. The forest would take over; the fields would become overgrown, unrecognizable, and then indistinguishable from the virgin woodlands that had stood unchanged for centuries.

By all the rules, by the code of the tribe, Balan had been avenged. This should have been a moment of sweet triumph.

But Tagart felt nothing of that. He felt only bleakness, desolation, and a vast gray weariness that no sleep could ever assuage. His one goal had been reached. All his strivings were over. He had spent himself, he had succeeded; and been left with nothing. Those corpses lying in the compound, those people: what did he care about them? They meant nothing to him; they never had. What were they? Could anything about them, least of all their destruction, bring Balan back? Or Mirin? Or the joy he had known with the tribe? Tagart had failed, bitterly and completely, to achieve anything of value or importance. What had he brought himself? Not the taste of vengenance, of satisfaction, but vileness, misery, and three weeks of the worst privation he had ever endured.

Yet out of those three weeks one glimmer had emerged.

Without it there could be nothing to relieve the emptiness of his future. It provided a chance, no more, but from chances he knew he could make much. And most of all it provided hope. The days were too fleet to be spent with a dead spirit. There was one more promise to fulfill.

Tagart stood and watched the village.

Swirling, making the sunshine brown and the grass on the slope dark, the billows of smoke and ash drifted toward the forest, particles returning to their birthplace, from five buildings and thirty-three stone and timber houses that rippled and belched an orange blaze and one by one disintegrated, the beams falling inward with showers and flurries of sparks. In twenty places the palisade was down or had burnt away. It would not remain standing much longer.

The roof of the Meeting House collapsed, too heavy for its weakened supports; the stilts and rafters and walls twisted sideways, and the whole structure fell in flames to a mass of burning wreckage on the ground.

Tagart entered the spinney. On the other side, in its neat enclosure of white stones, the head of the barrow showed newly dug earth. He took some in his fingers and crumbled it. At his feet he noticed a wilted wreath of campion and chamomile. He stooped and held it to his face. No hint of scent remained.

Tagart stood up, and hitching the pack on his shoulders, let fall the wreath and set his face toward Valdoe.

Part Four

1

Too quick for the human eye to follow, Blene's tiercel hobby swept into the twittering flock of migrating martins and came out on the other side. As it flew it bent its head and tore a morsel from the prize that Blene saw it now held in the clutch of one foot.

The mines Trundleman was out alone, two miles from Valdoe. He could see the black walls of the Trundle encircling the crown of the hill across the valley. The unmarked pennons of the Flint Lord flacked and strained at their masts above each guard tower and barrack house. Smoke from many fires was scattered by the wind. The gates stood open to admit the traders and itinerants: the preparations for the Crale had begun. In the valley below, the river looped and showed dark blue in a green pasture, among the nodding foliage of alders and willows. This was the last afternoon of High Summer, the eve of Harvest, and though the sun was shining brightly a chilly breeze turned the white undersides of leaves and made the trees along the field edge sigh.

Blene whistled. On rapid, shallow wingbeats the tiny falcon climbed to turn, and with a glare of both eyes directed at its master described a low glide that terminated in a jangle of bells as its talons took purchase on the gauntlet. The martin, white feathers bloody, fell to the turf; the hobby, sleek and unruffled, opened its beak and panted, riding Blene's wrist as he secured the jesses at its legs. He had trained the bird himself, and it was his favorite, his usual companion on these daily walks. It served no practical purpose, it caught nothing for the table, but to see it killing was to Blene a thrill incomparable to anything that the hawk mews in the Trundle could provide. Sometimes he took out one of the austringer's goshawks, for hares; in the winter perhaps a gyrfalcon for wildfowl; or perhaps an eagle to run at deer. Most of the Trundlemen favored peregrines, with their faultless control of wind and sky, but Blene liked his little tiercel.

It was late. Much remained to be done; Blene gave his thoughts to getting back. The reports from Stobas and the other day-shift overseers would have to be heard, and there was the season's tally to complete before its presentation to Lord Brennis the following day. After that, work could be forgotten, for a while at least. He smiled to himself. Even Trundlemen looked forward to a holiday.

The Crale Festival, marking the beginning of Harvest, was second in the calendar only to the first day of Winter, the new year. To people whose survival depended on their crops, on the abundance of the harvest, the ceremonies and sacrifices of the Crale meant everything. This was the time of adoration and prayer, litany and chant; in every village and settlement was heard a petition for Gauhm's continuing beneficence during the two crucial months of harvest. She had allowed the wheat to grow: let her now permit it to be gathered in, before the rains of autumn beat the fields and spread the grasses flat. The Crale was also the time of renewal, when the last of the year's stocks were almost gone. What remained would be replaced by the new and would otherwise be wasted, so for once even the thrifty could afford to be prodigal, squandering all in a few days of eating and drinking: an act of faith, a demonstration to Gauhm.

Both inside the Trundle and out, the feasting would begin at nightfall. The oxen had already been turning and sizzling for two days; scores of pigs and sheep had been slaughtered. For the soldiers and overseers there would be liquor and free access to the brothel. For the miners and field-slaves there would be extra meat and half a gallon of beer apiece, and the next afternoon a visit to their own brothel in the outer enclosure. The older and more tractable slaves might be permitted an escorted walk through the Crale Market. Tents and awings now going up in the shelter of the palisade held booths and stalls where the soldiers and farmers would be tempted to make bargains with those who had come from farther afield, bringing pottery and imported wares, toys, sweetmeats, beard-scrapers, talismans and periapts, wooden combs, needles, bone awls, carved and leather work, ornaments, effigies in stone and wood, miniature axheads of polished white marble, foreign woven goods, bundles of ashwood handles for every kind of tool, ropes, twines, and leather by the strip and in pelts, furs and untreated skins. Under the southwest gatehouse, next to the slave quarters, the animal market had already been assembled, with pens and stalls for cattle, swine, sheep and goats. Other stalls were piled high with wildfowl and game, and animals and birds for pets: goldfinches in sad little cages, badger cubs, squirrels with their hind legs tied. Brisk interest surrounded the traders of grain and vegetable seed.

The refreshmentstalls stood nearby, laden with clay dishes of blackberries, sloe and crabapple jelly, elder and parsnip wine in jars, fruit liquors, and ale and bread and cold meats.

"What is this?"

Blene had paused by an open table on which strange little bottles had been arranged in rows. The old woman behind it, a crone with stooped shoulders and swollen knuckles, had averted her eyes at the approach of a Trundleman and now scarcely dared look up.

"Rosewater, master."

"What is it for? Perfume?"

"Yes, master."

Blene could have taken the bottle without payment, but the idea of the perfume amused him and his sensibility would not allow him to confiscate it. "Four scrapers," he offered.

"Yes, master. Thank you, master."

"Are four enough?"

"Yes, master."

Blene dropped the flints on to the table and passed through the crowds to the gate, between the somber walls of the southwest barrack house. The shadows had grown perceptibly longer. The afternoon cast a dusty, golden light on the outer enclosure, on the craftsmen and soldiers and freemen moving to and fro among the sheds and dwellings; a hundred paces away across the parade ground, the sunlight made the burnt oak of the inner palisade look more brown than black. Here, standing just outside the ditch, and facing south across the parade ground, had been built the Trundlemen's quarters: long and low, a single story divided into many rooms and suites, roofed with planks, the walls half-timbered and finished with clay and flints. Blene threaded his way among the openings which appeared for him and crossed to the main entrance, which led through a tackle room where outdoor clothing and equipment could be stored. Beyond it a long, dark passage, decorated with the heads and hides of trophies, allowed access through skin-draped doorways to the common room, refectory, and through hinged wooden doors to the Trundlemen's various private quarters. Once inside his own suite, Blene handed the hobby and gauntlet to his attendant and went into his chamber to bathe and change.

Leaving the bottle of rosewater standing on a low shelf by his bed, Blene reappeared, freshly attired, in the sunshine, and strolling toward the mines to complete his day's business there, first stopped off at the slaves' quarters and spoke a few words to the overseer of the kitchens.

Moments later, a hand on Segle's shoulder marked the end of her employment at the caldrons.

That she had not been taken from the kitchens before was to her a source of dull surprise, for when a Trundleman, especially the Trundleman in charge of the mines, made even a mild request, the request was that in name only. But Blene seemed more distant, less imperious than the others, and it was not as if a kitchen-girl alone could serve his needs or ranked high in his preference. Each of the Trundlemen already kept several women. Some had wives here at Valdoe, even families. Segle guessed that Blene's interest in her would not be sustained; it was a whim, a small pleasure, a moment's gratification.

Whatever his attitude, it was of no consequence to her.

Whether she was violated in Blene's chamber or in the soldiers's brothel, Segle knew that what little remained to her was about to be finally taken by Valdoe, taken and ground underfoot. She tried to think bravely, to compose herself for the ordeal; but as the women slaves bathed and dressed her ready for the Trundleman's presence she was filled with a blind terror and for the first time in her sixteen years fervently and truly wished herself dead.

Tagart walked through the massive framework of the gateway and found himself inside the Trundle.

Beside all the elaborate plans, the devices and stratagems he had invented on the length of his journey from Burh, this was the only, the single possibility he had not considered, had not even thought of: that the gates would be standing open without the slightest challenge to his entry. The whole feel of the place had changed. Soldiers and strangers alike were passing in and out as if the Trundle were not a fort at all. There were silhouettes in the guard towers; and Tagart had been given a desultory scrutiny by sentries on the road up the hill and by the gates; but since entering the boundary limits no one had spoken to him, asked him who or what he was, where he had come from, or what he was doing at Valdoe.

It had taken him over two days to make the walk. The heavy exertion of the journey had left him weaker, with constant pains in his chest, and aching feet, legs and back; but in his mind he had begun to improve, to plan more clearly. The delirious, dreamlike periods had grown shorter and less intense, and now he was almost himself again.

He had kept to the roads, making detours into the trees only to avoid the ferry stations, swimming the rivers using the inflated water bag to help float across his pack and clothing. West of the Arun he had caught up with and, at some risk, joined the tail of a party of itinerant peddlers, chapmen on their way to the festival. In his speech and manner he found no trouble in joining them, for chapmen were usually descended quite closely from the nomad tribes: people who retained a wandering existence, working where they could, selling what they could, hawkers and petty thieves, despised and avoided by nomads and farmers alike. And in appearance Tagart was not out of place among them, and prompted no undue interest: after swimming the river he had cleaned himself up as best he could, washed his farmer's clothes, and forced his feet into the unfamiliar clogs. The chapmen, a dozen or so men with their families and flocks, questioned him briefly but seemed inclined to accept that a lone traveler would prefer to walk in company. In a group there was less chance of being captured and taken for a slave.

As payment for this protection, their leader demanded the whole contents of Tagart's pack. Tagart tried to bargain. He told them that he too was a peddler, that he had come from farther east, and that he was searching for his family, from whom he had become separated at one of the villages where there was only enough harvest work for himself. He said he thought they might have stopped at Valdoe or be there still; he was hoping at the least for some word of them. He could not spare his belongings: they were his livelihood, the tools of his trade. The leader insisted. After much argument he relented and accepted a compromise, and Tagart parted with all his spare clothing, most of his flints, his rope, twine, grappling-hook, and one of the axes.

It was extortion, but it provided a safe passage through the most dangerous part of the journey: the last few miles to the fort. Tagart fell to the rear of the line, walking beside a youth whose sullen capacity for conversation soon became exhausted, enabling Tagart to withdraw into his own thoughts and plans.

They passed through Eartham, below its fort, and Tagart traded a few flints for hot gruel and bread at the settlement there. Keeping his adopted companions in sight, he left the shed where gruel was being sold and sat down in the shade of a beech tree by the road. With the silvery trunk at his back he dipped his bread into the bowl. Above him the sky showed blue; the wind hissed in the beech-leaves; the branches swayed. The road here was wide and well trodden, an important route. It ran between an avenue of beeches, not planted, but two uneven and inconsistent rows of trees which had escaped the ax only because no one had seen any reason to cut them down. The houses and huts of the settlement, encircled by a palisade, stood on the south side of the road and backed onto a system of barley and wheat fields which sloped gradually downhill into a belt of woodland. Beyond this, just visible from the village, spread the low coastal marshes of reed-beds and saltings known as the Rifes, having their beginnings at the Adur in the east, and running for mile upon mile along the coast below the hills, below Valdoe, to Apuldram and Itchenor in the west.

Tagart finished his gruel. There were other travelers on the road, some stopping for refreshment, others going straight on, covering the last few miles to Valdoe. Most seemed to be peddlers of one sort or another, with bales and bundles for sale at the Crale Market, or animals led on ropes and halters. He saw a few soldiers, some in armor, and here and there a group of more properous-looking travelers: wealthy farmers or priests from the villages. A small crowd had gathered by the gruel shed, and by another shed where meat and fruit were on sale.

Tagart stood up. His companions were leaving.

A few hundred yards west of the palisade the avenue of beeches came to an end. On the right was the scrub- and tree-clad steepness of the hill, leading up to open ground and Eartham fort. On the left were the village fields. With Tagart again at the rear, talking to no one, the chapmen followed the road through fields and scrubland as it curved first one way and then another, accommodating itself to level ground beneath the hills. Less than an hour from Eartham, in the late afternoon, they came within sight of the Trundle.

Tagart's main worry was a fear of being recognized. He had worked at the flint mines and might be known, and although he half consciously pulled up his jacket to cover his neck and the lower part of his jaw, he put his trust in the anonymity of a slave. His features might cause a tinge of memory; he might be half remembered; but it was unlikely. An overseer took little note of a slave's face, caring only about the number of flints he could produce in a day. And out of the mines, in farmer's clothes, among the crowds, there was still less chance of being recognized. Nonetheless Tagart watched warily as he went, walking self-confidently as if he were a freeman and not a fugitive, with a ready rebuttal and feigned resentment on his lips if he were to be challenged.

On the outskirts of Valdoe the group was closely questioned and searched for weapons. Tagart repeated his story, the one he had told the chapmen. It was accepted without demur. The soldiers opened his pack and took the remaining ax, and he was allowed to pass on.

Tagart accompanied the chapmen for most of the way

up the hill, past the slaves' quarters, and leaving them, went on alone through the timber framework of the gateway and into the Trundle.

"Give me one of those," Tagart said, pointing at a leg of bustard on the stall in front of him.

"Five scrapers."

Tagart did not know that he was expected to bargain. He nodded and reached into his pouch. His flints were almost all gone, but he was hungry. Over two hours had passed since his arrival, and he had yet to be sure where Segle was. He had loitered for as long as he thought it safe, watching the kitchens at the slaves' quarters. There had been no sign of her. He saw the dayshift miners brought in for their food; he saw them led out again and into the cage for the night. Meantime, around the walls and inside the Trundle, the preparations for the feast were coming to a close. Tagart heard shouts and music, and one by one more fires were being lit. The sun touched the horizon and sank beneath it; the breeze dropped; and in the kitchens the overseers had departed and the slaves were beginning to clear the tables for the holiday. Desperately he wondered whether he could afford the risk of an inquiry. He decided he could not; but there was no other choice.

There was no other way to find her. He approached the edge of the kitchens and called to one of the women there, and asked for Segle.

"Who are you? Why do you want her?"

"I am her friend."

The woman, middle-aged, with lank brown hair, stood closer to the bars and looked from side to side.

"Blene has taken her," she said. "The mines Trundleman."

"When was this?"

"Today."

"Where is she now?"

She could not tell him, nor could she speak longer. The kitchen overseer from his corner had seen her slacking and called her back to work.

From the slaves' quarters Tagart had made his way to the stalls.

Tagart paid for the roast leg of bustard and tore off a mouthful of the rich, dark meat. "Do you know anything of the Trundle?" he said, as casually as he could, to the man behind the stall. "Do you know which part is which?"

They were standing near the gate; the parade ground and much of the outer enclosure were visible. A great bonfire had been torched by the knappers' shed, in the middle of the enclosure, well away from the palisade, and its flames threw an orange light on the crowds.

The stall-holder was a short man with fair hair, dressed in beaver and doeskin: a sleeveless jerkin, leggings formed of spiral strips sewn with seal hide. He was a fowler, a freeman who traded with the consent of Valdoe, giving a tithe for its protection.

"Why should it interest you, friend?" he said affably.

"I have never been here before. I would like to know. Where is the house of Lord Brennis? Where do the soldiers sleep?"

The stall-holder, aware of an opportunity to impress, pointed out the various features: here the barracks, there the deep ditch which had taken hundreds of slaves to dig, there the inner palisade surrounding the Lord's Enclosure, where only Lord Brennis was allowed to enter freely.

"And the Trundlemen? Where do they sleep?"

"See there," the stall-holder said, indicating a low building next to the inner palisade. "Their quarters."

"Do all the Trundlemen live there?"

The stall-holder frowned. "You seem strangely interested."

Tagart made himself smile. "All those who know me say I am too curious." He finished the last of the roast meat. "You cook this well," he said.

"My woman does it."

Tagart dropped the bones into a butt provided for the purpose. "I wish you good fortune in your trade," he said, moving away into the semi-darkness, but the stall-holder was already attending to another customer.

In the west, behind Bow Hill, the last of the day had become a mere paleness. Smoke from the bonfires and cooking fires and from the torches which had been set up on top of the walls, and smoke from all the night fires of the temporary settlement, the fair, rose into the darkness. Tagart turned toward the Trundle. From the high ramparts came a squeal of pipes and a loud, wild, rhythmic thumping of drums which persisted through and overcame the cheering shout of the crowd; instantaneously burning brands were held to a huge heap of brushwood and timber on the southern slope of Valdoe Hill, and the beacon fire caught light. An orange twinkling appeared on Bow Hill to the west, and Eartham Hill to the east, and on along the coast, one after the other, on every hilltop where there was fort or settlement loyal to Valdoe and the Gehans.

The door of the bedchamber shut with a clatter of pegs locked into place, and Segle was alone.

She looked around the room. The women slaves had conducted her here, into the Trundlemen's quarters, down a dark passage, and into Blene's suite. Light in the room issued from wooden lamps—clips holding rush-pith dipped in beeswax—standing variously on shelves, by the bed, on a table by the window; as they burned they cast weird shadows and made prancing shapes of the curtains and hangings on the walls. Under her feet she felt soft matting. A smell pervaded the room, a smell of rosewater.

Outside, she could hear shouting and music and the noise of the feast. She stood in the middle of the room and clasped herself, and, no longer wishing to witness any part of the bedchamber or its furnishings, closed her eyes.

Segle opened them again and looked up. A curtain was drawn aside: Blene came in. In the uncertain light she saw that he was wearing nothing; she forced her eyes not to drop, not to look down, to keep to his face. Blene came and stood behind her. She felt his fingers on her neck.

"You're trembling."

Segle said nothing as she felt his body pressed against her own, moving her toward the bed.

2

TAGART ELBOWED AND SHOVED AND SHOULDERED ASIDE the jostling crowd of people and pushed a passage across the parade ground to the door of the Trundlemen's quarters, his mind working at furious pace, not knowing what he was going to say or how he was going to get in. He had wasted too much time, hesitated too long, been too cautious, too timid; nightfall had come, and with it the Crale feast had already started. Segle was inside with the mines Trundleman.

As the pipes on the ramparts shrilled and the hard patterns of the drums grew faster, Tagart forced his way through the last of the throng and found himself in the main entrance. He was in a tackle room, hung with nets and bows, ropes, outdoor clothing and gear.

A man came from the side, out of the shadows and into the lamplight. He was more than forty, gray-haired, less tall than Tagart, with a thin doeskin jacket and leggings—an attendant of some kind.

"Who are you? What do you want?"

Tagart looked past him and into the dark doorway that led further inside, and unbidden the right words came to him and he was speaking them. "I bring urgent message from Stobas at the mines. I must see Trundleman Blene."

"Has there been an accident."

"I must see Trundleman Blene, in person. Immediately."

"He cannot be disturbed."

"Where are his quarters?"

"He cannot be disturbed!" The attendant stood barring Tagart's way.

Tagart thought of striking the man, of knocking him aside, but changed his mind and checked his hand. There would be other attendants.

"I would not be in your place when he discovers you've stopped me," Tagart said. "A year's work is in peril. The main-shaft struts and shutters are in danger of collapse. We're rigging jury props but even those are breaking up under the strain. We must have Blene's word. Only he knows what to do."

Faced with a dilemma, the attendant seemed to waver. "Blene is in his chamber with a girl. My orders are strict. I daren't disturb him. I daren't go in."

"Then let me. If he's angry I'll take the blame. I'll say you tried to stop me."

The attendant bit his lip.

"Which is Blene's door?"

The attendant hesitated, but then pointed at the opening to the passage. "Through there. Follow the passage to its end. You want the last door. Knock before you enter; he's alone with her."

Tagart was not fully aware of pushing past the attendant. He was in a dark passageway, moving down it toward a glimmer of lamps and the shapes of wooden doors. His hands fumbled with catches and the door was opening into a dimly lit room. Making big shadows he crossed it and thrust aside a curtain and there before him was a bedchamber and in the corner a bed and a smell of rosewater; Tagart saw a girl's fingertips touching the rush matting, fingers spread wide in agony of revulsion and submission, and in them and her slender arm he remembered Mirin and the burning shelters and the rain and Segle's beauty. Even as in alarm the man on the bed realized that something was wrong and began to rise, Tagart's double fists came down on the back of his neck and broke from him a low grunt: Blene's muscles went limp and he slumped, a dead weight that Tagart rolled aside and onto the floor.

Tagart looked down. He sat on the edge of the bed and in the feeble light of the rush lamps took Segle's small, pale hand. Her hair, soft and dark, framed a face made unfamiliar by strain, her eyes and lips shut tight. Tagart whispered her name; again. She opened her eyes.

"I am Tagart," he said gently. "Sit up. You will be safe now."

She could not speak; she could not raise her head from the deep fur covering the pillows. She watched Tagart without recognition.

Beside Tagart, Blene stirred. On the table Tagart found a roll of legging-straps. He tied Blene's ankles and wrists, and pulled them together from behind. With another strap he tied a gag into Blene's mouth. Blene lay defenseless. Tagart told himself that he should kill him for what he had done; he should kill a man who lived by enslaving others, who had no conscience about robbing them of their life and liberty.

But Tagart could not bring himself to strike. There had been enough killing, and there would be no more.

Segle slowly sat up, in a daze. Tagart wanted to comfort her, to reassure her, to put his arms around her shoulders and draw her to him; but after what she had been through it would be wrong; and there was no time. "Where are your clothes?" he said. "We must be gone."

Still she was unable to understand. Tagart noticed her clothes on the floor and crammed them into his pouch. Taking one of Blene's capes, he pulled it around her and helped her up, over to the window. He ripped the kidskin curtain from its bar and caught a glimpse of the view outside, the fires and lights in the outer enclosure.

Segle would not respond to his voice. With a hand on each side of her waist he lifted her over the ledge and let her down on the other side, then climbed through himself.

"You were killed," she said softly. "They said you were killed in the mine with Boak and the others."

"Can you walk?"

"Yes."

Tagart guided her away from the wall of the Trundlemen's quarters and into the crowd, the bonfire somewhere on their left, its glare rising into the sky, carrying up smoke and heat with burning twigs and glowing bents of straw. On the wind was the smell of roasting meat and cooking, and the smell of ale spilled on clothes. "Keep by me," Tagart said, and held fast to Segle's wrist as he drew her toward the southwest gate.

It would be at most only a few minutes before the attendant went in and found Blene. Tagart knew that he and

Segle would have to make the most of their start. He thought of taking a straight run for the forest. At night there, alone, he could not be caught. But with Segle it was different. She would slow him down; and from her things at the Trundle the hounds would hold a scent so strong that in dry woodland there could be no escape.

Close by the wall of the barracks, they came out of the gate and into the stalls and stands of the fair. He looked over his shoulder. Life was returning to Segle's face.

"This way," he said, taking her behind the fowler's stand, around it in a loop, under a tent where cooked venison was being sold, through a narrow gap between two tables piled high with the dead plumage of mallard and quail and snipe, and, coming out of the fair, he led her downhill, due south, past the throng of people around the beacon fire, following the road to the mines where many people were passing back and forth, talking, strolling. The crowds grew thinner; beyond the fires there was darkness. The moon, a perfect circle, hung in the glare over the fort.

With Segle's warm hand in his own, Tagart left the road and started across rough ground, scrambling down the slope of the settlement fields. They were trampling the crops. Vaguely the huts and houses passed them in the moonlight. The slope steepened and they were among hawthorn scrub. Twice Segle slipped and fell; twice Tagart pulled her to her feet and drew her on, putting distance between them and the summit. They reached a level on the hillside and Tagart halted on an empty path, unfamiliar to him, that ran to left and right, with more scrub leading down on its farther side, toward the marshes and the coast.

He glanced uphill at the Trundle. He saw the slaves' quarters illuminated by the firelight of the beacon, he saw the palisade and ramparts, the framework of the guard towers, black and linear against the smoke and an orange sky. He saw the loose awnings and canopies of the fair, the people and animals, the cattle in pens; he heard their voices and the music, and above them he heard the hounds give tongue and the shouts of their handlers as the teams came straining through the southwest gate.

Even as Tagart pulled Segle across the path he heard the shouts become angry and the hounds' voices become yelps as they tangled their leashes with the stalls: tipping over tables of venison and game, their muzzles confused and over-busy with the strong scent of quail and snipe and mallard. The pack was already broken in purpose, not fifty yards from the gate, the hounds running against their collars, eager to find the trace; the handlers dragged them to, and held for them again the bedding from Segle's quarters and the bottle of rosewater given by Blene. But still the course through the stalls and crowds puzzled them and Tagart heard more yelps.

The delay gave him no heart. He knew that dogs trained to hunt human beings were of a special kind. They would not be among the stalls for long.

"You must run with me," he told Segle. "When I am not carrying you, do as I do. Plant your feet in mine. We're going into the Rifes."

✢ 3 ✢

BETWEEN VALDOE AND THE SEA LAY THREE MILES OF unroaded waste: reed marsh and lagoon, wet thicket and underwood, acre after acre where the drainage of the hills merged with the wash of surf and the sluggish leak under an unstable beach. At night it was a dangerous place, a wilderness of water sounds, of sudden deep channels and rotten islands, and beyond them sparkled moonlight on ripples and the mace-swamps, and the open streams that twisted and turned and became choked and lost among shattered willows and decaying leaves. Where the rivers grew brackish the reedbeds began. For nearly two miles they stretched toward the coast, giving way at last within hearing of the beach, becoming a muddy creek and a line of saltings. After that, there was only shingle: pebbles, foreshore, stinking weed, breaking froth, and the open sea.

A mile ahead of their pursuers, two figures waded the last of the freshwater marsh and appeared in the moonlight by the beginnings of the reeds. Tagart had used all his knowledge to slow the dogs, and Segle, who knew wet ground better than he, had guided them through the worst of the willow swamps and osier beds; but from the hounds' voices they could tell that the gap was closing quickly, perhaps too quickly, and they knew that if they misjudged and blundered in the reeds they would stand no chance. By now they were both naked, covered in mud, their limbs bleeding and torn from brambles and broken branches. For some of the way Tagart carried Segle. Times beyond count he had fallen; they had both fallen; or sunk to their thighs in ooze and struggled clear.

There were three dog-handlers. The break handler controlled the leading team, and two brace handlers came behind. They were soldiers, experienced men who had served on slaving trips, both from the Trundle and abroad; each lived with and looked after four hounds, big, heavy animals chosen for their endurance and strength, trained to obedience.

The dogs knew the marshes. They knew the sounds of splashing, of breaking wood, and the sound of breeze in the reed stems. They knew the bird cries, and the smell of eels. By their breed and training they could taste scent as it lingered on the surface of the water, or in the filling footprints across an oily mudbank. A trail which had long since scattered among the spikes and fluffy heads of the reedmace could with a few stray molecules be regained and held and followed with renewed baying and hauling at the leashes.

Behind the handlers came four ordinary soldiers, cursing the way of the scent, south through the scrub and toward the swamps. They had been held up for a long time among the stall of the fair: the dogs had lost the scent completely, not once, but six or seven times. At last they had found it again just off the road, in the barley field.

They passed the deserted boundary line and followed the trace across a scrubby heath which dipped in slow stages to the lower road from Eartham. On the other side the heath became one with a dense stand of birch and oak, mingled with elms where the trees bordered the Apuldram road.

The dogs massed here in the moonlight, their noses close to the ground. The line of scent had been drawn beside the road for a hundred paces. Halfway along it, the trace of rosewater abruptly stopped, where Segle had climbed onto Tagart's back. But the hounds had already owned Tagart's personal odor: the vegetation by the road held it strongly and they followed without difficulty. The scent crossed the road, recrossed it, wandering and broken among the foul stench of the wayside hemlock, and turned back under the elms and through a broad bed of nettles that stung sensitive muzzles and eyes and flews. From the stamens of the male flowers powdery pollen got in the dogs' noses; the leaves and the ground smelled of dry hemp. The leading hound, a big black bitch, turned in bewilderment with her tongue held low. The scent had died. The other dogs came up. One sneezed; another whimpered. The brace teams spread through the nettle bed, searching from side to side.

"Where's it? Where's it? Where's it?"

The handlers spoke to the dogs, and to each other.

"Where's it, girl? Where's the line?"

The black hound sniffed at a particle, a hint, her wet tongue sliding at something in the air . . . roses; not roses . . . rose petals. She drew in air again, across damp membranes, but no fresh nerves fired: she had used up all the scent.

"Back it on! Back it on! Turn it!" the break handler shouted, anticipating by moments the black hound's own conclusion: that the prey had doubled back.

"Back it on! Back it on!"

They raced back to the roadside and the stink of hemlock. The hounds ran about, loose on their leads. Within moments they had regained the taste of Tagart's musk. And, ten yards on, at the place where Segle had climbed down, it was rejoined by rosewater.

The trail led due south. In full cry the hounds ran straight through the trees and after it.

They were checked by the first water of the marshes, at a stagnant ditch, a natural drain rank with willowherb and flags. To cross it in the easy wake of the scent they were awaiting the handlers' word—the dogs never went leashed where the handlers could not follow. The black bitch whined impatiently as the leading handler probed the ditch with his staff.

It was safe, waist-deep, and the dogs thrashed across. The water stank; smelly mud rose to the surface. The quarry had smeared themselves, to no avail. Their scent, barely disguised, appeared strong and sure on the other bank.

The soldiers crossed the ditch and dragged themselves clear.

They were in the marshes now: it was time to change the mode of chase. There were firm places for dogs that would not take human feet, shortcuts made obvious by the wanderings of the scent.

The hounds yelped and strained in excited frenzy to be

free. Fingers worked at straps and buckles, and twelve collars were unleashed.

Before them reached wet woodlands of sallow and willow, with open ground among the islands of trees and fallen trunks.

Mud-spattered and sweating, the men ran behind, skirting ditches the dogs had crossed, negotiating streams the dogs had leaped. With every yard the trail grew stonger, newer, fresher. As the dogs sensed it the pack's stride lengthened and its speed increased.

Just ahead of the black bitch the leading runner squealed. In the moonlight and darkness it made a clumsy, tearing somersault and slid limp-backed into the leaves. It had run onto a broken stake, hastily angled and thrust at dog's-head height into the ground.

The pack faltered. The black bitch smelled suddenly opened flesh and heard the handler's rage.

"Leave him, girl! Leave him! Go to!"

She turned and the dogs ran on, less one, the stream of rosewater growing. Together in a scramble they entered and swam a black pool; on its far bank they trod on thorns and tasted Tagart's taint. Snarling, growling, worrying what they had found, tearing it to pieces, they dragged something free, the strongest scent yet, rammed into the space below a rotten log.

The handlers came up.

It was Blene's cape, the one that Segle had worn.

"What do you think?"

"They're slowing. They must be tired."

"We're nearly on them now."

The hounds whimpered and panted. Some shook fur and made spray.

"Go to! Go to! In the water! Go to!"

Another black pool; a tangle of willow branches and old trees lying drowned and quietly rotting in the water with their limbs submerged. The trace wandered at its edge, and moved uncertainly, then went in. The quarry, both together, had swum the pool, so recently that the trace lingered in the air as well as on the film, destroyed by the hounds as they plunged and splashed, whining with frustration: for in deep water the scent went under, below the rise of a floating trunk, where the dogs could not follow. Wet pads and claws, legs not meant for climbing, scrabbled at rotten willow bark. The dogs found no purchase and fell back, unable to climb over the obstacle, unable to swim under. The brace hounds paddled to the side, exploring the tangle of old branches and withered leaves, looking for a way through. It was no use.

"Turn it! Turn it! Turn it!"

"Come out and turn it!"

Reluctantly, paddling, the hounds came out, while the handlers struggled to catch up and tried to find a route which circled the maze of streams and pools, to get to the other side of the floating trunks, to search among the osiers and willows for the line of scent that somewhere had to resume its course.

Pushing the reeds down flat, using the stems and leaves to help support their weight, Segle led Tagart first in one direction and then another, pushing southward in a passage of rustling and crushing and sucking. She carried a light pole, a broken sallow branch two yards long. By the feel under her feet, by the subtle changes in the rate at which the mud threatened to give in, Segle sensed her way along the seams of older and firmer ground: a skill she had been taught in the tribe, demanding speed, nerve, and experience. To stop once, to hesitate, would allow the mud to open and swallow them up.

Above the noise of their progress Tagart tried to listen, to ascertain how long the pursuit had been delayed at the pool.

It came again, the terrifying music of the hounds. They had crossed the pool and regained the scent.

In one hand Tagart carried a pole like Segle's. In the other he carried the bundle of his clothes—leggings and a farmer's jacket. Before entering the reeds he had taken them off. When Segle gave the word he was to drop them, leave them for the dogs to find; because once the dogs had stopped in their course to investigate, the handlers would do the same.

"Now!" Segle called out.

Tagart let the clothes fall.

In the brief freedom since leaving the fort, Segle had already recovered herself. From incredulity that Tagart had come back from the dead, and wonder that he had managed to overpower Blene, Segle had marshaled her feelings and now it was she who was guiding Tagart, using her knowledge of the reeds to help them both. And in the few words and tender gestures they had exchanged he knew that he was no longer alone; his empty days were over.

Suddenly there was no support for his feet and Tagart was sliding into the mud, slime rising past his calves, his knees, his thighs, toward his waist. Somehow he had lost his grip on the pole. Instinctively he threw his arms out and tried to grab handfuls of reeds: Segle heard his shout and turned to look. Without seeming to pause, she turned her pole horizontally and allowed herself to fall, spreading her arms and legs to distribute her weight.

"Lean back! Lean back and keep still! Struggling gets you in deeper!"

Tagart felt the mud rising over his waist. The reeds towered above him, the seed heads pendulous and heavy, obscuring the bright circle of the moon. In the clear space overhead the night sky was filled with stars. Before him was utter blackness; on the mud, bluish glints.

Segle, using the pole for support, crawled toward him. "Lean back! Lean back!"

He heard the hounds coming closer. By the change in their voices he thought they were entering the reeds.

"Lean back!"

Contrary to its every instinct, he forced his body to respond. He forced it to yield, offering more of itself to the mud; and as he leaned back he found his feet rising slightly and became aware that he was no longer sinking so fast.

"Spread your arms and pull on the reeds. Let the mud float you like water. Don't struggle against it, let it help you."

With agonizing slowness Tagart tried to obey, to drag himself backward and out of the mud. But now he felt his head sinking into the slime. He heard the dogs' voices become dull and faint as the slime filled his ears, its coldness rising up his face. Despite himself he knew that he was very near to panic; he knew that once he felt the mud closing over his nose and mouth he would thrash and flounder and be unable to stop himself from going down, on his back, with no hope of getting out.

The dogs were coming. He was trapped here, and they were coming.

He spoke, and his voice sounded strange to him; he heard the words filling his head.

"Leave me here. I can't move. Leave me here."

Not a word of Segle's reply reached him.

The soldiers splashed and waded knee-deep through the last open channel before the reeds. From the osiers and sallows they had each taken poles.

The brace handlers called their dogs in and directed them after the break team, into the corridor of reeds broken down by the prey. There was no longer any need of scent. The trackers could see where the quarry had gone.

One of the soldiers carried a bundle of thin rope; he took it from his shoulder and passed the end along the line, linking the men together. If one went in the mud, the others should be able to pull him up.

"Go to! In the reeds, girl! Go to!"

The black bitch, her feet sinking in the ooze, her tongue hungry for confirmation of the wide trace shown by mere eyesight, led the hounds into the forest of stems and along the zigzag of reed swath made only minutes before.

Below his head, Tagart felt a gentle pressure. Segle was lifting him so that he could breathe.

His fingers found something hard and relatively unyielding, out of place in the sea of slime and reeds. It was his sallow pole. Segle had found it and put it within his grasp.

Using the support of the pole, he began to win. Slowly, he freed more and more of himself from the mud. Beside him he was aware of Segle's help, her support, lifting first his arm, trying to raise his body, his legs; and then all at once the mud had released him and he was able to move.

Segle was speaking, her words unable to penetrate his deadened hearing. He pressed his fingers to his head and cleared some of the mud from his ears. At once he heard the hounds, three hundred paces away, less, drawing nearer through the reeds, and he heard the soldiers' shouts.

"Try to stand on the pole. Try to stand up."

Segle had risen to her feet, balancing on the precarious support of her own pole as it gently sank deeper into the mud. She extended a hand. With a slippery grip Tagart took it and he too was rising. His feet found the pole, ankle-deep in slime.

"Follow me!"

They had made a mess of the reeds and mud where Tagart had foundered, churning the mire into a black and watery bog. But Segle managed to pass it, and Tagart, covered in mud, placed his feet exactly where hers had been and once again was running through the reeds.

Almost as the fresh reeds opened for them, the dogs ran down the reek of Tagart's clothes.

The break handler shouted. "Go to! Leave it!"

"Go to!"

"Leave it! Go to!"

But in their excitement few of the hounds heard. Too late he shouted again; too late the other handlers shouted. Only the black bitch had heeded and gone through. The others, growling, gnarring, tussled with bared teeth for the jacket and leggings; and as they fought for them their feet began to sink deeper and deeper.

"Go to! Go to, you bastards!"

"Don't let them stop!"

"Go to! Go to! Go to! Go to!"

The break handler tried to change direction, to avoid the

pack of dogs in his way. With his pole held high, unthinking, he faltered, stumbled, and in the softest mud at once sank to his waist. The water soaked his jacket, his chest, covered his chin. He sensed the suction beneath him, all around him. The mud was almost a living creature. And as the break handler tasted swamp he knew the mud wanted him.

Another of the handlers hesitated, was made to turn; his left leg slid into the mud to the knee, and then the right. Behind him two of the soldiers were going down. The other men laid their poles and spread themselves flat as Segle had done, holding fast to the rope. One of them, desperate, threw himself onto the heaving backs of the dogs. They were sinking too; as he hit them they turned and snarled and tried to bite him. But their bodies were giving him support, keeping him clear, and however many dogs suffocated it did not matter.

The break handler felt the water rising over his forehead. He screamed. They did not hear it. The scream was the last of his air, his life, a silver bubble which wriggled its way to the surface and broke. His body involuntarily prepared to make another scream but as his chest expanded for it his lungs drew only mud.

The black bitch ran on alone, through the reeds, dipping her nose low. Her tongue touched the water and lapped the scent she had pursued all the way down from the fort. From the strength of it she knew the prey were only yards ahead, and she knew that she was gaining. She could think of nothing but the quarry. Her handler's voice had given an order: until countermanded it would push all else from her brain.

The scent stream turned and rose onto firmer ground, away from the soft mud. The reeds parted in front of the black bitch and her eyes dimly discerned running shapes against the moonlight and the night blue of the coastal sky. She heard them shout with fear. Power burst to her muscles and sinews and with her feet leaving the ground she sprang, throat-high. In the instant of her flight she tasted rosewater and then the full weight of her body struck and was bringing the human down.

Her training was not to bite the quarry, not to attack unless it showed resistance. She was merely to subdue and hold it until her masters came. But as the girl beneath her struggled and screamed, the black hound felt other hands closing below her jaw and the back of her head and she knew she was fighting for her life.

A strength like that of no human she had ever known jerked her head upward and back. Before her neck broke she saw white and smelled the welter of her own scents and those of the marshes and the prey. Vertebra parted from vertebra; her spinal cord tore and leaked fluid. Damaged tissues fired a blizzard of faulty impulses to her brain, fading, quickly going dark, and she received no more.

4

SEGLE HELD CLOSELY TO TAGART, HER FACE IN HIS shoulder.

"Are you hurt? Did it bite you?"

She shook her head.

In the marshes at their backs they could hear the calls and shouts of the soldiers. The plan seemed to have worked—the hounds had come across Tagart's clothes. But whether they had been stopped or merely delayed, there was no time to waste. Other teams might be dispatched from the Trundle.

"We must keep moving," Tagart said.

He helped Segle to her feet and pushed the lifeless body of the dog aside.

She touched his arm. "Listen."

Away from the shouting and the soldiers, to the south, sounded the distant crash of breakers on a sloping shore.

It could not be much farther to the sea.

They went on; and now it was Tagart who led the way.

The ending of the reed-beds was signaled by the fluting cry of a curlew disturbed from its feeding in the creek. For several seconds it had stood with head bobbing in uncertainty, alarmed by the approaching noise of rustling stems; and when Tagart and Segle came out of the reeds it saw them and took wing, twenty feet over the glittering mud, passing in front of the moon. Other birds in the creek and in the saltings heard its cry and shared the alert: redshanks, whimbrels, oyster-catchers, and their own distinctive voices were added to the curlew's as they too opened their bills and flew up.

"The tide's out," Segle said.

They left shin-deep footmarks across the width of the creek and entered the saltings, among the glasswort and sea purslane, stepping over gullies and gutters of wet mud. The glasswort gave way to seablite which scratched softly at their legs. Before them was the rising slope of the beach; behind them was silence, and no sound of pursuit.

Their feet crunched on shingle, climbing to the low crest of the moonlit shore; and there from west to east spread sparkling sea, the waves angled in broad sweeps and tumbling into surf, almost luminous where the foam broke and slid back into the oncoming crests.

Tagart wearily took Segle's hand and led her down to the water. Their scent could still be traced, even across the pebbles. It was time to make sure they would be followed no more.

It was time to slip into the sea, to swim beside the beach, to come out where it was safe and sleep an untroubled sleep; and afterward, with the sun on their bodies and the wind blowing subtly along the shore, to find food and clothing and make a start on all the questions.

The water was warm. A wave slapped at their knees; they went in further. Wordlessly they drew together. With the friendly sea swelling to their waists they let the water wash away the black mud from their skins, the filth of the marshes, clean and healing, gentle, soothing, billowing in a dark cloud, merging with the currents until all trace of it was gone.

About the Author

RICHARD HERLEY was born in Watford, England. A trained biologist, he has devoted himself to writing since his graduation from Sussex University. His interest in natural history inspired him to acquire a firsthand knowledge of the Sussex Coast, the setting for THE STONE ARROW. In this book he has tried to convey as faithfully as possible what the countryside of Sussex must have been like in the New Stone Age, thousands of years before Christ.